BURN DOWN, RISE UP

BURN DOWN, RISE UP

VINCENT TIRADO

sourcebooks
fire

Published by Sourcebooks Fire, an imprint of Sourcebooks
P.O. Box 4410, Naperville, Illinois 60567-4410
(630) 961-3900
sourcebooks.com

Cataloging-in-Publication data is on file with the Library of Congress.

Printed and bound in the United States of America.
WOZ 10 9 8 7 6 5 4 3 2 1

To Sharon Lee De La Cruz,
for teaching me the richness of my neighborhood.

To Tricia Clarke and Mark Fusco,
for always encouraging my writing.

To The Point, to the Bronx,
and to all the people in it who make it great.

PROLOGUE
THE ROT SPREADS

The Bronx was alive.

He was alive.

For now.

Cisco shot forward with a desperate urgency.

The hospital. Get there. Go.

The thought felt foreign to him, as though someone—or some*thing*—was whispering it into his ear, but he didn't fight it. He couldn't fight it. He was busy fighting something else, something that was working its way through his body and blackening his veins. Sweat coated every inch of his skin, and confusion clouded him, making him question where he was and why.

He tried to shake it off, fight it off as he walked-stumbled-ran. Desperation ebbed and flowed. Like a rubber band, he felt his body snapping between worlds.

SNAP!

Even in his daze, he knew something was wrong. The streets weren't supposed to be turning this way and that. That person wasn't supposed to be peeling half their face off. Was that building always abandoned? Always smoking? Always on *fire*?

He dug inside himself for answers, only managing to earn a half second of clarity.

His name was Francisco Cruz, he was eighteen years old, he was a student at Fordham University, where he met some people, played a game—or was it a challenge?—and then he...he...

He snapped his head up, sure he heard it.

Skittering.

An insect-like pitter-patter that was almost certainly getting close. He didn't know what it was, but he knew fear when it crawled up his spine.

Cisco pulled out his phone. No bars. *No bars?* He was in the Bronx. Why was there no signal?

He stared at the screen wallpaper, a picture of himself with a dark-skinned girl whose curls looked like springs. Her smile was bright and calming. Tears pricked his eyes as he thought about his cousin and his promise before he realized what he'd done.

"Charlize—"

SNAP!

A deep shiver ran through his core. A car honked, and he realized it was because he was suddenly in the middle of the street. He tripped—there was the curb. The streetlights were on, which meant it was night. He checked his phone again and finally had signal. Full bars meant he was safe.

The hospital. Get there. Go.

Cisco stumbled again and fell forward to grip a wrought iron fence. Missing-persons posters stuck loosely to some of the bars. He squinted. Some of these faces looked familiar. In fact, he was sure he had seen them at some point during the hellish night, but here they looked too...healthy. Alive.

The people he'd seen were neither.

There was a misshapen urban garden just beyond the fence with small compost bins. Brook Park. Not too far from Lincoln Hospital.

He held on to that knowledge like an anchor as he groped along fences and brick walls. A sea of confusion raged all around him, but as long as he made it to the hospital, things would be *fine*. The doctors would help him. That was their job, wasn't it? They would see Cisco, see the black veins coursing through him, touch his clammy skin, and know just what to do.

They would get it out of him—the *rot*—before it was too late, before it could take any more of him and his thoughts and memories.

Finally, he got to the emergency room. After scribbling through whatever paperwork they handed him, he found himself in an isolated room, a plastic bracelet sealed on his wrist. The nurse who came to see him had long dreadlocks and a familiar face. She stared at him like she knew him.

Did she?

"Okay, Cisco, why don't you walk me through what happened tonight?" She stood just a few feet away. "I promise you, you aren't going to be in trouble. We just need to find out if you took anything that could be making you sick. Was it Molly? Did you drop some acid?"

Even her voice sounded familiar, Cisco just couldn't place it. Still, he shook his head, eager to get the rot out of him. He just needed to explain, if only he weren't so *confused*—

"I *br*-broke the rules."

The nurse blinked, waiting for him to go on. He opened his mouth again, brain trying to put the words in a correct sentence, but all that came out was an agonizing screech. His entire body felt engulfed in flames, and when he looked at his arms, he could see his veins blackening again.

"Francisco!" The nurse jumped as he threw himself over the bed. "We need some help! Security!"

The room exploded with security guards and another nurse. They pulled at him and tried to flatten him against the bed, but he pushed back, tossing the other nurse against the wall and kicking a security guard in the stomach.

"What is this?" the first nurse yelled, finally getting a look at his veins.

Cisco's hands shook against his will before wrapping themselves around her arms. His nails pierced through her scrubs, and she screamed.

"I'm sorry!" he cried, vision blurring with tears. As she tried to claw his hands off, he felt the black rot pulsing out of him and into her.

The security guards descended on him. Cisco threw himself away from the nurse and into the wall. Then he turned and ran.

Forget the hospital, he decided. Between the rot and the snapping between worlds, nothing was making sense. Maybe his cousin could help him. Once he put a few blocks between himself and the hospital, he turned into in an alleyway and squatted for air.

Cisco shook with a quiet sob that made him sink to the ground. The game—the stupid game with stupid rules that he and his friends broke. It all went to shit in less than an hour and he was going to pay for it.

He sucked in a breath so deep, it hurt, and focused on his surroundings instead. The squeal of rats fighting for food, the pulsing red and blue lights of cop cars going by—was that for him? Probably. He had no way of knowing how many people he injured on his way out of the hospital.

This wasn't supposed to happen.

Cisco froze. He knew he heard it: a flurry of legs skittering around in search of its prey.

"*Fuck!*" he hissed, pressing himself farther into the shadows. Eyes darting around, he looked for signs of decay and ruin only to find the buildings around him still intact.

Cisco stilled his breathing and his shaking body. The skittering was suddenly gone. Or maybe it was never there. He hadn't snapped back yet.

But he would.

Cisco jabbed his hands into his pockets and pulled out his cell phone.

The ringing went on forever, and he whispered prayers into the receiver for his cousin to pick up.

"Cisco?" Charlize yawned. She sounded half-annoyed and half-sleep-deprived.

"*Ch*-Charlize!" He choked back a sob. "I need *he*-help. Please—"

"What are you doing calling me? It's like four a.m."

"*Th*-the game—" He tried his best to explain, to communicate that everything was thoroughly and deeply *wrong*. Words tumbled out before he could even process them, and he hoped he was making a crumb of sense.

"Whoa." Charlize hushed him. A spring mattress creaked from shifting weight. "What are you talking about, Cisco? What game?"

"Don't leave *th*-the train before *f*-four, don't-don't talk to the Passengers, don't *touch* the Passengers, don't turn around—" The rules shot off his tongue like firecrackers, sharp and all at once. "The game—the challenge, Ch-Charlize—"

"What? Cisco, I can't hear you. You're cutting out."

"Li-listen, I'm coming over to you now, Charlize, okay? And I ne-need you to bring a wea-weapon—a knife, bat, *something*, ju-just anything, okay?"

Cisco ended the call and shoved the phone deep in his pocket. The confusion was hanging low on his mind again, washing him in panic. He only had a vague idea of where he was. Just up the street was Rite Aid, and if he crossed it, there would be McDonald's. There was a train passing over him, which meant he had to be somewhere uptown.

Even more pressing was the familiar build of the snap before it happened. It was like something inside his chest began to stretch and when it reached its limit—when it *snapped*—he'd end up somewhere hellish.

Paranoia seized Cisco as the skittering returned. He screamed and took off toward Charlize's house.

He could only hope he made it before the creature caught up.

PART ONE

THE NEXT STOP IS

THE TRAIN WAS PACKED TIGHT THIS MORNING.

Aaron and I watched as it pulled into the platform. We quickly scanned each car for even a sliver of space we could squeeze ourselves into. Once the train slowed to a stop, we had only a few seconds to choose our fate or risk being late. Hyde High School was notorious for giving lunch detentions for even the slightest infractions, and neither of us cared to stay an extra hour after school in silence.

"Yo, there's space here, Raquel," Aaron said. I twisted my head in his direction and eyed the car he was heading toward. He was a thin guy as tall as a traffic light. It was next to impossible to lose Aaron in a crowd, but that also meant he could easily lose *you.* As soon as the doors slid open, an automated voice spoke clearly.

This is a Wakefield-bound two train. The next stop is...

A small trail of people emptied out the car, and that's when we took our chance. Aaron filled in the closest gap, and I was on his heel.

"Sorry. Excuse me," I mumbled, still having to push my way

into the crowd. I shimmied my backpack off and rested it on the floor between my legs. The train chimed again with a robotic voice.

Stand clear of the closing doors, please...

The train doors slid shut before it continued on its way. I sighed.

"I told you we'd make it," Aaron said. His eyes were already glued to his phone, Twitter reflecting in his glasses.

"Barely." I rolled my eyes. "You really need to wake up earlier. My mom is getting real serious about me not leaving the house without someone around."

Aaron made a face.

"So I gotta come pick you up every morning?"

"Well." I frowned. "Only if my mom is home. She really won't let me leave if I'm by myself." Today was one of the exceptions, though. When I woke up, Mami was still out, probably working another late shift at the hospital. I noticed because the shower curtain was still open when I went to use the bathroom. I always left the shower curtain open, but Mami insisted on closing it each time. It was one of the few things I did that drove her wild.

I felt a twinge of guilt about it, the word *wrong* going off in my head like a *Jeopardy!* buzzer. That happened whenever I chose to dodge Mami's rules. She called it a "strong moral compass."

I sent a quick text before going to school, letting her know I was on my way out and would likely see her after school. She didn't respond, but that was normal when she worked late.

"She's really that freaked out about the disappearances?" Aaron asked, yawning.

I nodded. "Her and the church people she hangs with have been thinking about setting a curfew for all kids just in case." I'd accidentally eavesdropped on her conversation about it just the night before. The walls were thin, and Dominicans never knew how to talk quietly.

Still, I guess I could understand her fear. The whole borough was on edge, unsure what was causing the disappearances. And since no bodies had been found, the police didn't want to call it a serial killer.

Aaron furrowed his brow and frowned.

"That sucks," he said.

"You know it's bad when they can't even find the white kids."

They were the first group to disappear. The faces of those four students from Fordham University were plastered everywhere, and the police damn near busted their asses trying to find them. There were a lot of protests in the street about it, unsurprisingly. Someone went digging around and found out the students had rich parents with connections, so rumor was cops' jobs were on the line.

They never did find them, though. Then every month, almost like clockwork, one or two more people would go missing. Homeless people or late-night workers, but sometimes it'd be kids. I'd feel my phone buzz with an Amber Alert, only for the police to later dismiss the idea that whoever abducted that particular kid was responsible for all the other disappearances.

"True." Aaron was never a particularly talkative guy. If anything could be said in one word or two, he would do it. Sometimes it annoyed me, but he'd been my best friend since we were kids and the good always outweighed the small pet peeves, so I got used to it.

The next stop came.

People shifted, either trying to get off or make space for new passengers. I tucked my shoulders inward and tried to make myself as small as possible with a winter coat. The automatic voice spoke up again, just as a young girl sat in an empty seat on my right.

"Why was Papi being so weird last night?" the girl said, leaning into an older woman next to her, maybe her grandmother. Their faces were oval-shaped and brown, and the older woman had a frown set deeper than the ocean.

"He just has a lot on his mind. Why?" The woman glanced down. "Did he say something to you?"

The girl nodded. "He said to never get on the train at night. That there was something in the tunnels that took people."

"And how does he know that?"

"He said it came to him in a dream."

The older woman cursed in Spanish under her breath.

I looked over to Aaron. He was still focused on the sudoku puzzle.

"Yo, you heard that?" I whispered.

"What?"

"They said something in the tunnels is taking people." I hoped the concept would freak him out enough to look up, but he didn't.

"Well, we don't have to worry about that," he said as the train went from the underground tunnel to the open air.

Light streamed in through the windows, and we rode above buildings where we could see illegible graffiti coating the top edges. Store signs and billboards were just as dirty, with grime inching along nearly every crack and crease. Out on the street, a shopkeeper swept the sidewalk, pushing fallen twigs and crumpled leaves out of the way of the store entrance. The wind would likely toss the debris back, but he was diligent in his cleaning, nonetheless. For some reason, it reminded me of a phrase my aunts and uncles would say about the Bronx: *It's not all that...but it* is *all that*.

People did what they could to take care of their home, and

the graffiti told stories about people who came and went with a desire to be remembered. Even the dirt and grime gave the message: *We're here.* The South Bronx, despite being looked down on by all the other boroughs and maybe even some of the residents, was a place where people lived, continued to live, and made their own way.

And that made it perfect.

Just then, Aaron leaned down, fidgeting with his backpack. "Imagine if there was really something in the tunnel." He snickered. "That'd be wild."

HISTORY ON PAPER

HYDE HIGH SCHOOL WAS NEW. IN FACT, IT WAS THE *ONLY* newly built school in the Bronx, as none were erected in the last fifty years, or so I've been told. It was a medium-sized building, with light-gray stones and polished windows. There were four floors in total, starting with the security lobby that shared the floor with a computer lab and the cafeteria. The cafeteria took up the entire length of the school, and as Aaron and I walked in for lunch, we jumped to the back of the line. It was already starting to reach the far back corner.

My eyes fell on the dean, who was making her rounds in checking adherence to uniform and other minor behavioral issues. Hyde was a charter school, so it had the luxury of making up new rules almost every year that we would either deal with or push against. I remember the year when they ruled all the girls could only wear the girl ties that crossed at the neck. Then the next year, because it was a useless rule, they repealed it and let us wear actual ties.

At some point, I stopped paying attention to all the rules they made up because if it were really bad, no one would follow it anyway.

"Please, Raquel?"

"No, Aaron," I said, moving ahead in the lunch line. "You and I *both* know that if we team up for the term paper, not only will we have to write more pages but *you'll* leave me to do all the work. I'm not about it."

"Oh, come on, give me some credit!"

I held up a finger, cutting him off. "The answer is no. You're on your own."

The term paper wasn't due for another few weeks, and while our history teacher gave us permission to work in pairs, it came with the understanding that it would have to be nearly twice as long. Truthfully, I hadn't started it, but at least I had a list of sources to look into.

Aaron probably didn't even know what the term paper was about.

Somehow he always managed to make this my problem.

"Pleasepleasepleasepleasepleaseplease*please*—" He tugged on my arm the way little kids did when they were trying to wear you down. Unfortunately, it was working. "Can you at least give me some help with where to start?"

"Ugh!" I pulled away as I got to the front of the line. I grabbed the first tray I saw and walked to the nearest table. "Fine! But you better write fast because I'm not repeating myself."

"Yes!" Aaron rushed after me. I sat down with my back toward the cafeteria entrance, feeling the burst of breeze every time someone pushed through the double doors. It was calming and I needed calming right then. I opened a carton of apple juice and watched Aaron dig into his bag for a notebook.

"First, Robert Moses."

He began scribbling the name across the top of his page.

"He was the public official who built the Cross Bronx Expressway."

"The one we literally pass by every day?"

"Do you know another Cross Bronx Expressway?" I asked, before continuing. "Just to build that, he went as far as destroying housing. And *then* made the expressway low enough that buses couldn't pass through."

"What, did he expect everyone to just get a car?" Aaron snorted at his own joke.

"He expected *some* people to have cars." I didn't elaborate on which people those were. Aaron could figure it out.

I watched Aaron's hand work fast and hard, to the detriment of his own handwriting. I couldn't tell his *R*s from his *H*s, and the grip he had on his pen made my own hand cramp up.

"Moses also built residential complexes designed specifically for veterans and then opposed Black veterans from moving in."

"Oh, so he was racist." Aaron nodded, writing in big letters *RACIST*. He wrote it with such ease, as though there were no reason to be shocked or upset. Which, I guess there wasn't— racism was so ingrained in our lives and in so many laws, what was one more discriminating policy?

Still, something in me wished he'd reacted much more strongly. I opened my mouth to say more but decided against it.

"All right, there you have it."

"What?" Aaron looked up, confused. "That's it?"

"That's all I'm giving you." I shrugged, picking at the corners of a slice of corn bread. "Good luck."

I expected him to try to fight me on this. When he didn't, I looked up. He was staring off into the distance behind me. I put down my corn bread and turned my neck.

Charlize was a short Black girl with Shirley Temple curls. She was in the grade above us, so we never had class together, but she was nice enough to talk to us anyway. She was the kind of girl who liked to share everything good in her life—whether it was news, advice, or just snacks.

And she also happened to be the love of Aaron's life—she just didn't know it.

People flocked to Charlize naturally. A crowd of students surrounded her like a bubble. If it weren't for Aaron's forlorn stare and the way her curls peeked up over the crowd, I wouldn't have known she was there at all.

I looked back at Aaron, who sighed quietly.

"Seriously? I'm trying to help you out and you start daydreaming?"

"Yo...I think she's crying."

"What?"

I twisted myself back around. The girls parted just enough to show a very distraught Charlize. Her eyes were red, and her cheeks were wet. Snot was flowing, and she wiped it away every few seconds with a white napkin. Someone held out a box of tissues, offering it to her in her time of need.

And she definitely needed it.

Charlize looked up just a moment to meet my eyes, her lips parting to suck in a deep breath. My stomach twisted.

"Wasn't she like, your bestie when we were kids?" Aaron said.

Charlize and I were childhood friends, like Aaron and me, but our relationship was...different. Sometimes, I would talk a little too loud about going to the park, and she would be there. Other times, she would talk about going to get an iced coffee at the Boogie Down Café, and I would find a reason to go. It was a weird relationship, I know, inviting each other but not *really* inviting each other.

Truthfully, it was an accident when it started and somehow it morphed into a game—a secret game like a secret language only the two of us could speak.

Swallowing, I shook my head at Aaron. "If you mean she and I would awkwardly sit together while her cousin and your older brother played games, then yeah, sure. We were besties," I said. There was also that time she and I played house, and we pretended to be a married couple—an idea that absolutely thrilled me for some reason, but Aaron didn't need to know that.

"Raquel?"

I looked up from my tray. Mr. Wade, the guidance counselor, stood a few feet away, hands shoved into the pockets of his slacks. It was his go-to move when he was nervous but didn't want to let it show. No one would be able to see him playing with his hands if he kept them hidden.

"Yeah?" I said, putting down my spork.

"Your father is here to pick you up." Mr. Wade took a step back, waiting for me to follow. My feet moved without permission, and I glanced at Aaron in confusion. He shrugged.

Did I hear that right?

"My...father?" I stepped after Mr. Wade. He pushed open the cafeteria double doors for me and led me into the lobby.

That's when I saw him.

"Papi?"

WHAT HAD
HAPPENED WAS

The official story was that Mami was in a coma. Papi had gotten a call from the hospital where she worked since he was still an emergency contact, and he ran right away to pick me up from school. (Part of me wanted to know why he was still an emergency contact at all, considering Mami and Papi never got along.)

I'd been to Lincoln Hospital more times than I could count, bringing Mami's lunch, work ID, and on a few occasions, a change of shoes after some unidentifiable body fluids ruined the pair she was wearing. I was familiar enough with her coworkers to know which ones were the hard-asses she complained about and knew the layout of the hospital well enough to know just how far I could get into the OR before getting caught by someone who knew I definitely didn't belong there.

But this was the first time I'd ever been there to see Mami as a patient. The hallways that were usually as comfortable as my own home suddenly felt much more foreign.

Papi and I stood outside of her room, only peering through the glass window.

"Last night, your mother was attacked by a patient."

All my blood pooled at my feet. Tentatively, the doctor continued.

"Now, the injuries she sustained weren't serious, but in the scuffle, we think he infected her with something—something we haven't been able identify yet, so it would be best if you stayed outside the room until we know for sure how contagious it is."

Mami lay in bed, covered up to her waist in a hospital blanket. A blue, plastic hairnet only marginally covered her dreads, as if someone were in the process of taking it off but decided last minute they couldn't be bothered.

A nasal cannula snaked across her face and under her nose. An IV drip penetrated the inside of her elbow, and several wires snaked under her blanket, sending electromagnetic messages to machines I couldn't identify. The steady beat of the heart monitor was the only thing keeping me calm. I glanced at the corner of the screen where her heart rate and temperature were displayed. They were both a little high.

"Do you have any idea what it might be?" Papi asked. I could tell he was digging around for whatever information his EMT background could give him.

The doctor sighed before shaking her head.

"Honestly? All we know is that it's an infection. And that it's very painful."

I wrinkled my nose and looked up at her. "Painful?"

Papi put a firm hand on my shoulder. From my periphery, I could see he was giving the doctor a pleading stare, as if he were asking her to please consider her next words with compassion.

"Yes, uh—" Her eyes darted from us to Mami. "Your mother

was screaming and thrashing, saying she was burning. We had to sedate her and put her in a medical coma."

My eyes started brimming with tears. It was bad enough to imagine someone assaulting her. But the sight of Mami thrashing and in pain? It was like a spear to my chest.

I tried to breathe through the lump in my throat. "Is there anything you need from me? Do you need like, a blood transfusion or a liver transplant?" My knowledge of medical procedures began and ended with the terrible medical dramas Mami and I watched together in her time off. Even though Mami was a no-nonsense nurse, she liked to scoff and roll her eyes, telling me why something one character did was breaking HIPAA or why a hospital would never allow such a risky procedure. This entire scenario felt as unreal as one of those shows.

"No, I—I don't believe so," the doctor said, destroying my hopes. "However, the police may want to contact you at a later date to talk about potentially pressing charges..."

Her voice trailed off as I stared at Mami's sleeping figure.

Until something moved from under her blanket. I shrieked in response and stumbled back.

"Whoa, what's wrong?" Papi said.

"There was something—something *moved*." Something small, like a creature. Maybe a rat. Rats wouldn't be around here though, right? Lincoln Hospital wasn't great, but it couldn't be *that* bad.

I stared at Mami's arm, right where it disappeared under the blanket. I could see something peeking out—a black fuzz that peppered her skin.

It looked like...*mold*.

"Is your daughter okay?" the doctor asked Papi. There was a hint of annoyance mixed with exhaustion in her voice. I recognized it from how Mami would speak after a long shift. It seemed to be a tone every healthcare professional inherited at some point in their career.

"She's fine." Papi waved her off and then leaned over next to me. "Listen, I know that this is going to be very hard for you, especially not being able to get close to your mother. But if you ever want to check up on her, at least you know where to find her." He squeezed my shoulder and then pulled me into a hug.

I felt hollow just looking at her, so I focused on the window. I could see my own reflection in the glass along with Papi still wrapping me in a hug. The colorful Yoruba beads he wore were bulky and pressed into me uncomfortably, but what caught my attention completely overshadowed the pain.

Right next to Papi was a man in a corduroy jacket, his dark skin cracked with dryness. He stared right at me in the reflection, sending a fierce chill up my spine. His chest rose with a wheeze, and I waited for Papi to notice we were not alone the way I thought we were.

The man reached out to me. His hand was covered with mold and black rot. It shocked me back to my senses.

I shoved Papi away and twirled on my heel. The man in the corduroy jacket was gone. I double-checked in the reflection, my heart racing and an overwhelming sense of doom washing over me.

No one was there. But I couldn't have imagined that.

"Hey!" Papi yelled, rubbing his chest. "That hurt. Since when were you that strong?"

"Can we go?" I asked, still watching the glass from the corner of my eyes. Papi's mouth fell in surprise, but I couldn't want for him to answer.

I ran out of there, the prickling sensation of a hand hovering over me.

RESGUARDOS

I STOOD IN THE MIDDLE OF MY ROOM, A DUFFEL BAG IN HAND and my backpack on my shoulders, and considered what I would need for the next few weeks. Some clothes, hygiene products, my laptop, library books, sketchbooks, two sets of pajamas, shampoo, conditioner, leave-in conditioner, a tub of gel, a brush and a comb...and, of course, all my textbooks. I didn't have anything at Papi's house.

I was about seven years old when Mami and Papi separated. Neither really explained it to me, but it didn't bother me very much. I still got to see Papi, and the separation meant I got twice as many gifts on birthdays and holidays.

I got used to the new arrangement fast, and by the time I got into high school, Papi was like a distant relative. I saw him whenever we were both free—which was rare. He was an EMT with constantly changing schedules, and I was a high schooler with several AP classes, an after-school art club and, until recently, the soccer team. Life was busy for both of us.

It never really struck me until now how separate our lives were.

My phone buzzed again. Papi promised me he wouldn't come into the house since we both knew Mami wouldn't like that, so he waited outside while I gathered my things.

Papi

are you okay?

Me

yea, almost done.

I wiped my eyes with the back of my hand. I didn't even realize I was crying.

The taxi ride to Papi's house was more than awkward. We sat silently, facing out the opposite windows with my duffel bag acting as a barrier between us. It had been months since I'd seen Papi, really. The last time we spoke, he was hitting that weird part of his middle-age crisis where he was trying to be the "cool" parent. He offered to let me drink beer or smoke weed as long as I did it at home and promised he wouldn't say anything about it to Mami.

Even if I believed that, I didn't care to do any of those things. Papi thought I was just putting up a goody-two-shoes front.

I glanced at him from the corner of my eyes. His skin was a deep reddish brown, and his hair was beginning to thin with specks of gray. He had crow's-feet around his eyes, which I heard was either due to lots of smiling or lots of crying. Either would be on brand for Papi. He was always the more emotional adult in my life. Mami was calmer and set in her ways. She had an inner strength that was unparalleled and unshakable. I liked to think I took after her in that regard.

The taxi rolled to a stop at a red light. "So how was school?" Papi asked.

I shrugged. I didn't finish the day. He knew that.

"It was fine."

"You keeping your grades up?"

"Sí, Papi."

Twenty silent minutes later, we pulled up to Papi's house. I waited on the steps with my heavy duffel while he paid the taxi driver. When he was done, Papi smiled at me playfully then jogged up the steps with his keys in hand. I trudged after him with my head down, my bag strap digging into my shoulders.

It wasn't that I hated Papi or even hated his house. He was, by most people's standards, a decent person. He didn't go to church like Mami, and he preferred to go to a botanica than a doctor, but he was kind and responsible. He paid Mami nearly twice the amount of child support that he had to, even when he didn't get to see me because of work. He was always there for birthday parties, holidays, and special events like my school's art galleries, where I showed off my paintings. He was an all-around supportive father. I knew I was pretty lucky to have him.

That being said, Papi could be absolutely ridiculous about other things.

I carefully stepped inside his apartment, wrinkling my nose at a strong and minty smell.

"Is that Vicks?"

"Close." He grinned, tossing his head back at me. "It's camphor. I got little cubes of it and broke it into pieces in every corner of the house. It helps clear your lungs and is a wonderful sleep aid."

I wasn't sure how much of that was true, but hey, he *was* the EMT.

Papi grabbed my duffel bag, destroying any excuse not to get into a whole conversation. No "Wow, I'm really tired from all this packing and unpacking, I guess I'll talk to you tomorrow." I would have to indulge his fatherly instinct to make me feel welcomed.

The hallway stretched from the front door to the living room, where there was a large futon couch, a desk area converted into an altar of some sort next to a TV, and a large library-esque bookshelf. The bookshelf was just an inch away from the ceiling and was crammed from side to side and top to bottom with books about astral projection, Yoruba religion, theories of multiple universes, and a few Marvel comics. Along the wall over the futon was a traditional West African painting of a woman dressed in gold and selling fish in a marketplace.

It was a stark contrast from Mami's house—*my* house. The most religious thing we owned was a cross that hung over the living room television, and Mami didn't care for furniture that looked like it was nearing its expiration date. We were tidy to the point where I thought she might have been a little obsessive about it. But now that I was in Papi's house, the sudden difference wounded me, and I didn't have the energy to hide it.

Papi followed my line of sight to the altar he made. "You want me to take that down? I know your mother doesn't like those things and you're not used to it, so if it makes you uncomfortable, I can just move it into my room."

The altar was a colorful display. A red-and-gold tapestry hung over a three-foot-tall portable coffee table. Small wooden statues in white dresses stood surrounded by several tiny blue bowls of water. Beads flowed in a straight line all around the table, hanging by inches off the edge. The display seemed entirely disorganized—a confusing array of worship that I knew meant a lot to my father.

Mami would've hated it.

"No, it's fine," I said. "You can leave it here."

I carefully walked over to it. The sets of beads were more color-coordinated upon closer look. Red with white, green with black, blue with clear beads, yellow with brown—something told me there was a clear meaning behind the colors.

"I remember when you used to be really interested in the resguardos."

"The what?" I frowned, looking up at him.

"Hold on, let me get one."

Papi walked away and into his room. Dresser drawers opened and closed, boxes were shuffled aside. He stomped around, mumbling to himself every few moments.

"I know it's around here somewhere!"

I almost told him to forget it, but then he hollered with excitement.

"Here it is!" He stumbled out of his room. Between his forefinger and thumb was a small, marble-like ball constructed of tightly bound beads. Like the ones on the table, it also had alternating colors of green and black. Papi held it out to me, and I could see two tiny seashells woven on either side.

"This is a resguardo," he explained as I picked it up. "When you were small, you used to play with these like marbles, rolling them around as much as they could go and throwing them. You laughed so hard at the sounds they made when they hit each other. I think at one point, your mother made them into little bobble hair ties so you could show them off at school."

I raised an eyebrow, trying to imagine the sound. "Okay, but what even is this?"

"It's like a little charm. A totem full of spiritual energy that protects you."

"Oh." I dropped it back into his hand. If I no longer remembered something like that, I must've been young, like a toddler.

Papi was quiet for a moment. When we ran out of things to talk about, it always got like this—uncomfortable. This was usually the point in the phone call when we would both make an excuse to hang up.

"You know, if you're ever interested in this stuff, I can always teach you a little here and there," he offered. "Or anything else. My library is always open to you." He gave a small chuckle, gesturing to his overfilled bookshelf.

I sighed.

"Something wrong?" he asked.

Everything was wrong.

"I'm just hungry." It wasn't a lie. I hadn't eaten since lunch a few hours ago.

"Oh right, dinner," he said, as though he'd forgotten I actually needed to eat. He sauntered into the kitchen and began opening and closing cabinets, the fridge, the pantry before poking his head out. "You want tostones?"

Fifteen minutes later, I sat on a cushion in the middle of the living room and picked the little fried plantains off my plate while Papi tried to figure out how to pull the couch out into a futon. He swore up and down that there was a switch or a lever somewhere but spent the better part of an hour trying to figure it out.

I turned the TV on and busied myself with flipping through the channels, trying to find something decent to watch. Reruns of *Will & Grace* nearly caught my attention, until I caught sight of a bewildering news headline.

"Bronx residents are calling for the firing of several NYPD officers after they allegedly shot thirty-three-year-old Hazel Boon fourteen times..." The anchorwoman went on to speak in passive language. I grimaced, remembering the video that circulated just a week ago. Hazel Boon was a deaf woman who didn't even hear the police officers shouting at her to get on the ground. And for what? Because they thought her Popsicle stick was a weapon.

"Allegedly? How else did she get fourteen bullet holes in her?" I mumbled.

It was the biggest bullshit I'd ever heard and just another reason in the long list of reasons I never felt comfortable around cops. The possibility of undue violence made my chest ache with despair.

As if that weren't enough, the news chose an unflattering photo of Hazel Boon. She was a hefty woman, and in the picture, she had what looked like oil stains on her shirt and a bad case of bedhead. It was like they were implying that she deserved to get shot. I moved to change the channel.

And then I saw a familiar face.

"Police are looking for Bronx native Francisco Cruz, who was last reported—"

"Watch your head, m'ija," Papi said, holding on to one end of the futon. "I finally got it out."

I shifted closer to the television and frowned when the news moved on to something else. But I knew it was Cisco. The misshapen head and freakishly long neck were uniquely his, and I recognized the photo they chose—I'd been there for it. Aaron and I ran into him at Rite Aid while he was sick with the flu and buying medicine. We snuck through the aisles to see how long it would take him to notice us, and Aaron took a picture of him once he turned around. In the photo, Cisco's eyes were glazed over, making him look mean and unfriendly, which couldn't be further from the truth. I wondered how far into his Facebook the news had to scroll to find that specific photo.

I guess I knew why Charlize was freaking out today.

The two cousins were thicker than most siblings. If something terrible happened to Cisco, then Charlize would be a wreck.

I didn't catch why the police were looking for him, but Cisco committing a crime seemed unlikely. Which meant... Was he missing?

I glanced over to my bag and thought about my cell phone. I shut it off after school got out, knowing that Aaron would blow it up with texts and questions.

Or worse—actual calls.

I wanted to know what was going on with Cisco, but I didn't want to open myself up to a barrage of questions. I couldn't wrap my mind around Mami's situation, let alone explain it to Aaron. He barely gave a person time to think when he was curious, always throwing out one question after the next. There were only so many times I could answer "I don't know" before I considered smacking him.

I went into my bag and retrieved my laptop instead. "Papi, what's the Wi-Fi password?" My eyes darted around the living room, looking for the router.

"Wi-Fi?" Papi scratched the back of his head, looking embarrassed.

Oh no.

"Sorry, m'ija, I don't even have internet."

Oh my God.

"There's a library not too far from here if you need to use it."

I slowly closed my laptop.

"Is everything okay?"

"*Mm-hmm.*" It was not. "I think I'm just tired."

"Okay. I'll let you get some rest."

Papi left for a moment and returned with a pillow and two sets of blankets.

"Here you go, m'ija. If you need anything, my room is open." He kissed me on the forehead. "Good night."

I sat on the edge of the futon with the blankets in hand and watched him disappear into his room. With a flick of a finger, the lights were off. Darkness fell over me, and I breathed in the camphor that was likely hiding somewhere underneath the futon. The memory of Charlize's disheveled look swam to the forefront of my mind. I hoped for her that Cisco wasn't missing.

Over twenty disappearances in the last year. The streets were practically littered with missing-person fliers and strange faces that somehow looked familiar. The Bronx was small enough that you could run into the same person enough times and never really know it.

None of the other missing people were ever found.

SWEET DREAMS
AND
SOUR NIGHTMARES

WITHOUT REALIZING IT, I DROPPED INTO A DREAM. It started off very calm, with a clear sky and the sound of small, thudding feet. Little kids screamed. Birds chirped loudly. Water poured out of the sprinklers.

I breathed in the warm summer air and sat quietly while the slightly older kids argued about who should start the game of hide-and-seek. At the very edge of the park, adults sat on the green-painted benches. They chatted and gestured to each other as if in deep conversation.

Everywhere in the park was loud. And yet, I couldn't parse out the words anyone was saying. Even while yelling, they sounded muffled, like they were trapped behind glass. Their faces were blank—not emotionless, but rather smooth, with no eyes, noses, or mouths. For some reason, this didn't feel odd to me.

I sat down and decided to pick at the grass.

"Hey, what's your name?"

I looked up, squinting to avoid the glare of the sun. The girl in front of me partially blocked it out with her tiny Afro. She was the only one with a face. And that felt natural, too.

"I'm Raquel," I said, feeling a gap between my teeth. I didn't quite have a lisp, but the way my tongue ran along the empty space made me feel self-conscious, since most other kids had already lost all their baby teeth at my age.

The girl smiled, revealing a gap where her canines should've been.

"I'm Charlize," she said. "I'm Francisco's cousin."

"Francisco?" I blinked and looked over to the group of older kids. Suddenly, only one of them had a face, and my eyes locked on to his. His skin was browning under the glare of the sun. Francisco had kind eyes, which was rare for a kid. Kids were inquisitive, in a way that was almost invasive. Their eyes poked and prodded with curiosity, trying to find the truth of things with harsh edges. But Francisco's eyes were softer. Compassionate.

"Yeah. We call him Cisco sometimes." She turned to look in his direction. "Wish they would hurry up and choose someone already."

"Me too." I frowned. I had come to the park with Aaron and his older brother, but at the rate we were going, the sun would be down before we even played one round of hide-and-seek. The other faceless neighborhood kids were already starting to get picked off one by one by their equally faceless parents. We were thinning out fast. As I cast a glance over to the remaining parents, I noted the appearance of one man. Unlike any of the parents, he had a face.

And he was wearing a dirty corduroy jacket.

He gave a pearly white smile and waved. I looked back to Charlize, but her attention was elsewhere.

The kids around us still argued, but their voices and screams and laughs and giggles all sounded even more muffled. Their bodies blurred, and I could no longer figure out who was whom. Suddenly Charlize ran into the distorted crowd and became just as blurred.

"Wait!" I yelled, trying to follow. But no matter how hard I pumped my legs, I remained in place, unable to take a single step forward. I watched the mix of kids laugh and felt a jab of loneliness in my chest.

"Raquel."

I jumped and twirled on my heel. No one was behind me, not even the faceless parents.

"Hello?" I called out. The voice sounded familiar—off, but familiar. I twisted myself around again, and suddenly all the kids were gone, including Charlize.

But then I saw him.

Outside the park and farther down the block, he was much taller—much *older*—than the child version I had just seen. He was the present-day version.

"Cisco?" My voice lodged in my throat. I started half jogging to him. He was familiar, yeah, but something about him was off.

Wrong.

The corners of my eyes blurred. When I blinked to clear it, there was something just above him, lined on the wall. Black words painted on white: *FALSAS PROMESAS*. The look of it felt ominous, so I focused my eyes on Cisco and tried to keep them from blurring.

As I neared him, whatever felt wrong didn't stop feeling wrong, it just intensified and sat on my chest, constricting my breathing. I stopped short of him and realized I was coughing.

"Raquel," he said again. His voice was off—raspy, layered with dust. It echoed too, as if we were in a tunnel. Something moved behind me, spooking him. His kind eyes turned terrified. Dust kicked up behind him as he ran, and I tried my best to keep up.

"Cisco, wait!" I yelled. Goose bumps and sweat covered every inch of my body. I was so cold and hot at the same time. My chest throbbed with pain under the stress until I slowed to a jog. Then I stopped—and whatever was behind me moved again.

It sounded like a giant insect.

"Cisco?"

Suddenly he was right beside me, grabbing my hand and forcing me into another sprint. His hand was so tight on mine, it pinched.

"Don't turn around!" He hissed. I didn't know when, but the skittering had stopped. "Don't stop, don't turn around, don't get off the train, just keep going."

"Cisco, you're hurting me!" I wheezed. If he heard me, he didn't let it show. He just kept frantically speaking over me.

"It needs a lure, you know? Like a fishing rod or a light bulb. I can't let it! But it's so hard, it's in my head, trying to empty me out, I can't let it, I have to protect her."

"What?" We slowed just enough for me to take in a deeper breath. A shadow fell over us, and he looked up, eyes wide and afraid. Then they met mine.

"Protect Charlize."

Right then, something black and slick dripped from his hand to mine. Slime.

Before I could react, it formed spikes and pierced my palm.

Pain shot up my arm in a blaze of fire.

And then I screamed until I dropped back down onto the futon.

BAD BLOOD

CHARLIZE WAS STILL VERY FRAGILE THE NEXT DAY. BY NOW, people had found out that something bad had happened to Cisco, but the stories varied. Some said he had a warrant for his arrest for assaulting cops. Others said he was involved in some biochemical warfare. Neither made any sense to anyone who knew Cisco.

I scribbled down notes from the smartboard into half-legible sentences. The last thing anyone needed was more speculation, so I kept my mouth shut to avoid feeding the rumor mill.

"What do you think, Raquel?" Aaron asked in a low whisper. "Do you think he's *missing* missing?" The teacher raised an eyebrow at him as a warning, and he pretended to look shamed.

"I *think* we shouldn't be talking about this." I scowled. "Cisco was a good friend of ours, and we shouldn't be slandering his name."

Self-righteousness looked good on me. It was just too bad I didn't *feel* good. Last night's nightmare still had its hook in me. I kept glancing down at the hand that was hurt as if I would see remnants of the slime.

"Was?" He looked at me smugly.

"You know what I mean." I sucked my teeth. "Just because *Mario* had a falling out with Cisco doesn't mean that *we* did."

Though technically, that's what happened. Aaron's older brother Mario was close with Cisco. That's how I met Charlize. Mario had to babysit Aaron, who asked me to come along. It was a train of friends meeting nearly every Saturday for video games, movies, and the park, if the weather was good. It went on like that for weeks, which turned into months, which turned into years. A tradition, practically.

Until, well, something happened between Mario and Cisco. It couldn't have been more than a year ago that the two weirdly split. The first link in our train of friends broke, and the rest of us just never attempted to fix it.

It was odd.

And now, Cisco was gone. But not *missing* missing. No, he was definitely coming back, at least for Charlize's sake.

It was just a nightmare. Cisco's not really in danger, he's just...

"Uh-huh." Aaron rolled his eyes, as if reading my thoughts. "I'm not saying I'd rather him go to prison—"

"Really?" I cut him off. "Because that sounds exactly like what you're saying."

Aaron went quiet for a moment, and I realized I'd snapped at him. "Raquel, are you okay?"

I looked down at my notes. Not a single thing I wrote made any sense. I sucked in a deep breath and let it out.

"My mom's in a coma."

Silence again, but this time, it was a stunned silence.

"You deadass?"

I slowly nodded.

"Oh. Oh, damn. Sorry. Do you know why..."

I shook my head. The doctors were supposed to figure it out, and part of me was content with that. It was the right thing to do. Right with a capital *R*. Besides, Mami wouldn't like it if my grades started slipping. I had to focus to keep them up.

For the rest of class, Aaron was quiet. He didn't say anything at all until the bell rang and we got on our feet to get to the next class.

"Hey, Raquel?" He put a tentative hand on my shoulder. "You know you can talk to me about like...anything, right?"

His expression was awkwardly concerned. *Everything* about this was awkward. I knew he was just trying to be a good friend, but his sympathy made me uncomfortable. When it came to Aaron, I was used to being annoyed, bored, amused, and entertained.

I was not, however, used to sympathy.

I shrugged him off carefully and backed away.

"Yeah," I said. "Sure. Come on, we're going to be late to the next class."

And yet, Aaron didn't let up with the sympathy. The next few classes, he seemed to be walking on eggshells around me. If there was an in-class project, he gave me the easier job. If someone bumped into me, he barked at them to apologize. He went straight to the vending machines to buy snacks when I mentioned I was hungry and then went back to buy a juice to wash it down with.

By the time we were in study hall at the end of the day, he kind of relaxed and turned his attention to the latest rumor about Cisco. Someone knew someone who claimed to know someone from Fordham who said Cisco had been playing with a Ouija board and gotten possessed and that he was wanted for assaulting a nurse at a hospital.

"Okay, none of that sounds like something Cisco would do," I said, raising a hand to interject. "How does Charlize even factor into this?"

Aaron and his friend Alex sat side by side, working on separate papers. Alex typed away on one of the school's laptops, with several tabs open. A cursory glance told me he was distracted by the updates of the Hazel Boon case.

"Oh, it gets worse," Aaron said. "Charlize said that after he left the hospital, he called her, all crazed about some sort of game he played and that he broke the rules. Even yelled about a monster coming after him."

"*Charlize* said this to *you*, or did someone say that Charlize said this?" I raised an eyebrow. I had a hard time believing Aaron would grow the balls to talk to Charlize completely unprompted. He got tongue-tied around pretty girls he *wasn't* interested in.

Which I guess said something about me.

I waved that thought away and waited for an answer. He floundered—and that was all I needed to see.

"Wait—" Alex raised his hand. "There's a video." He tapped a key twice and twirled the laptop around.

"A video of a monster?"

"No. Of Charlize."

The video was grainy, which was just what you'd expect from the MTA cameras. It was at the top of a website called LEAK'D!— one of those WikiLeaks wannabe sites that prioritized free information over authority. Alex pressed play, and an empty subway station came into view. A few seconds passed and nothing happened...until it did.

Cisco fell backward over the turnstile and rolled several times, then he fell onto the train tracks. My eyes widened as I watched him flail frantically. The video cut off for half a second before it came back—with Cisco nowhere in sight. Instead, Charlize jumped over the turnstiles and ran the length of the platform until it dipped into the tracks. I couldn't hear anything, but from the way Charlize was moving, I could tell she was screaming.

The video stopped.

"What the hell was that?" Aaron laughed, clearly uncomfortable.

"He's underground?" I asked.

"Probably." Alex shrugged. "But did you notice?"

"Notice what?"

Alex moved the cursor back to the beginning of the video, playing it again.

"The way Cisco's falling. It's like he's being dragged by something."

GOOD BLOOD

Charlize was hiding out in the bathroom. I knew because I was, too. Once the bell rang and Alex went to his locker, Aaron refocused on making me feel better, and I just couldn't handle being treated with kid gloves.

I sat in the middle stall, my backpack hanging on the back of the door. My phone buzzed with texts from Aaron, wondering where I was at. It was Tuesday, so he knew I had art club at The Point. I told him he didn't need to wait for me or walk with me— The Point was literally only two blocks over. Luckily, he didn't protest. I sighed with relief when I realized he wasn't texting back and shoved my cell phone into my backpack.

Once the rush of students leaving school slowed down enough, I stepped out of the stall just as Charlize did hers.

She didn't notice me, at least not at first. Her eyes were glued to her phone, replaying the same LEAK'D video over and over again as she walked.

I followed her—there was literally only one way out.

She sniffled quietly and kept her head down amidst all the students. Most of them barely noticed her, but she couldn't relax.

Eventually, she felt my eyes on her and looked up with an embarrassed grimace. "Hey."

Hey, I heard about Cisco. That sucks.

Hey, I heard about Cisco. Are you doing okay?

Hey, I heard about Cisco. What the hell happened?

Hey, I heard about Cisco.

Hey, I had a dream about Cisco, and he told me to protect you—

"Hey," I said once my brain stopped spiraling through responses.

Cold air hit us as soon as we stepped out of lobby. It didn't take long until I lost feeling in my fingers and Charlize fidgeted with her scarf. Even now, I could smell the peppermint leave-in conditioner she wore. It was calming, and I finally understood why Papi had camphor scattered around the house. I could practically bathe in the smell now.

"I'm guessing you heard about Cisco," she said sheepishly.

"Kinda hard not to," I said. Charlize chuckled, small and forced and losing steam fast. She tried to blink them away, but the tears came on too fast, and she had to settle for wiping them quickly.

"Do you think I'm making things up too?"

I shook my head and felt heat rush to my cheeks. This whole interaction was making me self-conscious. What was it about pretty girls that did that?

"Do you wanna talk about it?" I asked.

"No."

I somehow felt relieved and yet dejected. Conflicting emotions, but hey, what was I gonna do?

I looked down and sucked in a slow breath.

"Okay, well..." I started stepping around her.

"Wait."

And then she grabbed my hand. It was the same hand the black sludge tore into in my dream, but instead of pain shooting up my arm, it was lightning—a thrilling shock. My heart skipped a beat, and I pursed my lips in a line to keep from making a goofy smile.

"Where are you going?" she asked.

"The Point." And then, because I didn't want her to let go, I went, "You want to come with?"

———

The Point was a warehouse turned community development center near Hyde, just on the other side of a post office. It looked like the kind of building that once mass-produced paper clips or something, but these days a graffiti crew was paid to paint beautiful murals on each wall. Every few months, the murals would change from smiling faces of residents to an entire urban landscape with trains painted like they came straight out of the '70s— covered from top to bottom in colorful and expressive graffiti. The bottom corner would be tagged with the name of the graffiti crew in bright white against solid red. *TATS CRU, The Mural Kings*. If you walked the entire length of the Bronx, you were sure to come across more of their work.

On the inside, there were lots of different activities and services, from art club to book club to movie nights to childcare. It was almost like The Point couldn't decide what it wanted to do, so it did it all.

I sat Charlize down at an empty table off to the side, where a bookshelf met the brick wall. She shrugged off her coat while I ran to the café and ordered her a hot chocolate. That was what you were supposed to give people going through a hard time, right? A hot beverage?

I brought it back to her, ignoring how the heat singed my fingertips.

"Here, drink this."

Her mouth fell open. She blinked a few times, shaking off the surprise, and blew over the rising steam before taking a sip.

"Thank you," Charlize murmured. She fell silent, focusing on her drink as if that were all she could stand to do. Minutes passed before she put down the Styrofoam cup, and I fidgeted as I realized she was about to ask a question.

"Raquel," she began. "Do you know anything about a game?"

"Uh, you're going to have to be more specific." Why did I have to sound so callous? It was like my nerves couldn't differentiate between fight or flight, so it made everything come out harsh by default.

"Hah." Her lips curved upward. "That's what I told Cisco."

I swallowed, thinking carefully about my next words.

"What...happened, Charlize?"

She was quiet for a moment. Contemplative. She closed her eyes tight, and when I thought she would break down into another sob, she leaned back against her seat and breathed deeply in and out.

Inhale. Exhale.

"That's what I'm trying to find out, but so far, I think I'm just getting nowhere."

Charlize's eyes fluttered open, and she stared at the ceiling while I weighed the pros and cons of trying to touch her hand.

Pros: I'd be holding her hand.

Cons: I'd be sweaty and holding her hand.

They canceled each other out, so I stayed put.

"You can just ignore me." She stood up. "This is so stupid anyway—"

"No, it's not."

She stopped in her tracks. The fluorescent lighting of The Point was man-made and the same as every other day, but with Charlize in the center, it came down like it was purely celestial.

She slowly sat down.

"I don't know what else I'm supposed to do." Charlize toyed with a brass ring on her finger. She swiveled it right and left as she spoke, staring down at it with a hopeless expression. "Cisco came to me," she started. "He was all freaked out, crying, a whole mess, and he came to *me*. There had to be a reason for that."

"You two are close," I offered, as if that gave her all the answers she needed. She pursed her lips tight like she was considering this. Then she shut her eyes and swallowed.

"Yeah," she said. "We are."

There was something in the way she said it that made me wonder if there was something else going on. But would she tell me even if I asked?

Quietly, she reached into her pocket and pulled out her cell phone. I thought she was getting ready to call an Uber or something until she slid it across the table. Leaning over, I could see a picture she took of Cisco sometime at night.

"I know it's a bit blurry but..."

My face fell as I saw something like mold inching down his arm. *Mold or slime?* I couldn't tell what would be worse.

"At first I thought was pen ink, but then—"

My chest tightened as I interrupted her. "Did Cisco go to Lincoln Hospital at any point?"

"I'm...I'm not sure? I didn't ask. Why?"

"My—my mom has the same thing. They said she was attacked the other night at the hospital. She's in a coma," I blurted for the second time that day.

Charlize looked up at me, startled, and her mouth fell open.

"Oh my God." Then she reached across and touched *my* hand, and the act confirmed that yes, I was definitely sweaty. "I'm so, so, *so* sorry, Raquel."

I shook my head. "It's fine. You didn't do anything wrong."

"Wait, do the doctors know what it is?" There was hope in her eyes. I could see her thoughts clearly. Maybe Cisco was under some weird brain infection that was making him irrational. Maybe he could be cured.

I tried not to think about the nightmare I had with him. It was just a coincidence, a stress-related dream that took a turn for the worst. In fact, wasn't it better to know Cisco infected Mami? That meant it was something science could cure.

But what if it wasn't? Without meaning to, I squeezed her hand for reassurance.

"Not really," I said, now playing with the toy ring on her finger. The action was somehow calming. "Sorry."

"It's fine," she said in a way that told me it was not. She sighed audibly. "So, I guess we're sort of in the same boat?"

"The 'sudden absentee relative who is infected with strange black mold' boat?" I smiled, weakly. "Sure."

It was probably a little naive to call this "rekindling an old friendship," and I knew this. Still, unlike Papi, who was...Papi, and Aaron, who could be really weird when trying to comfort me, it was easy to talk to Charlize.

The Point was buzzing with childcare until about 6:00 p.m., when parents slowly trickled in to pick up their kids. Then the cafe started closing down, and then the clubs. Charlize and I sat in that corner, both silently wondering what we could do about our situations until our cell phones rang and our parents called us home.

Charlize readjusted her scarf and set out before me. As freezing as the November air was, my ears were overheating when she turned around and waved at me.

"I'll see you tomorrow?"

"Yeah. Tomorrow."

The winds were even colder in the evening, and I hustled quickly down the block to the nearest bus stop, only looking up briefly to avoid colliding with other pedestrians. I glanced over my shoulder every few seconds to watch for an oncoming bus.

Corduroy.

I blinked twice, certain I had seen him, only to slam into someone.

"Sorry!" I stammered. The pedestrian waved me off, clearly in a rush on their own. I focused back behind me. Any sight of corduroy completely disappeared.

"Must've been seeing things," I muttered to myself. "That's all. Just seeing things." I repeated this internally, forcing down the budding paranoia as I went on to the bus stop.

It didn't work.

THE BRONX
WAS BURNING

THE BUS JOLTED TO A STOP, JERKING ME TO MY FEET. I looked around, expecting to see annoyed faces cast in the direction of the driver, but there weren't. There weren't any faces at all. The bus was completely empty, and the skies outside were dark. It suddenly dawned on me that I didn't remember ever getting on a bus, and I peered through the window to see where I was.

It was a Bronx I didn't recognize.

Debris and rubble piled high for what seemed like miles, and the few buildings around were engulfed in flames. Old convertibles sat abandoned on every corner. Their windows, broken. Their tires, stolen.

Dust kicked up with every bit of wind, some of which somehow got inside the bus.

I tried to control my breathing and only gripped the bus pole. My chest got tighter and tighter, racked with something dark and thick.

Smoke.

Patting down my pockets, I quickly came to the realization I didn't have my asthma pump with me. My eyes burned with tears as I crouched down onto the ground. I crawled toward the bus door and pushed, only to be met with resistance.

"Help!" I cried, slamming my hands on the glass again and again. Even through the smoke, I could see there were figures outside. I screamed louder, hoping they would hear me.

"Please...help!" I choked. I blinked rapidly, trying to keep the smoke from burning my eyes, but it continued flowing, and everything around me shifted until I was no longer in a smoke-filled bus—but a building. Fire consumed the walls and raged all around me. The only sound I could hear was the scream of a child in the next room.

I busted inside using my shoulder and covered my mouth with my other arm. The smoke was even thicker in here, but it was flowing out of a window. The yelling was coming from outside.

"*Someone help!*"

It sounded like a small boy.

I crawled through the small opening of the window to get to him. He stood up, body hanging halfway off the fire escape as he waved frantically to the people below.

"Hey, I'm here," I said between violent coughs. "What happened? Where are your parents?"

The boy didn't answer me. Instead, he ran to the other side of the fire escape, still screaming for help. There were crowds of people, all standing around the building, murmuring something in unison. The smoke was too thick to see closely, but none of them moved. They only watched the boy struggle for air.

From the height of the fire escape, the wreckage of the Bronx was even more prominent. It seemed less like the neighborhood I grew up in and more like a war-torn country.

Suddenly the murmurs died down, and the eerie silence allowed me to pinpoint another thing that was off.

There were no sirens from either ambulances or fire trucks. What was going on? Why was there no help?

"Kid!" I called, stepping closer. The metal of the fire escape shook in place, nearly throwing the boy over. I reached out and grabbed his leg at the last second, then brought him down.

"It's too dangerous to do that! Why don't we just crawl down the ladder, okay? I'll help you."

He didn't respond. His body jerked forward with every hacking cough.

"Kid?"

The boy stopped and slowly turned around. Half his face was burned to a crisp. Pus flowed from his right eye and crusted over where his nose should've been. Even the side of his throat had a chunk of meat missing.

His voice became deeper. "Who are you?"

I threw myself back against the wall of the building. Suddenly it clicked into place.

This wasn't the Bronx. This wasn't *my* Bronx.

"*Th*-this isn't real," I stammered, trying to remember how I got here. "It's just a dream."

I wasn't really on the fire escape with a small boy who, by the look of his injuries alone, should've been long dead. I was sleeping on a futon couch, probably thrashing around. Any moment, Papi was going to shake me awake.

Any moment now.

"I'm not real?" The boy's voice dropped even deeper. He came closer and reached a steady hand to me. The moment his fingers made contact against my shoulder, I screamed under a sizzling pain that shouldn't have been possible.

I shoved his hand away and pressed myself farther against the brick wall. He crawled closer to me and cocked his head to the side like he was studying me. The part of his face that wasn't burned was twisted in an awful sneer.

"Did that feel real enough for you?"

Fueled by adrenaline and fear, I planted my foot square in his chest and kicked him back. The fire escape shook under the sudden slam, but I used the momentum to crawl back into the apartment.

The inside was even worse.

Parts of the floorboards were completely collapsed, and others were so weak that any step made a loud groan. A large section of the wall was broken through, revealing unfinished scaffolding and an electrical wire bitten to hell by rats. I ducked underneath the exposed circuits to the other side of the room. The next room was more of the same but with thicker smoke. The heat wrapped around me like a second skin, and my lungs struggled to find air.

It didn't take long before I heard small footsteps gingerly making their way through the previous room. I quickly hid in the nearest closet and looked around for decent weapons to use.

There were none.

"Raquel?" the boy said in a gruff voice. "Where are you? I thought you wanted to save me. Or was that just another false promise?" He let out a mocking laugh, and the sound of crackling fire intensified. The pitter-patter of his feet ran by the closet door. I held my breath even as my lungs suffered from the smoke.

"I've been burning here for decades." He sounded close. "Don't you feel bad for me? Don't you want to *stay* with me?"

My chest tightened, and I dug myself deeper into the closet. A weak spot in the closet gave a sharp squeak, giving away my position.

Fuck me! I stilled in the corner, waiting for the inevitable sound of small feet running over and the closet door slamming open. Seconds turned into minutes. Nothing happened.

I reached up to the knob of the closet door and slowly peeked out. The smoke had cleared. The apartment—whoever it belonged to—was empty.

Carefully, I came to my feet, and a rough pair of hands grabbed me from behind, pulling me back into the closet. I fought against them hard, throwing fists and kicking in every direction. The boy laughed loudly while my hits did nothing. He only sang a mock nursery rhyme: *Fal-sas prome-sas! Fal-sas prome-sas!*

"Raquel?" a familiar voice said.

"Papi?"

"Raquel!"

I opened my eyes—not even realizing I had shut them—and looked up into the jarring white smile of the man in the corduroy jacket.

"*Found you.*"

He grabbed me. I screamed and lashed out again. My fist finally hit something solid just as my feet slipped out from under me and I fell onto a cushioned surface.

"Ow! ¿Raquel, tu 'ta loca?"

I blinked quickly to clear my vision. The smell of camphor and various floral scents took the place of any smoke. Papi rubbed his shoulder, mumbling Spanish curses under his breath.

My chest rose and fell painfully, and I struggled to calm my heart down.

"Sorry," I swallowed. My throat felt rubbed dry. "*I*—I just had a nightmare. That's all."

I pulled the collar of my shirt up over my shoulder again and winced.

"You were fighting in your sleep," Papi said, watching me leap from the futon and run into the bathroom. My reflection pulled the shirt collar an inch to the right and froze.

Oh no.

There was a palm-sized burn mark right at the cusp of my neck.

"Raquel?" Papi knocked on the door. "You okay in there?"

I did my best to hide the burn without touching it too much. Upon opening the door, Papi looked me over with concern.

"You sure you're okay? No weird bruises?"

"No, why?" I said a little too quickly. "I mean, what makes you say that?"

"You were just thrashing so much," he mumbled, backing off. "Reminded me a bit of when you were younger, actually."

Mami never said a word about that. Hell, I didn't even remember having trouble sleeping as a kid. I followed Papi into the kitchen, carefully choosing my next words.

"I had sleeping problems as a kid?"

"Yeah, it was strange. One of your mom's friends was convinced you were being attacked by a demon in your sleep." Papi laughed, a fun little trip down memory lane. I tried not to be offended by it. "I remember she had to drag you kicking and screaming to the altar so the pastor would pray over you."

"Did it work?"

Papi pulled a gallon of milk out of the fridge and reached above it to get a box of Frosted Flakes.

"Sure. At least for a few days. Then you'd go right back to fighting things in your sleep." Papi handed me a bowl of cereal. His expression went sour, as if he just thought of something unpleasant. "And then it got kind of serious. You'd start screaming and wake up with bruises."

"What?" I said, between bites. The sugary breakfast was actually doing wonders in helping me forget about my wound.

"Yeah, it wasn't pretty."

"So what'd you do to make it stop?" Because as far as I knew, it didn't start happening again until last night.

"Hmm." Papi thought carefully. "Actually, I don't think we did much else. Your mother's solution worked, but it was kind of temporary, and I think she didn't like having to drag you back to church all the time to rinse and repeat the whole exorcism." He shrugged. "Eventually, you started sleeping with a few resguardos in your hands. You played with them so much that you always had at least one with you."

"That's...good. Right?" I couldn't tell.

"Pfft, tell that to your mother. Them old ladies at church got on my case for having the little beads around the house. They said it had to be inviting something." Papi paused to slurp down the extra milk. "As far as I was concerned, those beads saved us from a lot of sleepless nights."

I looked down at my bowl. Soggy flakes floated in circles.

"Papi, do you think I'm like...psychic?"

I wasn't sure what to expect. Maybe something like an impromptu lesson about how science only gets us so far and sometimes we had to put our trust in something that goes further. Or he'd burst out laughing, thinking I just made a joke.

"Honestly? Maybe. You have two spiritual parents in opposite directions, I can't imagine you didn't somehow pick something up."

CURSED OR PSYCHIC

"OH YEAH, YOU'RE DEFINITELY CURSED," AARON SAID, biting into a bagel. I slapped his arm hard enough for him to drop it on the table. "What? You asked me for my honest opinion, and I gave it to you. If a creepy kid hurt you in a dream and you woke up with that exact injury, how does that *not* sound like some *Nightmare on Elm Street* shit?"

It did, and that was the problem. My whole life was already uprooted by having a comatose mother—I didn't need to deal with vengeful spirits on top of that.

"That doesn't make sense. *I* didn't kill him. Why the hell would he be after me?"

I crossed my arms and rested them on the cafeteria table before glancing over at the clock. We only had another fifteen minutes before homeroom started, and Aaron wasn't even halfway through his cream cheese bagel. He kept most of the foil on, but I doubted the bread was still warm after dragging it through the cold.

"Maybe it's not about you," he said between bites. "Sometimes spirits are just angry. They want someone to feel their pain."

I've been burning here for decades.

Aaron was probably right about that. I didn't know any kid who'd died trapped in a burning apartment, much less torched a building myself.

Gingerly, I shifted my backpack strap away from the injury. My skin still burned even after pouring tons of aloe vera on it. Moving my arm in any direction was hell, and I breathed through the pain. It sure fucking felt personal, though.

"What the hell am I supposed to do?" I muttered.

Aaron looked thoughtful for a moment. "Start carrying holy water?"

I slapped him again.

"Can you *stop* that?" He was on the last bite of his bagel.

"Can you be *helpful* for once?" I checked the time again—we had another five minutes to hike it up the stairs.

"Well, I don't know, Raquel! It's not like you started messing around with a Ouija board or played that shitty Echo game." He shoved the last bit in his mouth, still trying to talk through it.

"Finish chewing and then talk," I said, disgusted. He followed me through the lobby and double jumped up the stairs. My thighs throbbed by the time we reached the top, but we made it to class before the bell rang anyway.

"I said I don't know why this is suddenly happening to you. Were you always practically psychic, or was this like, a radioactive spider bite situation?"

"Ha." I folded my arms over my chest.

"I'm joking—but seriously. You're like my best friend, and I wanna help you figure this out." He said it so matter-of-factly, my ears ran hot. "And if there's a chance we can turn this into a money-making business," Aaron went on, "I'd like to start sooner rather than later."

"Oh my God." I rolled my eyes and went to the farthest seat away from him. He followed anyway, of course.

"You said your dad's into Santeria right? Something in his house could have triggered it." Aaron took the seat next to me.

"Maybe? He said I was always 'sensitive' to this kind of thing. But I've been to his house before. Why would this happen after such a long time?" Something just wasn't adding up.

"Well, this is the first time you're in his house for a longer time," he proposed. "It could be a proximity and time-based thing. Which I guess would make sense since ya moms doesn't let you go into any botanica. You're hardly ever around that stuff."

He had a point. I thought it was more a conflict of beliefs for Mami when she forbade me from even walking by a botanica. She was Christian, and those places were like dens of the devil to her. But what if she was trying to stop triggering the same thing that happened when I was a kid? It wasn't like I ever thought to ask.

A loud ring chimed through the air just as most of the students plopped into their seats. We glanced at the door, still waiting for Mr. Franco to arrive, but when he didn't, we turned back to each other and continued our talk.

Aaron pulled his books from his backpack, pursing his lips tight. I knew what that expression meant, and I didn't like it.

"What?" I demanded.

He held up his hand defensively. "You have to promise not to get upset."

"I'm already upset."

"Then I'm not telling you!" Aaron said, shutting his book. I pulled the chair over to him before he could put it back.

"Wait..." I sighed, exasperated. "Fine. I won't get upset. Just tell me."

"What if...this is somehow linked to your mom?" He carefully looked up at me as I considered his theory. I could see the flow of his logic. I didn't start having these strange experiences until Mami was in the hospital—and even when I visited her in the hospital, I had yet *another* odd experience. The pale man with black rot just under his skin and mold sprinkling off his hand definitely felt connected to whatever the hell was going on with Mami.

Mr. Franco walked in as the second bell rang.

"Reading period starts now," he reminded us. "No one should be talking for the next forty-five minutes."

I shot Aaron a look, and he only shrugged in response.

Later, he mouthed.

Suddenly my phone buzzed with a text from Charlize.

Charlize

We need to talk. Can you meet me after third period?

My stomach flipped with both excitement and anxiety. I debated all the ways to say yes (yea, yeah, sure, ofc, kk) before just going with yes. Aaron gave me a funny look as I put away my phone, and I pretended like the guilt wasn't fighting my excitement.

It was suddenly impossible to focus on reading.

PRIORITIES

I CHECKED MY CELL PHONE FOR THE THIRD TIME TO MAKE sure I got the location right. A pack of freshmen girls crowded the bathroom mirrors, hogging the sink. Where was Charlize?

"I can never keep my hands steady for this shit," one of the freshmen complained, trying to apply eyeliner. "It's like a whole other level of skill."

"I told you to use a pencil eyeliner. It looks good even if it's a little smudged," said another as she tightened her ponytail and combed her fingers through it. Static made some of it stick up. She applied a fresh coat of lip gloss over her bottom lip and smacked them twice.

After the freshmen left, a stall door opened. Charlize's Shirley Temple curls were braided back, like she couldn't be bothered with it, and a light-pink scar showed under her eye. Her eyes darted around the bathroom before settling on me, and she pulled me into the accessible stall without a single word.

"Charlize, what happened? I got your text, is everything okay—"

She locked the door and looked back at me. For the first time in days, her eyes were dry.

"I saw Cisco."

My mouth fell open. Why didn't she seem happy? Her stare was glued to the stall door, and she pushed her lips out in a pout.

"Wow, that's great," I said, trying to read her expression. "Is he okay? What happened to him—"

"He disappeared."

"Again?" My shoulders fell, deflating. "What the hell do you mean—"

"I need you to listen carefully, and I need you to not judge what I'm about to say next, okay?"

I narrowed my eyes and studied her face. This emotional roller coaster was running me into the ground, but everything in her expression told me she was serious.

"*Y*-yeah, sure," I stammered. "Go for it."

She chewed on her bottom lip thoughtfully.

"When I saw Cisco late last night, he wasn't himself. He was babbling, confused, I had *never* seen him like that before, you know? He kept talking about a game and breaking the rules. At first, I thought it was drugs..." Her voice trailed off. "But he keeps vanishing—like a ghost."

"Like a ghost?" Aaron's theory flashed through my mind. The little boy might not have known me, but Cisco sure as hell knows Charlize.

Cisco's not dead, though.

"Yeah, you know, like he was there one minute, and then not there the next. I turned my back for just five seconds, and then he screamed like he was getting screws drilled into his head, and when I looked back, he was gone."

She stared at me as though I knew what to do with that information.

"You don't believe me?" She scoffed, shaking her head. I didn't say a word.

Instead, I pulled my shirt down to reveal the palm-sized burn.

"I got this in a *dream* last night." Charlize's face went slack at my admission. "My dad told me I used to...see things in my dreams. Like, *Paranormal Activity* type of things. I was really young, so I don't remember much, but..." I pulled my shirt back up to cover it. "Something's happening in the Bronx. I just know it."

Charlize slowly pulled out her phone and scrolled to a picture on her camera roll.

At first, I wasn't sure what I was looking at. The picture was blurred, with someone's hand partially covering the camera. But I could still see it was taken in a park. Streetlights shined off monkey bars in the background, and when I squinted my eyes, I recognized the figure in front.

"Is that Cisco?" I looked closer. His clothes were more than just torn—they were filthy, with dirt and blood caking the lining of his jacket. Parts of his pants were singed black, almost like he had run through a fire himself. But that wasn't what caught my attention.

Right where the jacket crept up over his stomach, I could see it—a black fuzz that dug into his skin.

"Shit." I zoomed into it.

Charlize shook her head and leaned into the door. "Is this the same thing your mom has?"

I slowly nodded and sucked in a deep breath. It was hard to look at Cisco and think about his role in infecting my mom. I still wanted to blame someone—*anyone*—but Cisco wouldn't have done something like that on purpose.

"Do...do the doctors know what it is now?" There it was, that hope in her voice. She wanted me to reassure her, to let her know everything was going to be okay. My eyelids fluttered as I struggled to hold back tears. We hadn't heard anything from them yet.

"I should get back to class—I…"

"Raquel?"

"My mom will be upset if I don't keep my grades up."

"Your mom is in a coma. I think she'll understand if you were too worried to study for once."

Would she? Just a week ago, I brought home a quiz from AP English. Though she was proud that I got a ninety-seven, she furrowed her brow and jokingly asked me what happened to the last three points. I knew she wasn't serious, but in the deep corners of my mind, a soft *Jeopardy!* buzzer went off.

Wrong.

I flattened my back against the wall and shut my eyes. Cisco and Mami were suffering from the same thing. Except Cisco was running around like his head was on fire while Mami was comatose. Those were two wildly different responses to the same infection.

The doctors wouldn't know jack shit about how to deal with it.

"Hey, um." I coughed. "Do you believe in, like psychic stuff?"

"What?"

"Never mind," I said, and we fell silent.

We stood only four feet apart in the stall, but it somehow felt like there were miles between us. Charlize made a point of only looking near me, and I stared at the lining of the tiled floor underneath us.

"So what do we do now?" Her voice was barely audible.

Now that was a great fucking question. The disappearances, the rot that was eating up Mami and Cisco, the man in corduroy, maybe even the boy in my dream—it was all weirdly connected.

"I think…" I furrowed my brow, considering my next words. "We should team up."

A PHOENIX FIRST MUST BURN

Tonight was an El Valle kind of night. The diner was half-full with people enjoying their Caribbean-themed dinner. Papi and I were in a short line of people waiting for their take-out, and everyone in front of us seemed to order enough to feed a parade.

I shivered every time the door behind us opened and let in a brisk rush of air. Papi pretended not to notice, which was bold. I'd argued we should have just had the food delivered, and he said the walk would be good for us.

"So how was school today?" Papi asked.

I shrugged. "It was okay." I felt bad on all accounts. Here Papi was, trying his best to be a supportive father, and I just couldn't give him much to work with.

But on the other hand, I didn't want to talk about how worried I was about Mami or the fear I was suddenly facing. It was all too much, and I was emotionally drained.

Papi hummed to fill the silence. My guilt doubled.

Just give him something.

I perked up and forced the next few words out of my mouth. "I'm working on a history paper about the Bronx."

And just like that, his eyes gleamed with excitement. He coughed, badly covering it up.

"Uh-huh. Gonna talk about the Bronx burning?"

"What's that?"

He laughed at this, and I frowned, a little annoyed he was taking my last bit of effort to connect for granted.

"Wait, you're serious? Wow, what are they teaching you in school? It was a rough time, went on for about a decade. The Bronx didn't used to be all parks and greenways, you know."

I raised an eyebrow. I only vaguely remembered a time before the greenways—the city's attempt at environmental protection by setting aside small trails of trees, grass, and shrubbery. It used to be nothing but concrete before the beautification. I was too young to realize when it had changed, but I appreciated it, nonetheless.

Papi and I shuffled in the line as indoor diners passed by. The savory smell of their to-go containers called to me, but I forced my attention back to Papi.

"Do you at least know what redlining is?"

I nodded. It was the practice of banks avoiding any investment in areas depending on the community demographics (which were usually Black inner-city neighborhoods). I remembered being shown why it was called *redlining* when Mr. Chan took a red marker to a map. Everything inside the red area he drew was shunned by banks, investment-wise.

Everything I had ever known was inside that red.

"Well, a lot of the Bronx was redlined. And after the urban renewal program happened—"

"Nuh-uh." I shook my head again, knowing that look in his eyes. He was jumping into a lecture, and if he threw too many terms at me, I'd never understand it. "Explain that. *Slowly.*"

As I waited, I glanced toward the kitchen. The buffet-style table behind a glass was nearly steaming with arroz con gandules, moro, pernil, and a whole host of other good Dominican-style food. The servers behind them dumped heaps of each desired portion in a Styrofoam container for the customer in front of us.

Papi frowned and tried again. "The urban renewal program was a project to redevelop large sections of Manhattan. It was an attempt to clear out slums and unfortunately displaced thousands in Black and Latino neighborhoods."

I pinched the bridge of my nose. "Was that by any chance led by Robert Moses?"

"Ha! They *are* teaching you something in school!"

I rolled my eyes and waited for him to continue.

"After all those people were made homeless, they had to go somewhere. So they started moving up here. Then white flight happened."

He stared at me, as if waiting to see a spark of recognition in my eyes. There was none.

"The government decided they would help subsidize mortgages for anyone moving to the suburbs—but only if you qualified. And guess who qualified?"

It finally clicked in. "*Ohh*. White flight."

"With the Bronx having already been deemed a bad neighborhood, it gave landlords an excuse to stop maintaining it. There was garbage everywhere, rats running the streets. A lot of landlords sold their buildings to slumlords who did nothing to update any of the electrical wiring...I'm pretty sure these buildings were prewar too, so they were *old* old. And the old electrical wiring couldn't handle new appliances." Papi's shoulders slopped downward. His face went blank as he spoke, as though he were in the middle of reliving it all. "By the time the fires started, New York City was on the verge of going bankrupt. Budget cuts meant entire fire companies were shut down."

"*What?*" My jaw fell open. He jumped at my sudden outburst and gave a nervous glance to everyone looking my way. "What sense does it make to shut down fire companies at a time when fires are everywhere?"

Papi only stared at me with saddened eyes.

"Not everywhere. Just the Bronx." Sensing my sudden grief, he tried to lighten up the conversation. "But hey, it wasn't *all* bad. I mean, at the very least, it was a great time for the Yankees."

It didn't work. My stomach dropped anyway, but before I could think to react, a long-haired server stopped in front of my father.

"What'll you have?"

"Let me get two orders of mofongo with a side of shrimp and salad," Papi said. He carefully thumbed through his wallet and produced a debit card to pay at the register. I stepped back, mentally digesting everything he said. It was a lot of information—way more than I was prepared to hear before ordering food.

White flight. Bankruptcy. Fire companies closed. Something about subsidizing. It was already started to fade in the background of my hunger.

Garlic. Sazón. Slow-roasted pork.

My mouth began to water.

And then, I froze.

Smoke. It was unmistakable. And the familiar smell made my lungs seize with fear.

When the diner around me didn't give a notice to the smell, I knew it was bad.

Was I trapped in another nightmare? I prayed I wasn't.

I reached out and tugged Papi's arm twice while coughing. I almost expected him to turn into the man in corduroy. That's what nightmares did, right? Turn something familiar into something terrifying.

Except he didn't.

Papi looked at me, brow knit together at my coughing fit. He sniffed the air before turning to the server.

"Señora, I think something's burning in your kitchen."

The woman packing our order quickly ducked through a swinging door. Moments later, someone yelled in Spanish and pots slammed together. Then the woman returned.

"Someone burned the pernil," she tutted.

Papi quickly paid for our meal and ushered me out the door. The fresh air, though cold and unappreciated, cleared out any hint of smoke in my lungs.

"You really scared me back there," he said, with a concerned look.

"Really?" I glanced at him. "Could've fooled me."

"Hey, I'm an EMT. I'm trained to stay calm in scary situations."

I bit back a scoff but couldn't stop myself from smiling.

"If it makes you feel better, I was scared, too."

I'd been terrified, actually. The thought that I could be stuck in a fire-and-brimstone version of the Bronx already made it difficult to breathe. I didn't know how Papi managed to survive it the first time around.

Speaking of which.

"Hey, do you have any newspaper articles about—"

"Samuel?" A voice called out. "Samuel, is that you?"

Papi and I turned slowly to see an elderly woman with a portable black shopping cart. She squinted as she came closer.

"Xiomara?" Papi gasped.

"Samuel!" She laughed, and the two embraced. They immediately fell into the sort of Spanish chatter that had decades of history behind it. Name-dropping, inside jokes, inquiries about entire careers. I stood off to the side, awkwardly waiting for them to be done with the whole exchange so I could go home and fill my rumbling stomach.

"Is this your daughter?" The woman pointed to me. "Rachel, right?"

"Close. It's Raquel."

I looked down at the paper bags full of our food. It was growing colder by the second, and my stomach was starting to wage war on itself.

The woman was old enough to be my grandmother, and it made me wonder exactly how Papi knew her. Like he was a mind reader, Papi said, "Raquel, this is Xiomara. She and I go *waaaay* back!"

"I practically adopted your father." She reached up to playfully tussle his receding hair. She was short enough that it was difficult, but that didn't stop her from trying.

"Come on, not in front of my daughter." Papi smiled, sheepish. "Actually, I think it's a good thing we ran into you. My daughter is doing a history report on the Bronx and wants to know more about what we went through."

Before Papi even finished that sentence, Xiomara's eyes lit up.

"What do you want to know?" she asked.

How to end this conversation and go home.

I swallowed my impatience before answering.

"The seventies, I guess. Papi told me a little about the Bronx burning, but he didn't tell me much about how it ended."

"Ah," Xiomara said, a wistful smile on her lips. "Come, let's walk and talk."

Papi fell into step behind us, as though we were getting ready to have "girl talk" or something just as personal. Xiomara eyed me carefully.

"How old are you, Raquel?"

"Sixteen."

"I guess you weren't around for when we protested the fish market."

I didn't even know there *was* a protest against the fish market. That side of the Bronx was so industrial that I couldn't imagine anyone going around there for anything other than the Fish Parade.

"Wait." The thought suddenly came to me. "Does that have anything to do with the Fish Parade?"

Xiomara snapped her fingers.

"Bingo! The Fish Parade used to be a protest against the Fulton Fish Market. We didn't want any more trucks coming into the neighborhood, tearing up streets and making it unsafe to even breathe. But, of course, we lost that fight, and the fish market came to stay. So instead, we hold a parade to celebrate everything that makes the Bronx what it is."

"Is that it?" I asked. She didn't give me any info about the Bronx burning. "What about the seventies?"

"Tell me something," she asked. "What is the heart and soul of the Bronx? What makes us *us*?"

Xiomara was starting to sound like my history teacher. I frowned as I tried to understand what she was getting at, but she wasn't giving me much to work with.

"Your father tell you how it was the slumlords and bureaucrats setting fire to buildings just to collect the insurance money?"

"Seriously?"

She nodded. "And they never got caught."

"*What?*"

She continued forward, and the wistful smile on her face got replaced by something stony and bitter.

"At least eighty percent of housing in the Bronx got burned down, all for insurance money. No one actually responsible was caught. Some people still lived in those buildings. Now, it wasn't a goal to kill people, but you can't really control fire. And those who managed to get out before being consumed, well, they were then homeless."

I stared at Xiomara's face. She was older than Papi and looked like it too, with wrinkles and loose skin hanging from her neck. Her hair was a bob cut and more than peppered with gray streaks. I tried to imagine what she looked like when she was younger—when she was dealing with all the fires. Day in and day out, for ten years. What was it like in the thick of it?

Was it something like my nightmare?

Right now, she looked nonchalant enough, lips curled slightly and eyes staring off into the distance.

Into the past. Somehow, I could see her grief, her anger at the injustice she lived through even though I couldn't know what that was like. I wondered if she was one of those people who lost their homes.

Or maybe she lost people.

We stopped in front of a gated building. Xiomara fumbled with her keys until she found the right one to unlock it.

"No one got caught, but if you read the newspapers, it was only ever our fault."

"So what did you do?" I asked.

She looked back at me one last time with a smile that looked like it held a secret.

"What else does a phoenix do when it's done burning?"

———

After we dropped Xiomara off at her home, Papi and I walked the rest of our way in silence. So far, I had a decent idea what my dreams had to do with the Bronx burning. The little boy said he'd been burning for decades—a hint that even in the afterlife, he's been suffering from the injustice that caused his death. That was one part of the puzzle about the disappearances. Now I just had to figure out the rest.

"You doing okay, m'ija?"

"Hmm?" I looked up. Papi looked worried.

"You've been really quiet. You haven't even complained about how cold it is for the last five minutes." He forced a chuckle. Then he straightened up. "I know Xiomara got a little heavy about it."

"Oh, it's fine," I said, shifting the bag of food to my other hand. "I mean, she wasn't wrong. Though I don't understand what she meant about the phoenix."

"Ha!" Papi let out a laugh. "Sometimes Xiomara can be cryptic, but what she meant was that we had to pick ourselves up. We had to rebuild the Bronx, *literally*. A few grassroots organizations formed. They taught residents carpentry so we could actually renovate our homes. We took special care of it because it was ours. And we had no one else—only each other."

That was depressing to hear.

"I know you don't believe in the spiritual stuff like your mother and I do, but I'd always feel like there was some underlying negative energy around. Like there were ghosts trapped in every brick."

I followed Papi in silence as if he didn't just say something poignant. He was right—I didn't believe in all that spiritual stuff. Not like him or Mami did. But just because I didn't believe didn't mean there wasn't something going on. A darkness that stained the Bronx and infected the people in it.

"You both mentioned slumlords—what are those?"

"Tuh, my landlord is a slumlord," he said, grumbling to himself. Then he cleared his throat and answered out loud. "It's a landlord who does nothing but collect rent money. Doesn't try to maintain the building, doesn't resolve complaints. Eventually the building gets broken down, a pest infestation starts up, and it gets disgusting very fast—so basically, a slum."

I frowned. The outside of his building wasn't maintained very well, but it wasn't terrible. Sure, the heating shut off in the middle of the night, which made the apartment freezing in the morning, the water sometimes ran brown, and the mold in the kitchen was spreading—

Ah. So that was a slum.

When we got inside, he grabbed the bags from me. "I'll heat up the mofongo."

I sat on the futon bed and watched him disappear into the kitchen, where the beeping sound of the microwave chimed clearly. We ate mostly in silence while watching a rerun of *Friends*.

When it was all said and done, he cleared the table and handed me a pile of quilts to help with the heating situation.

"Papi, wait!" I grabbed his arm as he turned back to his room. "Do you have, um, those resguardos?"

"A few, why?"

My thoughts went back to Xiomara and the look on her

face when she told me about all the people who lost their homes. Ghosts trapped in every brick of the Bronx, and how they were likely waiting for someone like me to pull into their pain. I didn't know how Cisco or Mami fit into all of it, but I'd be no good to anyone if I died in my sleep.

Resguardos are protection, right?

I could only hope so.

"Could I get one? Just to carry, I guess?"

He nodded. A moment later, I held a small, blue beaded resguardo in my hand. It shone in the light, and when I gripped it, a strange calmness washed over me.

WELL-RESTED

I WOKE UP COMPLETELY REFRESHED, THE RESGUARDO STILL tucked into my palm. No visions of burning buildings, no little boys with half-burnt faces trying to give me the same trauma. Just a deep and calming rest.

It felt a little silly to bring the resguardo to school. Even if it was for protection. One night of decent sleep couldn't possibly be due to something so small, right?

And yet, I jammed it into my pocket. All day, I would thumb it between my fingers every few minutes, just to make sure it was still there. The strange calmness was gone, but just the fact that the resguardo didn't mysteriously disappear on me was enough to keep me from being on the edge of my seat.

Well, almost.

Aaron and I were headed to our next class when he suddenly stopped short. I skidded into him.

"What the hell, Aaron?"

I carefully stepped around him and rubbed my face, then stopped, too. Two cops stood in the middle of the lobby, nodding along to something Mr. Wade, the guidance counselor, was saying. One of the cops responded, looking quite bored. The other one remained quiet and observed the students making their way to class. But that wasn't why Aaron froze in his tracks.

Charlize stood right beside Mr. Wade. Her eyes were glued to the ground, and she looked uncomfortable as all hell. No doubt the cops thought it was suspicious, because Officer Bored crossed his arms as he spoke. Officer Quiet took half a step forward, trying to block the line of sight of several nosy students.

"What is going on with Charlize?" Aaron mumbled to me. "First Cisco and now cops?"

I didn't have an answer, and the resguardo was no longer helping me stay calm.

Charlize glanced up in my direction, bringing Mr. Wade's gaze to me. He stopped midsentence and waved me over.

"Raquel, could you come here, please?"

Oh, fuck me.

"Aaron, in case anything happens to me—"

"You want me to make sure the news uses the photo of you with the Havana twists and yellow sundress?" Aaron said, under his breath.

"You're the only person who understands me."

I swallowed, following the group into Mr. Wade's office. I felt myself shrinking under the cops' stares. Charlize's stiff shoulder brushed against mine for half a second. She was just as nervous as I was.

Mr. Wade locked the door behind the officers and drew the blinds over the windows. Panic tightened my throat.

"Ladies, please take a seat." Mr. Wade gestured to the cushioned chairs against the walls. Charlize and I shot each other looks and then sat down.

"Now, Raquel, I've been told your mother is, unfortunately, in a coma."

He tried to say this with as much sympathy as he could muster, but I was having trouble maintaining eye contact knowing there were two guns in the room.

"And Charlize," he said, switching the focus of his stare, "your cousin is missing."

I glanced up to the cops, who were still scrutinizing me. Where was he going with this? Cisco was definitely not the first odd disappearance in the Bronx. In fact, until the Fordham kids went missing, the disappearance of anyone with Cisco's brown skin tone was routinely ignored. Sometimes, there would be Amber Alerts but nothing beyond that. It was always chalked up to gangs or drugs or both, even when neither made sense.

Why were they suddenly fixated on Cisco?

"These officers and some medical professionals have reason to believe that Francisco, who made an appearance at the hospital where Raquel's mother works, infected her with something dangerous." Mr. Wade looked between us. "Do either of you know anything about that?"

I tried not to fidget in my seat.

"Not really." I shrugged. Charlize didn't answer.

"You don't seem surprised," Officer Bored said.

Dread dug into my stomach. Was I supposed to be?

"We, uh, spoke about it," Charlize said. "With each other, I mean. We sort of connected the dots ourselves since our families know each other. I mean, if Cisco was sick with something, I'd think he'd want to go to someone he trusts."

She glanced over at me to confirm, and I quickly nodded.

Mr. Wade opened his mouth to say something but then turned around to the officers. "Uh, did you two have other..."

Officer Bored launched into an inquisition. "Charlize, you were the last one to see your cousin. Were you aware of any particularly biohazardous material he may have been carrying at the time?"

Charlize slowly shook her head. "I wouldn't know where he'd get any biohazardous material."

And neither did I. Where was anyone in the Bronx supposed to get something like that? Is that what they thought the black mold was that'd infected my mom?

"Are you sure he didn't at least mention anything about drugs or look strange during your encounter?" the officer persisted.

Charlize shook her head again. Cisco was a free spirit but he wasn't *that* free-spirited—at least not since I last hung out with him. The questions rolled on, all aimed at Charlize and her relationship with Cisco, making me increasingly coiled with anxiety.

I reached into my pocket, but feeling the plastic surface of the resguardo beads did nothing to calm me down. Eventually, I couldn't hold it anymore.

"Sorry, why am I here?" I blurted.

The two cops looked at each other and then back at me as though they'd forgotten I was here at all.

"We need your permission to get into your house," said Officer Quiet.

Which meant they didn't have a warrant, but that still didn't answer my question. In fact, it only made me more confused.

"Huh? Why?"

"If Francisco didn't infect your mother, the doctors need to know if something in your home could have possibly done it," Officer Bored explained. "It's not rapidly spreading, but that doesn't change the fact your mother can't be properly treated if they don't know what it is."

It was starting to sink in. I wasn't in trouble—I was just the only person with access to my house. Papi didn't even have the keys. If I let them in, it could give Charlize more time to help Cisco.

I peeked at Charlize from the corner of my eyes. Though she sat up straight and gave the appearance of a mentally stable teenager, I knew she had to be unraveling. She hadn't been hanging out with her crew lately, and it made me think that it was because she was hiding something. Not to mention, she and Cisco were thicker than thieves. You couldn't get her to give up any *real* information about him if you put a gun to her head.

Sitting up in my seat, I looked back to the officer. "If there was something in our house that got my mom sick, wouldn't I have gotten sick, too? I spend more time at home than she does."

A lump rose in my throat, hoping they would buy it.

The officers gave each other a look and shrugged.

"Probably. But it's your choice either way. We're just trying to rule out the possibilities." Turning back to Charlize, Officer Bored began, "I know you're probably scared for your cousin, but he is the only person who can tell us what is going on. If you see him again, you need to call us. That's all."

Mr. Wade got to his feet and unlocked the door.

"Girls, you should go ahead and grab lunch before the period ends." He followed the cops out.

Charlize's shoulders sagged even as she stood up. I grabbed her wrist before she reached the door.

"Listen, I know you're probably mad at me for not having your back, but I have a hunch about what's happening to Cisco and my mom, and I don't think it's something the police can deal with."

Charlize looked down at me with a glassy stare. She chuckled, low and tired.

"I'm not mad at you, Raquel. I wouldn't want a couple of cops snooping through my shit either. I'm just exhausted." She collapsed back into her seat. "What was that thing you were playing with? I saw you reach into your pocket."

"Oh." For some reason, the thought of showing Charlize the little beaded charm made me feel childish. Still, I couldn't stop myself from pulling it out to show her. "It's just a-a resguardo. Supposed to be something of a protective charm—"

"Can I have it?"

"What?"

She didn't seem like she was joking.

"It's my dad's."

She glanced away. "Cisco showed up again."

My mouth fell open. "What? Seriously?"

"Yeah, don't tell nobody. It felt like there was less of him in there. Like something's eating him from the inside out. He looked like he barely recognized me."

She closed her eyes, head leaning against the back of the seat. The memory of meeting him in my dream cropped up. He said something was trying to empty him out, use him as a lure. I'd forgotten about it because it sounded like absolute nonsense.

But was he actually trying to warn us about something?

"Did he disappear like a ghost again?"

"Yep," she reported. "One minute he's there—the next, just poof."

I didn't get it at all, but I guessed that was sort of the point. Things happening that shouldn't be happening was quickly becoming the theme of my life. I wondered if Charlize felt the same way. Life wasn't making sense anymore.

"Hey," she said, twisting in her seat. She leaned her arm over the back of the chair and rested her head on her hand. "You said you had a hunch about what was happening. Tell me."

"Remember that nightmare I told you about?" I asked, pulling the collar of my shirt down. "The one where I got this?"

Charlize clenched her teeth at the sight of my wound.

"Yeah."

"My dad told me about a time in the seventies when the Bronx was on fire. Like, almost all the time. If it weren't one building being reduced to ash, it was another one. A whole decade where landlords were just setting fire to everything they owned for insurance money."

Her face twisted into something like recognition. "I think I remember doing a history report on that."

"We all are. It's history class." I risked a small smile. "Lots of people ended up dying. People burned in buildings they couldn't get out of. And my dad told me about slumlords—you know what those are?"

"Vaguely."

"He said slumlords were people who were letting the buildings get disgusting. Not doing any maintenance, never dealing with pests and get this—*mold*."

Her jaw went slack.

"Your mom is covered in mold..." She drifted off and was quiet for a sec. "But wait, if Cisco infected your mom with it, how did *he* get infected? He's never been psychic, you know."

"You said there was a game he played and that he broke the rules, right?" I asked. "Maybe we need to find out what that was."

Charlize considered my words carefully then nodded.

"Alright," she said. "I think I might know where to start."

I hoped that whatever it was, we could do it fast. Cisco may still be alive somewhere, but there was no telling how much longer Mami had.

THIRD TIME'S
THE CHARM

AARON STARED AT ME FROM ACROSS THE CORNER STORE. His arms struggled to hold two bags of extra-hot Cheetos and two bottles of AriZona iced tea, and his mouth was agape, eyes searching me for any hint of a joke.

"You're lying."

I'd just told him about going to Charlize's house on Saturday.

"I'm not," I said, a little annoyed. Charlize's cousin was missing and my mom was comatose. Why was the idea of Charlize inviting him and me along for a private investigation so impossible?

Aaron took slow steps toward me, and my eyes darted around the store, looking for the nearest exit. Before I could jump for it, he pulled me into a tight hug, the bags of chips threatening to pop from the pressure. I struggled to push him away.

"You are the best wingman anyone could ever ask for." He finally let go and paced up to the cashier.

"Wingman?"

"Sorry—wing*woman*. What am I going to wear? I have to

look fly, Raquel. I gotta be drippin'. This might the one time I actually ever get to go to Charlize's house—"

He slapped a ten-dollar bill on the counter and turned to me while the clerk counted out his change.

"You've been to Charlize's house before," I said.

"Yeah, but she didn't invite *me*. I was just Mario's little brother then—now I'm Aaron. *She* invited *me* personally," he said, smile widening. "This is *huge*!"

I wanted to smack him upside the head. He was getting all excited about using a missing person's case to score brownie points with the person *related* to the missing person. Did he really lack this much self-awareness? Were all guys like this, deep down?

I followed Aaron out of the store, holding on to my anger with a death grip.

"Oh." He twirled around, looking at me with a hint of curiosity and mischief. "We gotta find someone for you, too."

"For what?" I asked, watching him backpedal and then walk away. "Aaron, for *what*?"

———

I'd been to Charlize's time a grand total of three times in my life. The first time was in the sixth grade, when I was hanging out with Aaron, and his brother promised our parents he would watch over us carefully. He didn't. Instead, he dragged us to Charlize's house so he could play video games with Cisco. At the time, the cousins lived together while Charlize's mom was applying for citizenship. I remember listening to the waves of Creole their parents would speak, fluid and natural, and wanting to learn just so my words could sound as pretty. But it was odd and jagged when I tried, earning me playful teases from the family until I stopped trying.

The second time was when she was moving into a new place and needed help moving boxes. We were in the eighth grade at the time, and Aaron was beginning to fall for Charlize. Since Cisco was helping Charlize move, Mario volunteered, which meant Aaron had to be there. And Aaron had a worse time talking to girls when he was thirteen than he did now at sixteen, so I offered to come and ease the tension. The move took less than five hours, and by the time we were done, I was starting to have weird feelings about Charlize myself.

The third time was right now. She lived on Southern Boulevard, just a few train stops away from where I was. It was a residential area, with large gray and brown buildings peppered with a supermarket and a bodega on every corner. It was one of those places that had damn near everything you'd ever need within a block of you. You would never really need to leave the boulevard if you didn't want to.

I walked with my shoulders hunched, ignoring both the cold wind and the pigeons overhead. The street was a particularly low hum of activity, only a few cars and a bus passing as people went about their business. I glanced up every few minutes to determine how much farther Charlize's house was and if maybe muscle memory was serving me wrong.

I dug my hands into my pockets and trudged along anyway. I tried not to look suspicious, especially since I was doing nothing wrong. But each time the wind blew too quiet or people would walk out of sight, I grew paranoid and walked faster as if being chased.

Eventually, I got to a red-stone building and pulled into the lobby. I quickly texted Charlize that I was here and waited. There were some early morning people starting their day up and down the street, either walking a dog or going for a jog. The sight made me feel better, so I kept my eyes on them until I heard the second door buzz open.

Inside, the hallway was eerily quiet. I figured most people would be at work, but I couldn't shake the feeling something bad was going to happen. I jumped up the stairs two at a time, ignoring the strain in my legs.

Charlize met me at her front door. She had her bonnet still on and wore a pair of Tweety Bird pajama bottoms.

"Hey." She smiled. "You got here quick."

It had been a while since I'd seen her eyes light up. Was it because she was slowly getting excited about figuring out the deal with Cisco...or was she just happy I had gotten there?

Let's not get ahead of ourselves, I thought.

"Yeah, I've been staying with my dad since my mom's, you know, comatose. He doesn't live too far from here."

Charlize's smile fell, and she turned back into her house.

Nice work, dumbass.

I followed her straight to her room. Aaron stood awkwardly by the doorway, both hands behind his back.

"Hey, just so you know." He swallowed. "Mario's here."

My jaw dropped. What the hell?

"Mario's *here*?"

"In the bathroom." Aaron jutted his chin out toward it. I struggled to put together words, completely bewildered, but gave up partway. I took a step into Charlize's room and only doubled back when I realized Aaron wasn't coming in.

"What's wrong with you?"

"Nothing, I just—" He glanced at the door. "Men shouldn't go into a single girl's room."

I scoffed and barreled past him. Charlize was busy applying gel to her hair and pulling it into two Afro puffs. It was the most work she'd done on her hair in days, a sign she had been doing a little better or at least was more energized. Hesitantly, I sat on the edge of her bed. There were piles of dirty mugs in the corner, used tea bags crusting around the edges. An empty container of cup ramen lay on its side next to a bottle of hot sauce.

"Sorry about...everything." Charlize gestured around the room. She kicked a collection of rolled socks under her bed. "I'm usually not this messy; things have just been hectic lately."

I didn't need any explanation. She quickly changed her clothes and did a second check in the mirror.

"You look like you're doing better," I offered. The bags under her eyes seemed lighter.

"Yeah, well, can't mope around for too long. Cisco's still missing, and as you know, the cops are on my ass about whether or not he's engaged in some biochemical terrorism. It's so fucked." She looked at me in the mirror. "Hey, how's your mom doing?"

"Haven't really heard any news, so I guess she's still stable." The doctors had been keeping Papi updated, but there wasn't much to report. Part of me knew I was well overdue to visit her again, and the other part of me was terrified of seeing her worsen. I wasn't religious, but I'd prayed more now than I ever had before, with or without the resguardo. I wanted to bring Mami one even though she would rather have a rosary. Either way, I knew the doctors wouldn't let me get close.

"And you?" Charlize asked. "No more handprint burns?"

"God, no." I shook my head then realized something. "Actually...I haven't been having *any* of those creepy dreams since I started sleeping with the resguardo."

I didn't think much of it at first, but maybe Papi was telling the truth when he said it was protective totem. It was definitely doing its part in helping me get some uninterrupted sleep.

She opened her mouth to say something only to be interrupted by a knock on the door frame. Mario entered, with a sheepish Aaron following behind.

"So where should we start?" Aaron asked, eyes on Charlize.

"Fordham." She said, applying a layer of ChapStick. She smacked her lips twice, reminding me of the freshmen crowding the bathroom sink. "We're starting at Fordham."

Fordham University had three campuses, with one of them being up on Rose Hill, near Fordham Road. The buildings were large, with nineteenth-century architecture and cathedrals. It was also a private university and the only place in the Bronx that seemed to be overflowing with white students. None of us were ever sure how Cisco managed to grab a dorm room at Rose Hill. Most New Yorkers hardly ever dormed at college, since they were close to home and home was so much cheaper. But Cisco did, not minding how much debt he'd be in as long as he could have the "dorm room experience."

I wonder if he ever thought the experience might get him killed.

The train ride over was disjointed, constantly stopping between platforms. When we had to transfer, there was at least a fifteen-minute waiting period before the next train arrived, and we shivered as we huddled for warmth.

"So, Raquel," Mario started. "You got any idea what college you want to go to?"

I blew into my hands and shot a look at Aaron. Where was Mario trying to go with this?

"Uh, no, not really," I said, leaning into Charlize. I didn't realize how close Mario was standing until he got closer.

"Well, if you need any help with applying, you can always ask me, you know." He gave me the kind of lopsided grin that made me wonder if he had a concussion, and I turned completely away, trying to keep from vomiting.

We got on the next train and took the first empty seats available. I sat between Charlize and Aaron. Mario decided to stand instead, swinging around the pole mindlessly. I watched him from the corner of my eye. He'd been best friends with Cisco but didn't seem to be too torn up about his disappearance. Then again, he didn't go to Fordham with Cisco. He went to Baruch College. And it's always been said that time away at college distanced even the closest high school friendships.

Charlize leaned into me, her hand sneaking its way into mine and squeezing. Whatever fluttered in my chest threatened to burst out *Alien*-style, but I was wedged so tight between her and Aaron that I couldn't pull away without making a whole scene. I could feel Aaron watching me through his peripheral vision, and it was the equivalent of a dirty look.

Bite me, pendejo.

The Fordham campus was practically barren, which was understandable. It was early Saturday morning, and it was freezing. I wouldn't be out of bed if it weren't for the current situation.

Charlize led the way, walking with purpose and only looking at each identical building once before moving on. Mario trailed at the edge of our group, and it was becoming obvious the campus itself made him uncomfortable. I wondered if it made him think of Cisco in a different way, like he was stolen first by the campus and again by whatever this thing was. Maybe he wasn't close to Cisco anymore, but he must have missed him.

He caught my stare and gave me wink. *Ugh.*

Charlize stopped at a building with a set of double doors and pulled the handles. It barely budged. There was a card scanner mounted to the doors.

"Shit. They must've fixed this. It used to be broken." She sucked her teeth.

I looked over to Aaron to see if he had any ideas, but he glanced away as soon as our eyes met. What the hell was his problem?

"Excuse me!" Mario suddenly yelled, flagging down a student. He jogged down the concrete path and stopped short of a guy wearing shorts and a sweater.

"Is that guy *not* cold?" Charlize clicked her teeth. "It's freezing out here."

"White people never feel cold," I said, watching Mario and the guy talk as if they were close friends. At some point both let out a loud roar of laughter before Mario pointed at us and started walking. The white guy smiled as he swiped us into the building. I waited until he was out of earshot to speak.

"What'd you tell him?" I asked Mario.

"That we were here to surprise a friend for his birthday party."

Charlize and I looked at each other, raising an eyebrow. "And that worked?" I asked.

"No clue," Mario replied. "He said he was really high off edibles."

Charlize led the way again, just down the hall and turning a corner into the right. Even inside, we couldn't escape the cold, having to pocket our hands or rub them together for warmth. We came to a door that had Cisco's name on it alongside some guy named Amadeus.

Charlize knocked on the door loud and hard then took a step back.

A short moment passed before she did it again, and this time, we heard someone stirring from their bed. "I'm coming..." a groggy voice said.

Another moment passed and the door was pulled open. For a

few seconds, I was sure the guy at the door was Cisco, but I realized I was mistaken.

The guy was tall but thin as a pole and had his hair dyed blond, matching his yellow gauges. Other than height and skin tone, he looked nothing like Cisco. He blinked a few times, getting his eyes adjusted to the hallway light.

"Yes?" he said. His eyes scanned us all and lingered on Charlize's face. It was clear he had a feeling he'd seen her somewhere before, but he just couldn't place it. Charlize didn't seem to mind.

"Hey, Amadeus. I'm Cisco's cousin."

He stared at her for a few more seconds. "I wanna say... Charlie?"

"It's Charlize," she said, pushing past him into the room.

Aaron and I were both too nervous and uncomfortable to do anything other than stand by the doorway while Charlize sat on Cisco's bed. The room was dark, with only a vague outline of furniture and books. Surprisingly enough, it smelled like pumpkin spice, as if a candle burned out of sight.

"Listen, I already told the police everything I knew."

"Yeah?" Mario said, entering the room. He flicked on the light. Amadeus recoiled from it like Nosferatu.

"Well, we're not the police." Mario smiled, strolling over to one of the wooden desks. There were sketchbooks and notebooks stacked everywhere, with Sharpies and other colorful markers scattered. He leaned against the edge of it and looked over to Charlize.

"Look," Charlize said quietly. "I really need your help. I can't tell you what's happening 'cause I know you'll think I'm crazy, and I don't need more of that in my life. I just need you to tell me what you know about the night Cisco disappeared."

Amadeus looked back at Aaron and me. He raised an eyebrow

as if to ask if we were planning to stand there the entire time. Aaron slumped over and walked in silently. I followed, closing the door behind us.

"Alright. Fine." Amadeus rubbed his eyes. "The night Cisco disappeared, he was going off to hang with some of them white kids from his theatre class."

I blinked and looked over to Charlize, who seemed just as surprised.

"Cisco was in theatre?" she asked.

"Well, not acting or anything," Amadeus said. "He just liked building the sets and painting stuff. You know, more of the background work."

She nodded. It sort of made sense. Cisco filled up dozens of sketchbooks with graffiti art and mural designs, though he kept all his ideas tucked away as if they were something to be ashamed of. Painting sets and graffiti wasn't exactly a one-to-one ratio, but I could see why Cisco would be drawn to it.

"He wanted me to come along, said it'd get me out of my shell more, but I had a test the next day that I needed to study for, so I couldn't do it. I asked him what he was planning on doing, and you know what he said?"

We all stared at him in silence.

"He said they were going to try to pull off the train challenge." Amadeus scoffed and shook his head.

"Train challenge? *Wh*—what's that?" Charlize's face twisted in confusion.

"It's one of those dumb internet trends, like Charlie Charlie or like the cinnamon challenge. But this one was about the subway and some ritual you have to pull off at three a.m. or whatever."

I glanced over at Aaron and did a double take. His face was slack, and all color leeched from him. But Amadeus didn't notice and only continued, "I told him that sounded like some demonic white people shit, and he laughed, saying it would help them get into character for some play they were trying to put on. He said he didn't really believe it worked, so he was going along for like, emotional support or something?"

"Heh." Charlize's face was pained as she gave a low chuckle. "Yeah, that sounds like Cisco. He's the kind of person who'd hold your hand through a haunted house experience even if he just met you a few minutes ago. Always wants people to feel safe."

"Yeah, and I think he felt bad for one kid who was having weird dreams," Amadeus said.

My shoulders tensed. "What kind of dreams?"

"I don't know, I didn't ask. But apparently, the guy kept waking up in a cold sweat around two a.m., feeling like he had to get on the next train for some reason."

Charlize leaned over and covered her face with her hands. At first, I thought she was crying, but then I saw the circular motion her fingers were making at her temples. She shut her eyes tight and took in several deep breaths before looking back to Amadeus, urging him to go on.

"When I woke up the next day, he was still gone, but I thought he must've gone out for breakfast." He shrugged. "That was the last time I spoke to him."

I stood silent for a moment, considering. Aaron and Mario likely thought it was all bullshit, but I wasn't worried about them.

I walked over to Charlize and sat on the bed next to her. She was almost a statue, absolutely still. I reached out and grabbed her hand, squeezing it a bit until she looked at me. Her glassy eyes were starting to tear up again, but she blinked them away.

"Sorry, uh." She sniffled. "Do you know the names of the white kids he was with?"

"Yeah, I remember the girl. Amanda Stones. The other two boys I never met, but I heard they dropped out. Went back to the Midwest somewhere to do some *Children of the Corn* shit."

"Where can we find Amanda?" Charlize asked.

"Oh, Amanda's in the hospital."

"What?" I jumped up. "I mean, why?"

"Dunno. Just heard she was frantic and crossed the street without looking. Got hit by a truck and now she's in the ICU somewhere upstate near her family."

We sat there, stunned. My insides went cold, instinct telling me there was a reason to be scared. Looking around, it seemed like I wasn't the only one getting the message: Charlize's eyes were wide, Aaron looked uncomfortable, and Mario's mouth was open.

There was something to be said about how Black people deal with the supernatural. We often avoided it, even if it was an odd superstition or myth. Not many people I knew would ever try to conjure Bloody Mary or use spirit boards. Even lacking experience, a deep conviction told us we were better off not messing around with that kind of stuff.

And yet, Cisco did anyway. It made no difference whether he was badgered by his new friends or not. He got himself sucked into something dark, and now we'd have to follow him to get him back.

"Look, I'd say y'all can stay as long as you need to," Amadeus began. "But I've gotta run errands, and no offense, Charlize, but I don't trust your friends enough to let them stay in my room unattended."

"Okay. Thanks anyway."

We left just as quickly as we came. Charlize walked in such a dazed state that even the cold air rushing through the door didn't faze her.

"Well, that was pointless," Mario said, digging his hands into his pockets as we walked. He curved his shoulders inward, trying to protect himself from the wind. "A train challenge? Who does something like that?"

Cisco, apparently. But none of us said it. We just walked down the path in silence.

What the hell were we supposed to do now?

I blew into my hands again and rubbed them together for warmth. There was no way we were going to do the train challenge since it caused Cisco's disappearance. That wasn't even an option. But what else were we supposed to do with that information? The cops weren't going to use it, that was for sure.

Aaron's cheeks flushed from the cold, but if it weren't for that, I knew he would still be pale.

"Aaron," I said. "What's going on?"

"I think..." He sucked in a sharp breath. "I think I've heard of the thing Cisco did. But it's not called the train challenge—or maybe it is because it's different everywhere. Most people call it the Echo Game."

A game.

Cisco had been talking about a game and rules he broke.

The revelation should've thrilled me, but it did just the opposite. Charlize cut across the grass, and I followed her until she suddenly turned around.

"We have to do it," she said. "We have to do the train challenge."

Mario scoffed. "It's just another internet trend. What good would that do?"

"I need to know what happened," Charlize said. "I know you and Aaron don't believe me, but there's something really messed up happening, and it happened to Cisco, and I need to know why. You don't have to join," she said, turning back around. "But Raquel and I are doing this whether you come with us or not."

Aaron looked at me like I just killed his brother in front of him. I threw my hands up defensively and ran after Charlize. Whatever meltdown Aaron was about to have—he could keep it. I still had my mom to think about, and Charlize needed me. She was really that set on finding out what happened to Cisco.

I needed to make sure she wouldn't end up just like him.

RULES OF THE GAME

Tuesday, Aaron's text came in the middle of class.

Aaron

> I need to talk to u about the challenge

He'd been avoiding me left and right since Fordham on Saturday. He was hoping to get in good with Charlize but then ended up being left behind by both his crush *and* his best friend. Though I'd been annoyed about Mario's presence, I couldn't help but feel maybe I hadn't really done my part as Aaron's "wingwoman."

Then again, I'd never agreed to that role.

But we wanted to do the train challenge soon, and Aaron hadn't said whether he was coming. Since the whole challenge had to be done at 3:00 a.m., Charlize and I'd agreed we'd have to wait to try it the following weekend. The delay only made me worried. Finding Cisco seemed to be the only way to help my mom. I could tell she was getting worse because Papi was being very weird around the house. It got to the point where he couldn't hold eye contact for long and went to bed earlier than usual.

Instead of texting back, I just shut off my phone and paid attention in class. Schoolwork was the only thing that kept my hands from shaking, and I would be damned if I let myself get distracted.

We would have plenty of time to talk after school.

The last bell rang, and I jumped down the steps two at a time, ignoring the yelps of students I bumped into or pushed past. I got to the lobby right when Aaron sent me a second text. I tapped his shoulder and he spun around, his phone still in his hand.

"Oh, you're here," he said. I led the way out of the building and down the street. Students started crowding the first bus we saw, so we skipped it and decided to walk for a bit.

"Actually..." He slowed to a stop. "I'm thinking we should sit down and like...talk about it."

I furrowed my brow. It wasn't like him to be so cryptic. "Okay, how about the library?" It was only a few blocks away from here.

He nodded and resumed walking. The cold November air burrowed its way into my bones, but I ignored it as we continued quietly down the long hill, towards the Bruckner Expressway. Rows upon rows of cars zoomed by, only disrupted by a large truck turning at the light. We stopped as the truck crossed onto the corner, and I glanced behind me.

My breath froze in my chest.

The man in the corduroy jacket stood a few paces back with a wide smile. The people around him didn't give him any notice, as though he didn't exist. In fact, one person passed through him, and he dissipated just as easily as smoke. The smell of it filled my lungs enough to cause a hacking fit, and as my eyes began to water, I heard his voice loud and clear.

"Remember, Raquel..." he said with a chuckle. *"If you're going to play the game, you have to follow the rules..."*

"Raquel!"

Aaron grabbed my arm and waved his other hand in front of my face.

"You okay? You looked scared."

I sucked in air and looked around us again. The man was gone. Aaron didn't seem to have noticed him at all.

"Raquel?"

I quickly nodded my head.

"Yeah, yeah I'm fine," I lied.

What *was* that?

Once the traffic light turned red, we quickly crossed the expressway and made our way to the library. It was a large, red-brick building that stood tall next to a plaza and just in front of a modest cathedral. Across the plaza was a garden of sorts, protected by a black gate and several tall trees. Behind it were a few busts of old priests, all creepily smiling with their hands in various prayer-like gestures.

We ignored the busts and walked through the double doors of the library. It wasn't as quiet as libraries stereotypically were, but that was to be expected. No one was paid enough to enforce an "absolute silence" rule. Instead, adults typed loudly on the two rows of computers the minuscule funding allowed, and students chatted happily while studying or doing homework.

Aaron sat at the last available computer and quickly logged on as a guest. He pulled up a browser and typed furiously.

"Okay, so, this is going to be weird."

"Aaron." I looked at him. "Nothing could be weirder than waking up with injuries from a dream."

"Yeah. Sorry," he said, clenching his jaw. "But look, remember when we were at Fordham and Cisco's roommate said he was doing the subway game?"

"I thought it was a challenge."

"Same shit. Anyway, it wasn't the first time I heard about it."

Aaron brought up a Reddit web page. A few more clicks opened a subreddit about something called the Echo. The forum was similar enough to the usual horror or creepypasta subreddit—a black background with words in stark white. The font resembled a Gothic typewriter, only more legible. On closer look, the background wasn't consistent black. It was a collage of photos—all seemingly taken in the dark. The brightest one was a darkened gray that featured a twisted, spiny creature blurring along the side. None of the photos seemed to repeat.

"The hell is this?" I murmured, reading some of the post titles.

BLITZ ECHO DOCUMENTED

NEW CREATURE IN CATACOMBS??

Чорнобильськевдлуння допомога

FRIEND LOST IN UNDERGROUND BEIJING

青木ケ原エコ はやらないで!!!

Some of the posts were typed in languages I could barely recognize but contained the same sense of urgency. Aaron scrolled the mouse over to the pinned post and opened it before leaning back.

"Go ahead," he said, giving me the space to read on.

The Echo Game / The Train Challenge / The Underground Challenge—whatever you want to call it—is NOT for the faint of heart. If you're here because you're curious about what this means about the fabric of our reality, have been having related dreams, or want to swap theories about what it really is—read on. If you're here because you want to try it yourself—RECONSIDER. Many people have gone missing and presumably died because of this challenge. Those who survived wish they hadn't.
Either way, you have been warned.

***For the sake of theorists, any and all information about each Echo will remain up for speculation. Do NOT spread misinformation as this could get people killed.

I pulled back and rubbed my eyes. They were beginning to water from the glare of the screen.

"Aaron..."

"Keep reading." He sighed. I leaned forward again and continued to read.

To play the game, here are the rules:

1. Before 3 a.m. (but no earlier than 2:45 a.m.), flip a coin three times to decide between two directions.

2. Begin the journey the minute it is 3 a.m. and chant "We are Echobound" three times; continue in the direction chosen.

3. Do not end the journey before 4 a.m. Do not turn around. If you try, you will become part of the journey.

It is our belief that the Echo is living distortions of our past. That means IT KNOWS YOU'RE THERE, so act accordingly.

And that's where the post ended. I scrolled farther down the page, but it only fed back into the other posts. All of them seemed either panicked or contemplative for reasons I didn't understand.

The only thing I did understand was the time restriction. It seemed so odd that anyone from the Bronx would bother being up at 3:00 a.m. if they actually had a choice. The white kids from Fordham were more or less an anomaly, but it fit in with their sense of reckless adventure.

"Well, this wasn't helpful." I frowned, sinking back into my seat. "This doesn't tell me anything about what Cisco went through or why he disappeared." It also didn't explain why he was suddenly bananas, according to Charlize. If Cisco's mind was unraveling, then there had be a reason why. A game-related reason.

"You have to read the rest of the posts."

"The *rest of them*?" I yelled, startling the people around me. I gave them apologetic glances and lowered my voice. "Dude, there are like, hundreds of posts on this website. And a lot of them aren't even in English!"

"I know that," he said, nudging me to look at the screen. "That's why you should just read the posts by the theorists." His finger tapped against a question mark icon. He clicked on it and opened an entirely new page that listed everyone with the icon, along with how many posts they wrote and when they were last active.

"These are the people who really try to make sense of it all because, well, everyone's experiences seem to be different depending on where they are. In fact, I could probably try and contact one..." Aaron bit his thumbnail, a habit he had whenever he was thinking hard about something. "Oh, but definitely ignore any theorist who say they're part of the Called. They're a group who have dreams about whatever Echo they're near. They think their dreams make them special, like they're chosen, but other theorists think they're just being lured."

There was that word again. Lure. Was that why people were disappearing in the Bronx? Because they were being pulled with dreams toward the Echo?

I ran a tired hand through my braids. The more I looked at these names, the less sure I was about the whole thing. Cisco said he broke the rules, and now that I knew what they were, I could see how. They were incredibly vague.

I took a mental note of the website address and collected my bag.

"Wait, I need to talk to you about...something serious," Aaron said.

I raised an eyebrow.

Well, that sounded ominous.

"This is going to come off really stupid."

I waited for what seemed like an eternity before he finally spit it out.

"Why did you blow off Mario?"

"Blow off Mario?" I cocked my head to the side. "What are you—"

And then it hit me. When Aaron brought his brother to Charlize's house, I thought it was because Mario was genuinely concerned about whatever happened to Cisco. But he wasn't. Mario came along because Aaron lied and told him I was into him.

That was why he winked at me.

We need to find someone for you, though.

I was going to fucking kill Aaron.

"You tried to set me up with *your brother*?" I shouted. The library froze, and several pairs of eyes fell over us. I lowered my voice and leaned closer to Aaron. "Are you *trying* to be obtuse?"

"Well, what was I supposed to do? I didn't want you to feel like a third wheel—"

"That wasn't a date!"

"And it's not like you've ever had a boyfriend before!"

I opened my mouth to speak but struggled to know what to say to that. Aaron tried to set me up with Mario. Mario, the kind of person who had a brutal honesty period where he insulted just about everyone who crossed his line of sight. And then, when he got punched in the throat, he cried about people not being able to handle it. He set me up with *that* kind of asshole all because I've never *had a boyfriend before*?

"Or girlfriend!" Aaron said, as though he could see my thoughts connecting. The fear in his eyes told me he was regretting his actions.

"Listen, I just thought this would be a great time for me to try and get closer to Charlize, but I didn't want to leave you high and dry." He swallowed. "You've never even been interested in someone before, so I just thought, I don't know, you'd have more chemistry with a person you already knew. And that was wrong of me to do without any input, but, I mean, it's not like you like Charlize or anything, right?"

I froze. My brain scrambled to find an answer that didn't sound suspicious or out of character, but it was drawing blanks. Nothing could have prepared me for that question. Luckily, my impulse took over, and I slapped Aaron upside the head.

"We were there to help her find out what happened to Cisco, not have a fucking matchmaking session," I said, one hand still clenched in a fist. "And honestly—*Mario*? Of all people, you had to choose the most obnoxious person in the history of the world? That was the worst possible decision you could have made. I cannot believe the absolute gall of you right now." I crossed my arms and stared him down.

"You're right," he said, nodding. "I wasn't thinking. I'm sorry."

A text came in from Papi.

Papi

Meet me at the hospital.

Bile rushed up my throat, but I was thankful for the sudden distraction.

"I've gotta go."

PART TWO

ASTRAL PROJECTING YOUR FEELINGS

Papi was late. I stared across the hospital lobby, waiting to see his bumbling figure come through the front entrance only to be disappointed when a complete stranger walked in instead. Where was he? I checked my cell phone for the fifth time.

"Miss, can I help you?" the security guard asked. He was an older Jamaican man, with only the hint of an accent and a face that was perpetually unsurprised. I shook my head.

"I'm just waiting for my father."

And I was only going to wait for another five minutes. Any longer than that and I was going to call CPS on him for child abandonment.

Ha. Tasteless joke. A very normal response in the very normal situation I found myself in—needing emotional support to see my comatose mother.

I rolled the resguardo between my forefinger and thumb. Just like with the cops, it did nothing to dispel the nausea that rolled in the pit of my stomach.

After another five minutes of Papi being a no-show, I sighed and signed myself into the visitor's log.

"You know where you're going?" the security guard said, in a bored drawl. I nodded and turned down the hall. Somehow, the hospital seemed busier than usual, and it wasn't due to the number of sick people or visitors. It was the doctors. They huddled together with thick packets in hand and prattled off medical jargon as they considered a case. Nurses ran here and there with carts of tubes and gauze, and someone pushed around a sharps container that was nearly reaching the *full* marking.

At some point down the hall, there were fewer people in scrubs and more people in full-on hazmat suits. The hallway was separated with a thin blue line of tape across the floor. Before I could think to approach it, a short woman stopped me.

"Excuse me, do you need help?" she asked. The only part of her I could see were her eyes, peering out of the mask.

"Uh, what's going on?"

"This area has been quarantined due to an infection that may be spreading."

"What?"

A taller hazmat suit called out to her from down the hall.

"The patient seems to be getting restless—"

"Is that my mom?" I said, feeling as though I swallowed my heart. The hazmat suit stood in front of the door to Mami's room. My legs suddenly became lead, rooting me to the ground.

"What's going on with my mom?" My panic rose just as I watched a cart get wheeled out of her room. Splotches of red lined the corners, and my stomach lurched at the sight of it. The woman in front of me cursed under her breath and began to hurry down the hall.

"If that's your mother, we may need you to provide a few samples," she said, tossing her head back. "Stay put and someone will come get you."

The world swirled around me, and my lungs refused to open to the air. I curled my fingers into my arms and tried to steady myself. I needed to stay calm. I needed to keep my cool and stick around because *clearly* I was needed for something. Samples—maybe a blood donation. Did Mami and I share the same tissue type? Was Mami going to need a new kidney? A partial liver?

Did the mold already spread to her heart?

I started to shake uncontrollably as I pulled out my cell phone. But it wasn't Papi I called.

"Hello?" I sniffled. "Charlize?"

———

I curled up in the corner of the bed, hugging my knees to my chest. It was odd to know that I'd be sleeping on one again after all these nights on the futon—and it was even odder to know I'd be sleeping on one that didn't belong to me.

Charlize paced back and forth in the hallway of her home, speaking low on my cell phone. Papi was likely driving her crazy with all sorts of questions. I'd hightailed it out of the hospital before he arrived. I almost felt bad, but he should have just been honest with me about Mami's situation.

I leaned my head against the wall and wondered where Charlize's mom was at. I couldn't remember what her job was, much less her shift hours, but there were likely going to be questions when she got home and saw her daughter decided all on her own that she should have a sleepover. Scanning the room, I realized Charlize had gone out of her way to clean up. There were no more dirty mugs and used tea bags collected in a corner. Her carpet was well vacuumed, and there was even a light touch of Febreze in the air. If Charlize's mom was anything like mine, then she would be happy enough that her daughter had cleaned her room this well.

The door creaked open, and Charlize appeared, looking as haggard as if she'd just fought her way through the Amazon. Knowing Papi, she might as well have.

"Sorry," I blurted.

She shook her head, handing back my cell phone. "It's normal for parents to be worried. He just wanted to know that you're safe. You look like you're deep in thought."

Charlize propped herself up on a pillow. She reached over to her nightstand and grabbed the plastic bowl of candy. It was her version of give-hot-beverages-to-calm-upset-people and, if I had to be honest, I liked it better. I popped a Tootsie Roll into my mouth and focused on the sugar rush it gave me.

"There's just a lot to think about." I shrugged. "It's clear that Cisco tried the train challenge and broke the rules—which may or may not have been the reason why he's—"

"Deranged?"

"I was going to say *losing his mind* but potato, po-*tah*-to." I swallowed the candy. Even the man in corduroy tried to warn me about the game.

If you're going to play it, you have to follow the rules.

But who was he? And what did he want with me? I had a hard time believing it was for anything but a malicious reason.

"Oh, and Aaron found something online that *could* be the train challenge, except it's called the Echo Game. I'm still not sure, but whatever it's called, it's really hard to understand. Has Cisco said *anything* to you that might give us more of a hint about where he is?"

Charlize shook her head, looking down at her single Reese's

Cup. She bit it in half. "Said something about a monster in his head, but he was barely coherent."

A monster in his head—the posts on the Reddit page mentioned monsters, but I didn't read enough to know what kind. The Echo Game seemed to differ by a lot depending on what part of the world you were in, so maybe the same could be said about the monsters. Or did he mean he was being made into a lure, to trick others to play the game? Was he still fighting it?

I sighed.

"What about you?" she asked. "Your dreams reveal anything? Or are you still sleeping with the resguardo?" I'd felt silly about it, like I was sleeping with a security blanket or surrounded by an army of stuffed teddy bears. But Charlize made it sound normal, and I wasn't sure if I felt sillier for sleeping with the resguardo or for thinking something like that *should* be embarrassing.

Either way, I only shook my head.

Charlize looked thoughtful as she savored the other half of the Reese's Cup. There was a slight spark in her eyes, and she glanced at me with a questioning look.

"What?" I said.

"Would it help if we did a séance?"

"*What*?" She started to repeat herself, but I stopped her. "I heard what you said. I want to know if you suddenly lost all the melanin in your skin because that was the whitest suggestion you've ever made."

"Just hear me out!" she said, jumping to a seated position. "Clearly there are ghosts involved. And *you're* basically psychic. What if instead of waiting for Cisco to come around back to us, we tried to reach out to *him* instead?"

Her logic was sound, but there was a slight problem.

"Cisco is *alive*, Charlize. Séances only work with dead people, and the last dead person I interacted with gave me a second-degree burn." I tugged my shirt over my shoulder for stronger effect. The aloe vera I slathered over it was doing its job, but I knew I'd still be sporting a scar in its place. "Besides, how would you even make sure the one we contact doesn't take over my body? We don't know what we're dealing with—if even one more thing goes wrong, we're fucked."

Charlize chewed on her bottom lip, ruminating. Without another word, she got up and sprinted in the direction of the kitchen. I listened to wooden cabinets creaking open and slamming shut before she returned with a one-pound container of iodized salt.

"I heard that if you sit in a salt circle, it'll keep you safe while you astral project."

"I'm going to astral project? What happened to your séance idea?"

"Well, like you said," she began, "séances only work when you're trying to contact dead people, and Cisco is still alive. If you astral project or shift into another dimension, you might be able to find him and figure out what's going on."

I stared at Charlize in bewilderment. She was fully committed to doing whatever we could to help Cisco and my mom.

"Fine." I grabbed the salt out of her hand. "But good luck explaining to your mom why my head is literally spinning if anything goes wrong."

I took my time laying down a salt circle and casually looking over at Charlize, hoping that she would backpedal. She didn't seem to care about how she'd have to vacuum her carpet all over again. She only unwrapped a Jolly Rancher and sucked on it noisily.

"Wait," she said, the moment the salt curved into a semicircle. She stood up and grabbed the salt, extending the length of the line. "You gotta make it big enough for both of us."

My face burned as I realized the meaning of her words and looked around. Her bed took up most of the room. If she planned on being in the circle with me, she'd have to be close, and I wasn't sure my heart could deal with that.

Charlize didn't notice how flustered I was and smiled.

"What, do you think I want some ghost or demon latching on to my body while you stayed safe? Fat chance."

Then she sat within the other end of the salt oval.

We spent the next half hour sitting in silence while I tried to concentrate on the idea of stepping outside my body. It was hard to focus with Charlize's knees pressed against my own and her soft hands holding mine. My palms became sweaty and gross. I wondered if she noticed.

My heartbeat was so loud, it drowned out every one of my thoughts. Even when I tried to remember the smell of smoke and burning charcoal, my lungs only took in the scent of lavender, making me all too aware of where I really was. Even when I envisioned stepping out of my body, I couldn't think of where I would even *want* to go. The only mystical place I had ever been to was the burning Bronx, and I wasn't eager to revisit.

Eventually, we stopped trying. Charlize left to grab the vacuum and I pretended like I wasn't feeling pathetic.

"Sorry," I mumbled.

"What? No, don't be sorry. It's fine." She waved it off like she wasn't actually set on her idea. Like it was just a joke. She kept a polite smile on her face as she ran the vacuum, and I scrambled to find something to say or do that would comfort her.

"A-Aaron said he's going to try and contact someone about the game that Cisco played," I stammered. "The train challenge, or the Echo Game, which is what the subreddit called it."

"Can I see the subreddit he found?" she asked.

I ignored the stab of jealousy as I pulled up the page on my phone. "It's different everywhere, so we might not really know what we're getting into."

Smooth. Why not tell her the game is a portal to Hell while you're at it?

"Why's it called the Echo Game?" she asked, resting her chin on my shoulder.

"The challenge makes you go through an echo of the place you do it in," I mumbled, cheeks heating up hotter than the sun. "Each one is supposed to be specific to the location and a moment in history."

She let out a sharp breath. "Okay," she said, pulling back. The polite smile was gone and replaced with a contemplative one. "So, Aaron's going to contact someone who might know more about it. That's...nice of him."

She disappeared to put back the vacuum cleaner, and I sat on the bed, racking my brain for any idea of what she might be thinking. When she returned, she joined me with a funny look on her face.

"Hey, just wondering, I hope it's not a stupid question, but like..." Charlize crossed her legs. "Have you ever *liked* someone before?"

I choked on a Jolly Rancher.

"Sorry!" She smacked my back as I coughed.

"No, no," I said. "I mean, it's okay. I'm just—why would you think that's a stupid question?"

"I don't know." Charlize let out a nervous laugh. "I guess it's 'cause you seem, you know. Like you're above it all. Romance, the drama—you seem like, really neutral about it. Am I wrong?"

Dead wrong.

But I couldn't say that. Her large eyes were glistening, and the longer I looked into them, the more my stomach fluttered. It was distracting.

"Well, if it's okay, could I just ask you for some advice?"

The alarm in my head rang loudly. Charlize wanted to ask me for advice. *Me.* The same person who couldn't get over myself long enough to be honest about my feelings. The same person who would sooner hand her over to Aaron because that's just how things are *supposed* to be. There's a bro code, you know, and how could I, Raquel, go after the girl that my best friend has been in love with since forever?

"Uh—"

"I have this friend that, uh. I kind of like. And I say *kind of* because we haven't spoken in a long time. Not deeply anyway, not since we were kids."

Was she talking about me or Aaron?

Obviously Aaron.

"And I just don't know if they're into me. Like, maybe I'm misreading all the signs, because lately they've just been so nice to me and going out of their way for me."

Me or Aaron?

It's Aaron.

The voice in my head was rational. The pulse in my hands, which were getting sweatier by the minute, was not.

"But what if they're only being nice to me because of the whole situation with Cisco? I don't want to mess up the opportunity to get to be friends with them again by assuming they have any feelings for me."

My heart was now lodged in my throat. What was I supposed to say to this? That I could relate? That I was going through the same thing? That would only out me in a second, and in the worst way possible—to the source itself.

"Um, how about you just…don't say anything?"

If it's Aaron.

"Really?" she said, her expression unreadable. Was my mind playing games, or did she sound crushed? I scrambled to pick up the pieces.

"Well—not *verbally* or anything. You could express a lot with your actions, and if the person is smart enough—" *Aaron is not.* "Then they'll pick up on it and show you back."

Was this solid advice? I hoped this was solid advice. Considering how fast my pulse was vibrating, I was having trouble concentrating on breathing, and my lungs were struggling to catch up.

"Wow," she whispered. I waited for her to respond or say anything else, but she didn't. She just fell silent, brow knit together in deep thought. Then without warning, she pulled me in for a hug. The smell of fresh mint filled my nose, and it dulled my own senses when I took it in. I awkwardly patted her on the shoulder until she pulled away.

"I'm glad we're friends again. Like we used to be, I mean. I wasn't sure it was possible."

"I think it is," I said, forcing the synapses in my brain to quit firing so damn loud.

"I don't know." Charlize laughed. "It's just that you and Aaron always have this…vibe around you. Like you two are the closest people to each other and no one else can get between you."

"Oh," I said, the guilt spilling over into my stomach. "Sorry."

"No!" Charlize shook her head. "Don't be sorry. It's nice. It kind of reminds me of…"

Her and Cisco. She wouldn't say it, but it was obvious in her eyes.

"Yeah," I said. "I know." I squeezed her hand before I even realized I was holding it. I froze in midpanic, but she didn't seem to mind.

A long moment passed before we decided to get to bed.

LIES AND CONSEQUENCES

THE WALK TO MY DAD'S PLACE THE NEXT DAY BEFORE school was almost more anxiety-inducing than the walk to the hospital. I clenched my cell phone in hand, well aware Papi had sent several text messages through the night. I didn't answer a single one and eventually shut it off for my own sanity. Now I was realizing what a bad idea that was.

Papi's apartment building stared at me as I approached, the windows wide with judgment. I ignored the way my legs shook and hopped up the steps. I lifted a tentative fist to the door and knocked a few times.

Seconds went by with only silence. I knocked again, and this time, I heard Papi thump around until he swung the door wide open.

He looked worse than I thought. He stood at the door with red eyes and a deep-set scowl. The smell of beer clung to his shirt, which was stained at the collar.

"*Entras,*" he said in a gruff voice.

I tried to walk in with my head high, but my spine quickly

weakened at the sound of the door slamming. My pace quickened as I entered the living room. Beer bottles collected in sets. The stink of the alcohol masked any remnants of camphor.

"I cannot *believe* the nonsense you pulled last night. Do you have any idea how worried I was?"

"*You* can't believe?" I snapped back, my anger rearing its head. "Papi, how long have you known about the quarantine at the hospital?"

His mouth clamped shut.

"You were *so* worried about me that you didn't think to tell me anything about Mami's condition worsening."

"Do not turn this around on me—"

"Why not?" I stepped to him. "Papi, I can deal with not having any internet to do my homework. I can deal with eating nothing but takeout every single day. But I will *not* be lied to about Mami."

I shook my head, tears pricking at the corners of my eyes. I didn't want to cry. I didn't want to be upset at all. How was it that Papi had a way of pulling my emotions out of me like entrails until I was a mess?

He was right about me being sensitive—he was just wrong about how.

I wiped away my tears with the back of my hand and sniffled loudly. A pair of gentle hands fell onto my shoulders and pulled me into an embrace.

"I'm sorry, m'ija." Papi kissed the top of my head. "I didn't mean to keep things from you. I just didn't know how I was supposed to tell you."

"You c-could have warned me," I said with a hiccup. "At least said something about her being quarantined."

I looked up at Papi's grimace. Regret shined in his eyes as he rubbed my back. The motion reminded me of the time I got the flu as a kid. My nose was so stuffy, I cried because I was certain I was going to suffocate in my sleep. Papi had rocked me in his arms, rubbing my back until I drifted off, and when I woke up, the congestion had subsided.

"You're right. I could have tried." Papi patted my head and pulled away. "From now on, I'll be one hundred percent honest even if I'm one hundred percent awkward."

And he would be. But it was better than nothing.

"So, your mother is...well, she's not doing too well. Whatever she's got is getting worse, and it's contagious, so they really have to limit the amount of people who interact with her. Because they don't know how to treat her, the last thing anyone needs is more people in her state."

I took in a deep breath. "What are they doing?"

He sharply exhaled. "A lot. More than I even know as an EMT. Trust me, the doctors are doing everything they can to save your mother."

They're doing everything they can.

"Papi, I'm scared."

"I know, m'ija."

No, he didn't. The doctors were doing everything they could, but I was just sitting by, twiddling my thumbs, letting everyone else do research and prepare for the scariest freaking challenge I'd ever heard of.

"It's okay to be scared, but you have to know that you're not alone in this. The worst thing you can do is believe you're alone in this. It'll paralyze you. You can be scared as long as you know you don't have to face it alone."

Christ, Papi didn't even know what he was telling me. I went from feeling bad about Mami to feeling bad for keeping Papi in the dark.

The guilt would have to be dealt with after the challenge.

"Okay." I sniffled, wiping away the last tear.

"Also, you're grounded."

"*What?*"

PRETTY GIRLS AND WICKED GAMES

I HAD TO HAND IT TO AARON. HE'D COME THROUGH. NOT only did he find someone who had done a version of the challenge, but he managed to convince them to talk to us about it. After he had shown me the subreddit page, I went into it myself and tried to ask around for veterans of the game, but no one was willing to step forward.

Unlike me, however, Aaron was persistent.

On Thursday, Charlize walked close to me as we approached Aaron's building, making it hard for me to concentrate on anything other than her. My only other thoughts were on whether Papi would find out I lied about going to the library today. Him having no Wi-Fi was my saving grace in getting out of an early curfew, but I didn't want to use that excuse too much.

"So I've been thinking about the Echo Game," she said. For most of the journey, she was silent or humming to herself, but now, she piped up as if this were a normal comment about homework. Then she looped her arm in mine, and the action was so sudden, I nearly stumbled.

"Y-yeah?"

"Like, are there *good* Echoes? Are there some games where its literally just a walk in the park, maybe a memory of someone's wedding?"

"I...don't know."

Charlize nodded and bit on her bottom lip thoughtfully.

It made me wonder what it would be like to bite it.

Focus.

I cleared my throat. "All I know is, it's not exactly like traveling to the past because that would just be time traveling, which would have a whole laundry list of implications. Paradoxes and all of that."

"Paradoxes and all of that," Charlize repeated in a teasing voice. "But it's something *like* the past, right?"

I nodded. "It reflects a period of time over and over again like a broken record, only distorted."

Which made it worse.

On the subreddit page, I'd read posts about Echoes at Aokigahara Forest, Chernobyl, Paris's catacombs—none of these were particularly cheerful places to visit. And what was an internet challenge without the very real possibility that one could die?

There were dates of when people attempted their individual journey to the Echo and dates of when whatever the horrific incident in history occurred. Aokigahara Forest was surrounded by question marks for the simple reason that suicides continued to happen there almost daily. But Chernobyl, like so many other places, had a specific point in history where everything changed.

There weren't any posts about the Bronx Echo, which made

me wonder—at what point in history did the Bronx change for the worse?

Just as we reached Aaron's building, Charlize turned to me, and the corners of her mouth turned up in a small smile.

"Thank you." She leaned in and placed a soft kiss on my cheek.

I suddenly felt like soaring through the clouds and kicked myself for it. What was it with pretty girls that they could make you feel on top of the world with just a simple kiss?

Charlize didn't seem to notice I was frozen. She leaned on my shoulder and filled my nose with the scent of her peppermint conditioner. It was minty, something that normally calmed me, but not right now. It made me think of camphor, which made me think of Papi, and thinking of Papi made me think of Mami...

I blinked rapidly and tried to shoo the thoughts away.

Aaron's was one of those apartments that looked like a single-family house, except it wasn't. It was two apartments in one small building, separated by a single hallway and a staircase. The staircase smelled moldy even when it was spotless due to leaky pipes in the ceiling above. I always passed around it, paranoid it would one day collapse.

Almost as soon as I knocked, Aaron opened the door.

He was still in his sweats and looked like shit. A disposable face mask sat under his nose and his eyes were bloodshot. He sniffled loudly and coughed into his elbow.

Charlize entered first, smiling at him but keeping her distance.

"Are you sick?" I asked, although it was obvious. He shut the door behind me and coughed again.

"Yeah," he replied. Even his voice was hoarse. "Flu season."

There were loud gunshots, and Mario's laughter rang through the living room. We walked in to see him clutching a PS4 controller. Charlize gave a half wave, but he didn't even notice we were there.

"Mario, we got company," Aaron said.

"Huh?" Mario glanced at us. "Oh, hey. Didn't know y'all were coming." He made no move to end his game. Aaron sighed and led us into his bedroom. It was obvious Mario wasn't taking this seriously.

The only empty seat in the room was a chair at Aaron's desk. His bed was a mess of used tissues and various shounen manga. The clutter of empty mugs on his nightstand sat right beside a stack of old PlayStation 2 disks he never bothered to preserve in the original cases. They were all probably nonfunctional as a result of all the scratches, but even if they could be scavenged, Aaron's PlayStation 2 broke years ago. He only kept the video game disks out of nostalgia.

Despite being an awkward conversationalist, Aaron was and would always be sentimental.

"Would've cleaned up a bit, but as you can see, I'm sick as fuck," Aaron said, collapsing into bed. He crawled under the blanket and curled into a ball. The only exposed part of his body were his eyes.

"You don't look so good," Charlize said. "Are you sure it's just the flu?"

Aaron shrugged. "I just feel like I'm dying."

I winced at his words but tried not to let it show. Instead, I walked over to Charlize and grabbed Aaron's laptop from his desk. He slowly sat up as I brought it over.

"Did I miss anything today?" he asked.

"No, not really," Charlize said, hugging her backpack on her lap. "Though I *did* hear that if even a single student at Hyde disappears next, they'll be implementing some sort of curfew."

It was the newest rumor floating around, and normally I would've ignored it, but the source was a teacher. The teachers were just as concerned as the parents about the sudden disappearances. They had their own theories about why it was happening though, and it had less to do with kidnapping and more to do with kids running away.

Anyone who acted up in school was sent straight to the counselor's office instead of detention. It was their form of trying to solve the problem instead of treating the symptoms.

"*Pfft.*" Aaron chuckled. "As if anyone is going to follow that. They're doing too much."

"Right?" Charlize laughed. Heat rushed to my cheeks. It was the first time Aaron was actually being somewhat normal around Charlize—and Charlize *liked* that.

My heart plummeted to the ground. Sure, pretty girls could make you feel like you were flying with a kiss...but they could also kill you with a laugh.

I struggled to keep a straight face as Aaron twisted his laptop around to us.

The laptop showed a paused video, with a young brunette frozen in fear. Her eyes were wide, and tears ran down her face. Her jaw was set, as if she were trying to keep herself from screaming. It was hard to make out what was going on around her. It was dark, and she looked like she was in some sort of a tunnel.

The image was grainy, but there was no mistaking the terror in her eyes.

"This is Olivia. I watched her video the other day," he said, speaking mostly to Charlize. "There wasn't much in this video, since most of it was blacked out, but it starts with her and her four friends and then ends with just her in a corner."

"This is the girl who agreed to talk to us?" I asked.

He nodded. "She's from London and was trying the challenge in their own subway. Obviously, it didn't end well."

Aaron turned his laptop back to himself and typed again. "She's agreed to talk to us on Skype, but try not to freak her out. Apparently, she's been real anxious lately."

She and I both.

I exhaled through my nose and wiped the back of my neck just as beads of sweat started to form. The heat was blazing, likely for Aaron's benefit, but for us it was torture. I glanced at Charlize, tempted to take her coat from her and offer to hang it up somewhere, but that felt like something Aaron should do.

"God, it's so hot," I said, pulling off my coat dramatically. "Aaron, I know you're sick and everything, but it's practically a sauna in here." With a nervous laugh, I tossed it on the floor.

"Oh." He blinked. "Sorry, uh. I can take your coat if you want," he said, turning to Charlize. Any guilt I had was overcome by a sense of irritation. I wished Aaron had more common sense. Then maybe I wouldn't be suffering like this.

"Sure." Charlize pursed her lips in a smile as she shed her coat. She didn't know that Aaron was in love with her or that her smile was all he needed to be happy.

I bit the inside of my cheek and turned my head to Aaron's screen. Skype was booted up. Olivia sent a message that she was ready anytime we wanted to start, so I stepped over and pressed the call button.

"Hey!" Aaron said, with Charlize's coat in his hands. But then the call went through.

Olivia was a wreck. In the video, her hair had been much longer and curled in beautiful waves. But now, it was dull and stringy, like she couldn't be bothered to keep up appearances. She had deep bags under her eyes, and her lips were badly chapped. Thin lines of red etched into where her lips split.

Her room was encased in shadows, but her pale face was

illuminated by her computer. Every few seconds, her eyes would dart around as if she were seeing or hearing something that scared her.

"Hello?" she said, forcing her eyes to face the screen. Her voice was even more ragged than Aaron's. "So, I'm guessing this is Raquel and Charlize."

"Hey." Charlize stepped forward. "Thanks for talking to us about it. We're feeling a little bit out of our depth."

"That's because you are." Olivia coughed. Her arm jolted up to scratch her shoulder, revealing short, bloodied nails. "You are *way* out of your depth. If I were you, I wouldn't even do the challenge. It's cursed. Worse than any urban legend or scary story you can find on Reddit."

"We—" I glanced at Charlize. "We don't have a choice. People have been going missing. We need to bring them back, but we don't really know what to really expect. There's not a lot online about it except for the rules. What can you tell us about the train challenge?"

Olivia chewed her bottom lip, looking off to the side. Her eyes were wide and clear enough to see our reflection in them. She took in a slow breath and spoke.

"Everywhere is different. I don't know the history of your location, but maybe you do. If you don't, you need to learn it. When I did the challenge, I was in the Tube with my friends. The tube only operates here from five a.m. to midnight, so when we started at three, we jumped onto the tracks and started walking. We didn't think anything was going to happen, just a bloody hour-long walk and—" Her voice cracked, dipping into a breathless sob. She covered her mouth and looked down as she cried for a few minutes.

Then she looked back up. "You're only supposed to go in one

direction for the entire hour—did you know that? We didn't. My friend Erin decided she was going to turn back. She was drunk when we started, but I guess when she sobered up, she realized how creepy and awful it was. But you're not supposed to stop or turn around before four a.m. If you do, if you try, the Echo—it *keeps* you."

Olivia broke down into another quiet sob.

Aaron glanced at me, with a look that said, *What is she even talking about?* and I shrugged.

Olivia sucked in a deep breath. "We started running into other people. Thought it was a prank at first because, why would anyone walk along the tracks at three a.m.?"

That was literally what you did, I wanted to say, but she continued.

"It started off with maybe one or two people. It was dark, because it's a bleeding tunnel—so we couldn't see them clearly. Then there were ten. Twenty. Every couple of minutes, we heard children laughing. My friends and I started holding hands because we were so scared—except one friend. Miles. He started going up to people, trying to talk to them. He even pushed one and that's— that's when he realized he fucked up."

She dragged down another breath. "When he touched them, when he really *felt* them, he could tell they weren't alive. It was like touching a water balloon, he said, that's how waterlogged these people were. And because he touched them, they knew *he* was alive—and they went after him." She shook her head several times.

"There are the people who are a part of the Echo, almost like ghosts. And then there are the people who tried to play the game and got stuck here. Do you know what happens to people who stay there too long? No matter what happens, they don't die—not really. But they're never the same again. The Echo already claimed them, so they don't need to eat to survive. Their personality gets warped. They're either too violent or too skittish, they don't notice when they're bleeding, they don't notice how much time passes by. They could spend a whole year there and never know."

"Why are you telling us this?" Charlize asked. She sounded chilled.

"Because I need you to understand that the Echo, *your* Echo, isn't just going to be a walk through a silent graveyard. There are things in there that shouldn't exist—monsters that will hunt you *down*, and the worst thing is you won't even know what it is until it stares you in the face." Olivia sniffled. "In the Echo here, I rediscovered the Blitz personally. I have *nightmares* about bombs dropping—I literally feel it pulling my bones apart. I don't sleep anymore. I'm too afraid to shower because I think I'm going to drown. And guess what?"

She looked straight me, and I realized just how dry my throat felt.

"What?"

"I followed the rules. I got out alive—but just because you do doesn't mean it's over. The Echo will keep following you, keep trying to call you back, to *warp* you. All the theorists say the Echo is like a pocket dimension or whatever—but really, it's more like a wild animal."

She stared at us with dead eyes.

"And you never want a wild animal to have your scent."

FUCK AROUND

There was another thing I had to figure out fast before any of us could play the Echo Game—namely, how I was going to sneak out of Papi's house without a set of keys. The plan went against every fiber of my goody-two-shoes, follow-the-rules, get-perfect-grades being. Was it so bad to just sit around and hope the doctors would figure it out? Maybe even Cisco would come back on his own, fully cured and with an explanation that did not defy logic.

Deep down, I knew that wouldn't happen.

I wasn't proud to admit I considered crawling out the window like a misbehaving suburban teen in a movie, sneaking out to a party. Except, in the Bronx and just about every single apartment in New York City, windows came with thick, metal window guards. I sure as hell wouldn't be able to get past that. And even if I could, I'd have to crawl back in the same way and hope no one would call the cops on a suspicious Black person attempting to enter an apartment window.

I'd have to figure out another way to go without Papi noticing.

It had only been a few days since I'd been grounded, but I

could tell my punishment was a double-edged sword. No TV meant an unpleasant meal in silence followed by me pretending to read a book I had already read.

This time, Papi didn't even try to ask how my day was or what happened in school or if I was *sure* I didn't need more help with my presentation. He just ate his fried plantains and tossed our plastic plates away when we were done. I lay back on the futon and cracked open *Heart of Darkness*.

"Ahem," Papi coughed. He held something out in his hands, and when I looked, my eyes widened. "I, uh, thought it was time to get you your own set of keys to this house."

It was just three brass keys connected by a silver ring. Papi pointed to each key and explained which lock they were for before he handed it to me.

"Oh, thanks," I said, a little caught off guard. Part of me was glad I didn't have to suffer in the cold anymore, waiting for him to open the door. The other part of me was wondering if this was a sign that I'd be staying much longer than I'd like.

"I'm proud of you, m'ija," he said, kissing the top of my head.

My face twisted in confusion. "For what?"

"Well, I know this change in your life hasn't been easy. Aside from your little stunt the other day, you've been taking it all in stride. You've certainly been keeping it together better than I have."

"Keeping it together?" I said, incredulous. I didn't like to acknowledge my crying stints, but that didn't mean they didn't happen.

"The operative phrase is 'better than I have.'" He laughed. "When I was your age, any slight stressor could have sent me into a drinking binge."

At my age, his whole world was falling apart. I couldn't even imagine leaving one country for a borough where the buildings were always in flames.

I outlined the keys with my fingertip and smiled. "Thank you, Papi."

"You're welcome." He stepped over to the TV and snatched the remote before clicking it on. "And now I officially declare your punishment over!"

That was fast. If Mami had been in charge, my punishment would've had no end in sight. I blinked, knowing what I had to do.

"So...does that mean I can sleep over Charlize's house?"

"Again?" He frowned but kept his eyes glued to a rerun of *How I Met Your Mother*.

"She and I are good friends," I pleaded. "And it's nice to be around another girl again."

Papi tried to hide the flash of hurt he got from the low blow. To save him the embarrassment, I pretended not to notice.

"Okay, fine," he mumbled. "But you have to let me know in advance."

"How about tomorrow? It's Saturday."

———

It was time. Tonight, we were going to play the Echo Game.

When Charlize's mom swung the door open, she was still dressed in a blazer and dress shirt. She was sort of like my mom, in that she was a busy woman who was rarely home.

She stared down at me for a few seconds before turning her head back and yelling into the hallway.

"Charlize! Your friend is here!" Then she turned back to me. "Come on in..."

"Raquel." It felt odd smiling, but every impression with her was a first impression.

"Raquel." She smiled back. "Nice to meet you."

She wore her hair even shorter than Charlize's and just as curly. Her accent was just as thick as when she moved off the island.

I walked into the house, my duffel bag slung on one shoulder. A dull pain radiated through it, a testament to how much I was carrying. Inside were a bunch of snacks, a single change of clothes, a few empty beer bottles I stole out of our trash can, Papi's good knife, and a small metal bat for good measure. Carrying weapons made me anxious down to the last atom. My inner moral compass felt smashed to bits.

I'm going to save Mami and help Charlize, I tried to convince myself. *That's always the right thing.*

I held the duffel bag tightly to my side, quieting any amount of noise the bottle and the bat could make, and walked briskly to Charlize's room.

"Hey, you made it," she said, opening her door with a smile.

"Yup," I said, pushing past her. The bag was killing me worse than the social niceties. I all but moaned with relief when I finally put it down.

"Okay, we'll be in my room, Mom!" Charlize called out as she closed the door. She dropped her voice to a whisper immediately. "What the hell are you carrying?"

"Weapons," I hissed, opening my bag. I pulled out a few of the beer bottles and set them aside. Her jaw dropped open. "What, you think we're just gonna waltz in and out without any problem?"

"I thought that was the plan!" She crossed her arms. "Remember what Olivia said about her friend, Miles? He started messing around and got got! If the monsters see us with weapons, do you think they'll just decide to play nice? They're *monsters*."

"Okay, well, do you wanna be caught running around the Bronx Echo without the ability to defend yourself?"

She eyed me carefully, glancing between the weapons and me like she was damn well considering it. Then she saw reason.

"Okay, well don't have them all out like that, put it back!" she said, running over to me. We sat side by side and rearranged the contents until the bottles no longer smacked against each other. The sound of the clacking reminded me of the resguardo Papi gave me—and I realized I had accidentally left it at home. I sucked my teeth at my own carelessness, and Charlize looked at me with worry.

"I forgot my resguardo."

"Would that have helped?"

"Well, it couldn't have hurt." I pouted. I wasn't brave enough to start sleeping without it in case those nightmares came back, but even I couldn't be sure it wasn't just the placebo effect. I pulled the handle of the metal bat up. "I got a bat, too. What are you gonna bring?"

Charlize looked around her room, probably trying to find something weapon worthy. Her nightstand had an array of perfume bottles and lotions, and three teddy bears sat in the corner of her bed. The only thing that carried any weight was a textbook left open on her pillow. She walked over and picked up a body spray and looked at me sheepishly. I rolled my eyes and grabbed the knife from my bag.

"Here, use this," I said, unwrapping the towel from around the blade.

Her jaw dropped. "Why do you have that?"

"Because it's the only knife in my house that actually cuts. I like to live, so I brought it with me just in case," I said, throwing the towel on it. I was growing a little concerned that Charlize might not have my back in the face of monstrous uncertainty. I wasn't even sure if she'd been in so much as one fight.

"Okay. Fine." She exhaled, still eyeing the knife. "I'll take the knife when we go."

"Good." I smiled. "In case something goes straight after you, you'll need something that'll do the most damage."

"Can't argue with that," she muttered. She sat back down on her bed and grabbed the nearest teddy bear. It was white with a red ribbon tied around its neck, and she squeezed it in a tight hug. "Still can't believe Aaron's not coming with us. I thought that as involved as he was in finding Olivia, he'd want to be part of this."

I ignored the guilt rising in my throat. I was sure he *did* want to be a part of it, but we were running out of time. "He can't help the fact he's sick. The way he is now, he'll just be a liability."

Charlize twisted her lips in thought and nodded. "So what do we do now?"

"I'm glad you asked," I said, going into my bag once more. I quickly brought out a bag of Oreos, Tostitos chips, and salsa. "I brought some snacks since we'll need to keep our energy up."

Charlize smiled softly. "That sounds great," she said in a low voice.

I cast my eyes down at the snacks and let my shoulders drop. Somehow, it felt less like a fun sleepover snack and more like a shitty last meal before an execution. My chest tightened, and I moved to put the food away.

"Sorry," I said with a nervous laugh. "I didn't even ask if you liked any of this stuff."

"No, it's okay," she said, grabbing my wrist. Heat rushed up my arm and settled in my cheeks. She pulled my hand gently and took the bag of Oreos. "I was just thinking...Cisco loved Oreos."

She froze.

"Loves. *Loves* Oreos." Her voice hitched in her throat, and she turned away from me, trying to hide the tears.

"Charlize?" My heart fell into the pit of my stomach.

"He hasn't come around in days." She waved her hand frantically over her eyes. "The last time I saw him was in the park, and he was *really* losing it, Raquel, like, he was worse off than Olivia." She wiped away a single tear, sucked in a deep breath, and forced a smile. "Sorry."

"No, don't be sorry." I turned to her. "This shit is *real*. You know that, I know that. I'm not going to judge you for being afraid or crying. But I *will* judge you if you decide to back out now after I did all this research."

She laughed and smiled a real smile. Charlize pushed me over, and I reached up to jab her playfully in the side. She fell on top of me and tickled me back until we were a mess of giggles and wiggling bodies. Eventually our momentum slowed, but Charlize didn't move. She stared at me, her eyes half-lidded. The gentle look sent my chest exploding in flutters.

She leaned down ever so slow, watching me watch her. Our noses touched.

And then I pulled away.

Her expression became unreadable as she helped me up.

A tornado of questions spun around my head.

But I didn't ask because I was a coward.

Instead, I opened the bag of Oreos and took one before offering it to Charlize. She grabbed one, and we sat in silence, twisting our cookies in half and licking the cream center.

"We should get some rest," she said.

PART THREE

PART
THREE

IT BEGINS

THE ALARM WAS SHRILL AND LOUD NEXT TO MY HEAD, nearly jolting me out of my skin. I forced my fists to uncurl as I slapped at it repeatedly.

After the third swipe, my phone silenced itself, and I let out a deep sigh. I checked the time. 2:10 a.m.

Time to get going.

I slowly rose to my knees and crawled over Charlize's sleeping frame.

In other circumstances, I might've felt happy. The last time we were this close was during our soccer team's training camp. We slept on hardwood floors in the middle of a cabin, all in a circle. Now, Charlize slept deeply with a hint of a smile on her lips. Her hand was just next to her face, curled with her nails just grazing her cheeks.

I reached my hand out and—nothing. I stopped in midair. Then I slid my socks on.

Turning back to Charlize, I whispered, "Hey," and pressed my hands into her back. "Hey, it's time to go." She rolled to her other side until I applied more pressure and shook her.

Her eyes peeled open, and she groggily pushed herself up onto my shoulder. Her forehead was cool against my neck, and I tried not to shiver.

"Come on," I whispered again. "We can't be late." She said nothing for a few seconds but then became more animated. I focused on tying my shoes on and collecting my duffel bag. The beer bottles still clanged against each other but less so, and I carefully lifted the bag as we tiptoed out of Charlize's room.

Her mom's bedroom door was closed, but we could hear snoring through the walls, loud and consistent with each breath. Charlize undid each lock on the front door in slow succession, pausing each time to hear for evidence of a waking mother. When the snore didn't interrupt, she undid the next one until we could step out of the house. She locked the door in slow succession again and then we bounded down the steps without another word.

It shouldn't have surprised me, but the world seemed to drop thirty degrees at 2:00 a.m. After just ten minutes of walking down the street, I was less concerned about the rattling of the beer bottles and more concerned with the rattling of my bones. My teeth clattered, and I immediately regretted not layering up more efficiently.

Charlize eyed me. "You okay?" She was dressed much warmer with a scarf on top of her jacket and a wool hat.

"Yeah, I'm fine," I lied. I pumped my legs faster, willing my body heat to travel as much as my blood. Charlize struggled to keep up with me, but she didn't complain. Once we reached the bus stop, she grabbed my arm and pulled me around.

"*Wha—*"

I was instantly cut off by her wrapping her scarf around me. She used the leverage to pull me in.

And then she kissed me. I froze at her soft skin against my lips. Time slowed to a complete stop. I didn't want to move for fear of shattering the reality of the situation, but I didn't have to. When she pulled back, Charlize continued to tie her scarf around me, even tucking it into my jacket for extra warmth.

A loose strand tickled my nose, and when I breathed in, I could smell Charlize around me.

"I can't believe we're actually doing this," she whispered.

"Me neither." I didn't know what she was referring to, but the sentiment was still the same.

"You really should invest in a scarf," Charlize said. She wouldn't look me in the eyes.

"*I*—I have one," I stammered.

"Uh-huh."

The bus rolled to a stop just then, and we climbed on, one right after the other. The bus driver nodded at us as we paid our fare. They either didn't think two high school girls being out past 2:00 a.m. was strange or just didn't care. There were worse things to be concerned about at this hour.

Charlize and I sat in the back. I gently placed my bag down on an empty seat and basked in the toiling heat of the bus. I tried not to notice how Charlize's leg pressed against mine. I fiddled with the straps on my duffel bag and fought the impulse to glance over at her. If she even looked like she was having second thoughts about the Echo Game, I'd wimp out and neither of us would get the answers we'd been stressing over.

For a moment, we were both silent, and then Charlize shifted in her seat.

"I'm tired. Wake me up when we get there." She rested her head on my shoulder and looped her arm around mine. I all but became a statue, keeping so still that I had a hard time believing I was even breathing. The kiss had only lasted half a second, but I could have sworn I experienced cardiac arrest in that half second.

I wanted to ask her how she felt, what did this *mean*, was she open to talking about it, and also was I a decent kisser?

But first we had to survive the challenge.

I mentally apologized to Aaron and sucked in a deep breath.

Charlize kneaded herself into me and yawned.

"Can't sleep?" I chuckled.

"Can you blame me?" she said with a jab. "We're literally on our way to hell."

I stared out the window with a sigh. Finally, the bus rolled to a stop.

As we exited onto the avenue, I thought about the rules of the game.

1. Before 3 a.m. (but no earlier than 2:45 a.m.), flip a coin three times to decide between two directions.

"Let's choose between the two train stations. The six train and the two or five train," I said. "The rules aren't too specific, and I think that's just so people can adapt them to their own location like with Olivia and the Tubes in London." She said they only ran between 5:00 a.m. and midnight, and so the only way to enter the Echo there was to walk along the tracks in one of two directions.

Charlize quickly nodded as I checked the time. The minute it became 2:45 a.m., I pulled out a quarter.

"Heads or tails?"

"Heads on six, tails on the two or five line," she said, just as it smacked the pavement. We cornered the coin, peering in the dim streetlight.

"It's tails," I said. "Guess we're heading up to Simpson."

Avenues were always long in New York, but Hunts Point Avenue felt like the longest in the cold dark. We walked in total silence and huddled close against the wind. I slid my phone out a few times, checking the time. We were going to make it just fine. The wind chill was torture, and by instinct, we elongated our legs to rush out of it.

Charlize bumped into me a few times until I realized it wasn't an accident. Even with her hands in her coat pocket, she held her elbow out toward me, nudging me repeatedly until I looked at her. Then she smiled reassuringly as if her life weren't in danger at all.

Something in me recoiled from that. It seemed stupid to pretend like we weren't afraid. I felt it in the thick of my bones and the pit of my stomach.

Maybe she is afraid, I thought. *But she's not alone. She's facing it with me. Like Papi said.*

My teeth clattered, and she laughed again just as we made it to the end of the boulevard.

I looked up, only partially surprised at how fast we made it to Simpson. The subway stairs were rusted with chipped paint, and while that was the normal for any subway station, tonight it felt like an omen.

We climbed the stairs and made our way to the turnstile, hopping over it with ease.

2. Begin the journey the minute it is 3 a.m. and chant "We are Echobound" three times; continue in the direction chosen.

With just two minutes to three, I squinted my eyes down the tracks at a moving body. In the distance, the train gearing up to us was lit with a green circle. It was a five train, and at the rate it was moving, I knew it would arrive right at the start of the challenge.

"Hey," Charlize whispered. "Let's flip the coin again."

I blinked at her. "Why would we—"

She smiled, but in the dark of the night, it was less comforting and more alarming. "I just want to see something. Do it before it comes!" she urged, and I impulsively tossed the coin in the air.

"Heads is the two train, tails is the five train!"

The quarter bounced off the ground twice before clattering flat. I hurried over to it, hearing the train approach the platform. George Washington's rusted head shone when I picked it up, and I twisted myself around to announce the result.

"Well, this says it's going to be the—"

"Two train," Charlize said from far behind.

"How'd you—"

I followed her line of sight to the approaching train. The green circle that lit up a five was now red with the number two in the center. Charlize's smile hardly faltered, and I realized why. She wasn't being nonchalant. She was terrified. She wanted me to toss the coin again to assuage her fears and prove this was all bullshit—but it wasn't.

The Echo was real, and it wanted us to visit.

The double doors slowly opened with a chilling beep.

This is a Flatbush-bound two train... The robotic voice spoke clearly over the wind.

Despite my fear, adrenaline shot through me, and my feet took quick steps forward until I was safely inside the train car. I looked back at Charlize, who was rooted to the platform. She was still smiling, but her eyes were brimming with tears.

"Charlize, hurry," I said, holding out my hand. Her lips began to quiver and curve downward. She shook her head, and I held my breath, waiting for the beep to signify closing doors.

It never came.

The realization hit us both—the journey had already begun.

Charlize couldn't turn around without risking death—or something even worse.

Don't turn around.

"Charlize, come on," I choked. "*Please.*"

Her entire body shook as she slowly placed her hand in mine. I pulled her into the train car and glanced down at my cell phone.

The time was 3:00 a.m.

"We are Echobound," I began chanting in a hushed voice. To my surprise, Charlize immediately joined me. "We are Echobound, we are Echobound."

For a second, nothing happened.

Then the automatic voice spoke again, clear as a death sentence.

Stand clear of the closing doors, please…

The doors slid shut.

There were only three rules. Three rules to live by for the next hour if we wanted to survive.

3. Do not end the journey before 4 a.m. Do not turn around. If you try, you will become part of the journey.

My mind ran through several things. Olivia managed to escape the Blitz Echo only to be plagued by terrors she couldn't have ever imagined. Her friends were never found, consumed by the Echo and part of their own journey forever.

As Charlize and I sat side by side, I wondered which was worse. She glued her eyes to the ground, fearful of what was coming. I stared out the window and watched as the train ran straight into darkness.

One minute down, fifty-nine to go.

3:02 a.m.

THE TRAIN CAR WAS EERILY EMPTY. I FIGURED IT WOULD always be empty at this time, but that didn't make it any better.

I gripped the end of my bat as Charlize sat next to me. She unzipped her coat and pulled out the towel-wrapped knife I set aside for her. Her hands shook, but her face was stoic—ready for anything.

"What happens now?" she asked, peering up to the windows. Our faces reflected in the darkness.

"We have an hour." I swallowed, remembering the rules. "We stay on this train for a whole hour. We don't say a word to anyone who gets on the train or do anything to them."

In fact, the less we interacted with any otherworldly passengers, the better. I couldn't begin to imagine what Olivia's friend went through the moment he started getting chased through a dark tunnel, and here, there was only so much space to run through. The weapons I brought were really just a last resort kind of thing. Hopefully we wouldn't need them at all.

The train left the station, but the world outside the windows stayed dark. It shouldn't have been possible—this part of the line was aboveground. After Simpson Avenue came Intervale, and the Intervale stop overlooked a supermarket on one side and a wall of apartment buildings on the other. At the very least, we should've been able to see the projects peeking up over the horizon and graffiti decorating the top of other buildings, but there was none of that. It was just consistently pitch black. A darkness that wouldn't exist in New York even in the dead of night.

We slowed to the next platform, and the train doors slid open with a beep. Charlize and I held our breaths, and despite the unknown sitting on the other side of the tracks, it made me feel better to know that I wasn't the only one feeling apprehensive.

"Do you hear that?" Charlize said. I listened closely. There was nothing. "The automated message is gone."

Goose bumps flared on my arm. She was right. There was no automated voice telling us where the train was headed or where we were currently. I looked up to the blinking line map, but the lights on it were off. Not even the usual *this is a Flatbush-bound two train* message scrolled across the top. We might as well have been off the tracks.

Maybe we were.

The train doors closed before taking off again. I noticed how smooth the transition was. It was normally a bumpy ride, with sudden jolts and jumps, but now, we were gliding.

The next stop came with something new.

A passenger. Her heels clicked onto the floor, and she hummed a song to herself, unaware of our presence. She wore a lightly stained navy-blue jacket. The sleeves were singed black, and the smell she brought with her made it obvious why.

She smelled like charred meat.

"Is she, you know..." Charlize whispered to me, trailing off when the humming stopped. The woman's head slowly turned to our direction, sending a new wave of fear through every inch of our body.

Her face was partially melted off. Her ear was welded into her cheek, and it was hard to see where her lips ended and where the lining of her gums began. The part of her smile that was still intact curled up, and she continued her song. It took me a moment too long to recognize it as "The Girl from Ipanema."

3:18 a.m.

THE TRAIN RIDE CONTINUED JUST LIKE THAT, WITH DECAYING people getting on and off at various stations. Some were burnt to a crisp, others were melted, and some had bones poking well out of their skin, twisting and turning in ways that should've made it impossible to move.

"Falsas promesas..." the Passengers hissed every few minutes. They were quiet until a switch inside them flipped, and it was all they would mutter. "Falsas promesas...falsas promesas..."

For a while, we sat frozen, but once it was obvious the Passengers would do nothing to us as long as we did nothing to them, we relaxed, our bodies sinking farther into the seats in an effort to keep to ourselves.

Charlize's leg jiggled in anticipation. It was obvious the whole train ride was just going to be that—a train ride. We would get off within the next hour, no worse for the wear but shaken by the senseless deaths people in our own hometown had experienced.

At some point, a Passenger brushed by my leg. Their memories flooded through me—bullets tearing through my body, rough hands slamming me against the ground. The last memory I was left with was the image of a police badge.

The person moved on and my stomach lurched the minute I could take a breath. Charlize wrapped her arms around me. She was frowning, startled but confused by my intense reaction. She didn't know. She wasn't experiencing death every time someone so much as grazed her shoulder.

God help me if the train ever became crowded.

I kept my eyes on the ground, watching every pair of feet get on and off the train car. I silently hoped a pair would belong to Cisco. The sooner we found him, the sooner we could get some answers. It would be great if we didn't have to suffer through another trip. I just wanted to exit the train at 4:00 a.m. and pretend like the whole challenge didn't exist.

The train grew silent as it emptied. Another person got on, and I knew immediately the worn-out loafers didn't belong to Cisco. Eventually, my eyes wandered up the feet and onto the full figure.

Like every single time before, he was emaciated. The skin on his bones somehow hung off and clung to him like bedsheets wrapped around a person. His eyes bulged out, and his hair grew matted and in patches. Bits of white peppered his dark skin in an ashy display and balls of lint were coming off his clothes.

If it weren't for the fact I knew that corduroy jacket, I would have just assumed this was another homeless person.

He stepped to the seat right in front of us. A large roach crawled out of his pocket and onto his pants, and when he sat down, an audible crunch and short squeal sounded.

"What was that?" Charlize whispered. The man in corduroy shifted his eyes from me to her. I pulled her closer, gritting my teeth in anticipation.

"You don't want to know."

When I looked up, the man smiled at me.

"You're here, Raquel."

3:22 a.m.

CHARLIZE'S FINGERTIPS DUG INTO MY ARM. I DUG MINE into the bat.

"And who's this?" He looked back to Charlize, baring his pearly white teeth.

"What do you want?" I asked.

"Wish I could say." He leaned forward. I did the same. "I just don't remember."

He laughed. The brief thought of slamming the bat into his temple crossed my mind. I shook it off, knowing it would just make matters worse.

"Raquel, who is this?" Charlize whispered. The knife she held was pointed outward, ready to stab if it became necessary.

"This is the guy that's been haunting me," I said, grinding my teeth. The image of me bashing his head in over and over again wouldn't leave my mind, and he laughed again as though he knew it.

"Did you think Olivia lied?" he asked. "You're never really done with it, even when you're done."

"What is he talking about?" Charlize said. "Raquel?"

I shook my head, clearing it as best as I could. Fear and paranoia swam through me, making it hard to focus.

Is this what happened to Cisco? Did confusion take over his mind?

"Raquel?"

Charlize's voice pierced my thoughts. My hands formed fists instinctively. I struggled to loosen them.

"What the hell is going on?" I growled. Even my voice sounded violent.

"What do you mean?" The man in corduroy said. His smile disappeared and malice collected in his stare. "You wanted to enter the Echo. Well, here you are. Try not to get lost in it."

My body twisted forward, dumping the contents of my stomach between the man's feet. Charlize fell to her knees next to me and pulled me close. She held my head firm between her hands and looked into my eyes.

"Raquel, say something," she pleaded. "Please."

"Something..." I said, and the man's laugh tumbled out again.

"Something's not right." I said, nausea taking hold in the pit of my stomach. "I feel sick."

"Don't worry!" The man's voice came out like a chime: light and ringing in my ears. "Even if you die here, you'll never really *die*. People always come back. Like me. Like Cisco."

Charlize jumped to her feet, and I wrapped my arms around her waist, pulling her back. She struggled hard, and I immediately regretted the knife I gave her.

"Let go!" she screamed. "I'm going to kill him!"

The laugh was like an echo itself, and it rang through my head again when I tossed Charlize back. She scrambled to her feet, huffing and puffing, with the knife still in her hand.

"Thank you, Raquel," the man said mockingly. "But you should know your friend can't kill me. I'm already dead."

I used the train seats as leverage to stand up. Charlize slowly shuffled over to me, and I gripped her hand tight, bringing her eyes to my stare.

"Don't...do...that," I breathed. Neither of us knew what would happen if she attacked him, even if he *did* technically come to me first. The Echo's rules were vague, but the consensus was still the same—don't touch anything if you could help it. The people—or monsters—here were vicious.

"Why did he say that about Cisco?" she said, sucking in air. "Cisco's not dead."

Charlize sounded so sure of herself, and for some reason, that filled me with rage.

"Do you think Cisco could *really* survive this?" I yelled. She stared at me, mouth slack and frightened. I blinked and shook my head as I stood back. "*S*-sorry, that wasn't—that wasn't *me*."

But it sounded like me, and that made all the difference. Charlize nodded, but I couldn't look at her.

The man beside me chuckled. It started off low and built up to a full laugh, the same as before. He hardly took a breath and even clapped his hands, the most fluid his motion had ever been.

"Charlize!" the man gasped. "I apologize. I've been so rude. Thank you so much for beginning this challenge, it's been a while since I've had some fun."

"How do you know my name?" she asked.

He's been in my head. But I couldn't find the strength to say it.

The man cocked his head to the side but cast his eyes back down to Charlize.

"Charlize." He repeated her name like he was tasting it, rolling it around in his mouth like a bite of chocolate. It made me uncomfortable, and some part of me knew he knew that, but I fought every impulse to lift my bat.

"What do you want to know? You get three questions and you better hurry—the next stop is mine."

"Three questions?" Charlize's eyes clouded with both confusion and curiosity. "Since when?"

What the hell happened to not interacting with the people from the Echo?

My anger licked up like a flame, and I took in a deep breath. No one online had mentioned anything about getting to ask three questions.

Was it only because he'd already been haunting me?

The man chuckled. "The Echo isn't just a place, it's a creature. A wild animal. And animals have to adapt—to change if they're going to survive. It's the same with the Slumlord. The great thing about rules is you can change them whenever you want and however you want. Today, you at least get three answers for your trouble. Tomorrow, who knows? Does that answer satisfy you?"

It didn't. And who was the Slumlord?

"Come on, come on," the man goaded. "Do you really want to waste the one chance you have to get answers from a direct source?"

Charlize sent me a panicked and confused look. I shook my head, knowing she wasn't going to listen to me anyway. But I wasn't sure we could trust him.

"Where is Cisco?" Charlize whispered.

The man blinked, and his gaze became a glare. "Oh, haven't you heard?" he asked, in a mockingly concerned voice. "Cisco's left the building."

Charlize's face twisted in absolute bewilderment and grief. Her shoulders shook, and she covered her mouth as she sobbed quietly. The sight of her tears made my chest puff up with rage.

"How do we kill the Echo?" I asked.

The train stilled. For once, the man didn't laugh, and he didn't smile. His eyes bored into me, and as the doors slid open, he completely disappeared. His last words were whispered in the cold breeze that flew into the train.

"You don't."

3:26 a.m.

CHARLIZE AND I LOCKED EYES, FEAR ROLLING THROUGH every inch of my body.

"We have to get off this train," I said.

"No! We can't end the journey!" she yelled. "That's literally one of only three rules!"

I opened my mouth to argue that but couldn't. I didn't have a reason why we should get off the train—I just felt it, like instinct. Something wasn't right.

"What time is it?" Charlize asked. I looked down at my phone.

"It's three twenty-six."

We had another half an hour to go before we could safely get off. I sat back in my seat and tapped my bat against the floor. Everything about the train felt like your typical subway train. Heat rolled into the car. It smelled like an amalgamation of everyone who had been on it. There was Sharpie graffiti on parts of the walls and stale gum stuck to the side of the seat I was on.

The automatic voice never came on, and the train ran smoothly, only stopping at platforms, but, other than that, it followed the basic expectations for a New York City train.

"What do we do now?" Charlize asked, making me think back to the man in the corduroy jacket. He only answered two questions before leaving. Even something about that felt like a hint. "What do we—"

"Jesus, Charlize!" I snapped again. "I don't know, okay! I don't know what we're supposed to do if we can't get off the train. Do *you* have any other ideas?"

She pursed her lips together and glared at me. She didn't. She only turned away, sitting farther down the train from me. Some part of me wanted to apologize, but I couldn't figure out why. I just knew I blamed her for being here.

You're just as much a part of this as she is, my own thoughts hissed back at me.

Mami was infected by Cisco, a fact I could no longer ignore. Why did he go after my own mom like that? Part of me knew these thoughts weren't my own—that it was the Echo getting into my head—but they still made me angry.

I sank back into the corner seat. The train ran on, stopping intermittently, but no one appeared to get on at all.

Suddenly, Charlize ran to the window.

"What?" I asked. She didn't answer until I called her again.

"*I thought*—I thought I saw Cisco." She stared out into the darkness, mouth ajar. I tried to follow her line of sight, but I couldn't see a platform, much less a person.

"I think the Echo is just messing with you," I said, looking away. "That seems to be the theme for the night."

"I know what I saw. Cisco's out there."

The train doors closed and moved on. Her shoulders dropped with a sigh. I didn't have to meet her eyes to know they were full of regret.

She slid down into a seat and continued to stare out the

window even while the train moved. In the reflection, I saw her narrow her eyes as if convinced of seeing something move in the darkness. The train stopped again, and she held the knife at the ready, but no one climbed on.

"There!" she yelled. "He's right *there*! How can you not see him?" Charlize turned to me and pointed straight ahead. I slowly got to my feet, seeing something entirely different.

Charlize's eyes were dulling in color. The Echo was really getting into her just like Olivia said it would.

"Raquel, look at him, he's—he's—" She did a double take, gasping into the dark before jumping to her feet. "Cisco, *wait!*"

I dove toward her. Wrapping my arms around her waist, I dug my feet into the ground and pulled her backward. "Charlize, you *just* said yourself that we can't get off this train, that it's one of the only three rules!"

"Let me go!"

Charlize struggled and twisted herself around. She jammed her elbow into my nose. Pain exploded in my face, and I fell to the ground. Her pounding footsteps took off into the dark.

The doors started to slide shut before I shot my hand out.

"Charlize, come back!" I forced the doors open. "Charlize!"

There was nothing in the dark but silence. The blood in my head rushed loudly, from the pain and the surge of adrenaline and fear flooding my mind. The rules were clear—do not end the journey before 4:00 a.m. Do not get off the train. If you attempt to, you'll be part of the journey forever, just like Olivia's friends were.

But what did that even mean?

"Charlize, *please!*" I choked out. I didn't even realize I was sobbing. Blood mixed with snot ran down my face. I wiped it away with the back of my hand. If it weren't for the thick fluff of her winter coat, she might have broken my nose.

The doors finally slid all the way open. Even with the light of the train, the platform was entirely encased in darkness. I took a shaky breath and closed my eyes before stepping forward. A shot of air flew out with the closing doors. And then the train started up again, rolling on by and leaving me in the dark. I opened my eyes, and any sense of safety and relief died.

I broke a rule.

I left the train.

3:36 a.m.

I LOOKED UP AND DOWN THE PLATFORM. THE LIGHTS WERE cut off, making the tunnels feel less like tunnels and more like voids where everything disappeared. Something slimy grew along the walls, and as I breathed in, I was choked by the smell of gasoline.

I covered my nose and headed toward the turnstiles.

"Cisco, if you can hear me, I would *really* appreciate some guidance considering I'm risking my neck to save *your* cousin." The only sound I heard in return was rats squealing in the dark.

I took the stairs two at a time until I was completely aboveground. The view made me stop in my tracks, breathless.

It wasn't just burning buildings. It was people with their guts hanging out, blood on every intersection, and a deep sense of dread. Piles of brick and rubble stretched on through the streets, and the stench of sewage and rotting meat rolled through the unrecognizable sight. Even the anger I felt was small in comparison to the absolute horror of the burning Bronx.

I forced myself to snap out of it and twisted around. There was no way to tell where Charlize went.

"If there was ever a time for my supercool psychic abilities to kick in, it would be now…" I mumbled to myself, but of course, it didn't. Because that would've been *too* convenient.

A sharp scream rang through the air. It was high-pitched and sounded like it could've been her. Every Passenger turned in the direction of the scream and started walking. I stayed low behind a car, following as fast as I could, cutting through alleyways and climbing fire escapes to get a better view. The chanting of the Passengers was low but clear.

"Falsas promesas…falsas promesas…"

Right in the center of a five-car pileup was a girl—but definitely not Charlize. Her strawberry-blond hair waved around frantically as she held a bleeding person in her arms. In front of her was a hulking man in a long, black trench coat.

Unlike the Passengers closing in on the girl and her friend, the man seemed untouched by the decay of the Bronx. His clothes were spotless, at least from where I stood. I couldn't see much other than his black slacks and black wing-tip shoes, but the look of them was out of place in the scene.

Somehow, it reminded me of the inhumane, pearly white smile of the man in corduroy. So perfect, it was trying to convince you of something, though everything in me told me I shouldn't trust either of them. I narrowed my eyes and leaned in to get a better look.

Then he grasped the arm of the motionless, bleeding person. And where he touched them, something that looked like black mold formed, traveling up the person's elbow.

I gasped. "What the hell are you?"

The longer he held on, the more black fuzzy spots grew on the kid's arm.

The girl refused to stop screaming, even though Passengers were beginning to surround her. She buried her face into the person's neck just as the man reached out to her. And then the Passengers descended.

I gripped the handrail tight and felt rust cutting into my skin.

This was messed up—and yet I was salivating. This was bad, this was cruel, and this was not something I should've been watching with sickening delight.

But I couldn't look away. The carnage that came next was gory and brutal. The snaps of bone cracking and meat being torn apart were only partially drowned out by the sound of screaming.

Until the screaming stopped. I dropped to my knees and took in deep shuddering breaths.

It wasn't me. I had to believe that—that I didn't like that, and if I did, well, it wasn't *me*. It was whatever the Echo was making me to be. I never liked violence. I never felt like I was snapping before this challenge. I was a calm and logical Bronx girl who was never swayed by *any* emotion, much less anger.

And I wished it didn't feel like a lie.

As soon as my legs stopped shaking, I turned to descend from the fire escape when a sudden movement caught my eye.

"Charlize?"

I ran down the fire escape, eager to meet her and get on the next train out of the Echo. It was going to be okay. As long as I could get Charlize on the train and put a little distance between us and the Echo, it would all be over.

I got ready to jump from the last step and onto the ground. Adrenaline flooded my body as I leapt—and accidentally hit my metal bat against the railing. The sound of metal striking metal rang clearly through the air and brought every pair of Passengers' eyes to me.

Shit.

I pumped my legs hard and took off running.

3:48 a.m.

I WAS QUICKLY RUNNING OUT OF TIME. THE ECHO WAS
doing a great job of filling my mind with violent imagery—every
time I so much as laid a hand on a building, images of bullets
and gangs and badges and fire shot fast through me. Littered
everywhere were newspaper articles, all disparaging the Bronx. I
couldn't be sure why it was showing me all this or what it hoped to
accomplish. I just knew I didn't have the energy to keep fighting it.
The Passengers wouldn't let up, and Charlize was still nowhere to
be found. The reality of the situation alone made me want to put
my head through a window.

Unfortunately, all the windows around were already broken,
which made the idea much less satisfying.

I zipped around corners and through alleyways until I lost
about half of the Passengers. The ones with broken limbs—who
could do nothing but stumble and shuffle slowly after me—were
very easy to lose. But the able-bodied ones were keeping pace, and
I was losing my patience. Part of me wanted to get at them until
my bat was bent and broken, but I knew I'd only be signing my
own death certificate.

I hid behind a large dumpster fire and listened for the sound of shuffling feet growing distant. All my adrenaline plummeted, turning into exhaustion as my chest ached. How the hell did I manage to not avoid an asthma attack in this heavily polluted hell-hole? It would be a pretty pathetic hunt if I succumbed to death via really shitty lungs. The Echo probably knew that. I could feel it digging around in my mind, like a wild animal did for scraps.

I was starting to really hate that analogy.

"It's the most accurate one."

I jumped back, startled by the sudden appearance of the man in the corduroy jacket. His grin spread from ear to ear as he looked down at me.

"Aw, did you really think you could get away with not being fed on by the Echo? You're special, Raquel, but you're not *that* special."

I gripped my bat tight, finally giving in to the thrilling sensation of anger.

"Careful," he laughed. "You don't want to alert the Slumlord—or the Passengers you finally just lost, do you? It's a shame, really. Had you listened to your father a little more carefully, you might have had more, ah, *protection*."

I glared at him for a moment, seething. He was mocking me for forgetting the resguardo, for being so stupid to think that it might have been useless when it had been anything *but*. I squeezed my eyes tight and took in a deep breath before looking back at him.

"You owe me another answer," I finally spat.

He spread his arms to the side. "I'm waiting."

A pair of feet scuffled just beyond the dumpster. The man didn't seem to care—and why would he? He was already dead. Dead and so lost that he couldn't even remember what he wanted me for in the first place. I listened to the scuffling feet grow more distant before speaking.

"Are you—"

"What does it want from me?" I asked, rolling the bat around in my hands. "The Echo—if it's like a wild animal, what makes *me* so special that it wants me?"

The man crouched down, slow and unblinking until he was at eye level.

"You can feel it, can't you?" he said, grin turning into a sinister scowl. "In the pit of your stomach."

I didn't know what he was talking about. The only thing I felt was rage with a side of nausea. The smell of burning flesh and smoking buildings left me physically ill, but I couldn't leave without Charlize.

"You've always had this...*innate* ability to see things others can't. A power buried deep inside. Since you were a kid. But you've had people shield it all this time. With prayers and trinkets, things you might have taken for granted. It's been waiting for you, Raquel."

"How do you even—"

"*Ah, ah, ah.*" He wagged a finger. "That was your last freebie. But I'll give you a warning."

I watched him lift, eyes still boring into me when I heard it. The sound of something skittering.

"*Run.*"

I peered out from behind the dumpster and froze. A large, centipede-like creature crawled fast toward me, its mandibles snapping in the air. When I turned around, the man was gone, so I did the only thing I could do.

I booked it down the street.

3:54 a.m.

I COULDN'T TELL WHAT IT WAS OR WHAT IT WAS SUPPOSED to be. The creature following me was worse than the Passengers. Its long, slithering body was covered in shifting black spores that broke off in pieces and fell into the air. I couldn't look at it long without feeling like my mind was literally being peeled apart— another aspect that made it more dangerous. It was definitely a monster, and I couldn't let it get to me.

I only had one option.

As soon as I was able to get away, I doubled back in the direction of the subway station. The Passengers were crowding the streets, so I had to get creative.

I collected stones, glass bottles, and other small-but-heavy-enough objects before chucking them as far as I could in another direction. The Passengers would turn and walk, and I'd crouch behind cars while moving. The system worked long enough to get to the end of a street, and then I had to reassess how much more time I had and what resources were still available.

The only thing that made it more difficult was the odd

placement of certain buildings. It was all wrong, like mismatched puzzle pieces forced together.

"That's not even there anymore," I mumbled, staring at an old corner store. I remembered the first time I walked past it—the *actual* corner—and had felt perplexed it had turned into a tailor's shop. Corner stores were a staple of the Bronx. How the hell could any go out of business?

The building shuddered, grabbing the attention of every nearby Passenger.

"Oh fuck," I said, crawling under the broken-down Cadillac. Bricks fell in quick succession, throwing up thick dust clouds. I could still hear the Passengers coming, undeterred by the falling debris. When the dust cleared, the Passengers quickly stepped away. I poked my head out from under the car.

The store was turned into a tailor shop.

I stared at it in disbelief. "Did *I* do that?"

Shuffling steps nearby caught my attention. I needed to leave—*now*.

"This don't make no damn sense," I muttered, staring back at the shop as I sprinted down the street. I eventually came to the top steps of a subway tunnel and quickly ran to jump the turnstiles. A rush of air blew through the tunnel, and when I checked the time, I knew this was my last chance.

It was 3:59 a.m. I made it just in time.

I gasped. I'd actually made it! The train slowed to a stop in front of me.

A blast of cool air fell over me—so did guilt.

Tears welled up in my eyes. I turned to look back at the decrepit train station even though I knew I couldn't stay there.

But was I really going to abandon Charlize?

"I'll come back," I promised. It came out in a shuddering

breath like I was trying to convince someone of something. "I'll come back for you."

I stepped onto the train with my bat still in hand and sat quietly in the center of the train car.

PART FOUR

FIND OUT

I CAME BACK HOME COVERED IN SWEAT AND GRIME. DRIED blood flecked my coat. Despite feeling feral, a kind of instinctive anger that made me curl my hands into fists—I collapsed into bed. I was drained of so much energy, my sight blurred at the edges.

Luckily, with the blanket covering my entire body, Papi couldn't see how wrecked I was. I could hear him attempting to walk quietly around the room in the morning, lightly cleaning up before he tried to shake me awake.

"M'ija, did you forget your duffel bag at Charlize's house?"

I didn't answer. My bag was probably found by a regular commuter and either taken or tossed. Either way, I'd have to buy a new one.

I listened as Papi stepped away briefly. He yelled something about breakfast, but I was too dazed to understand. Knowing our track record, the breakfast in question would be bought outside and not made fresh in our kitchen.

I didn't get up until I heard the front door open and close. The final clicking of the lock was sharp, and even though my sore muscles protested every bit of movement, I made my way to the bathroom. The water ran cold, shocking me awake.

I spent at least twenty minutes trying to scrub every bit of last night's mistake out of my skin. The choking smoke felt like it had bonded to my clothes and to me. Maybe it was the camphor, but I didn't understand how Papi hadn't smelled it.

Once I put on fresh clothes, I stepped out of the bathroom just as Papi came home. He held two large paper bags with grease stains. The smell of bacon overpowered the camphor.

"You're finally awake!" He grinned and held up the bags. "I got us some BLTs. You hungry?"

My stomach answered him before I did. He gave a nervous laugh as I plopped down on the futon, already tearing into my breakfast sandwich. A mix of grease and mayonnaise dribbled down my chin. I was using every bit of energy to devour the sandwich.

"Are you okay?" Papi asked. He looked worried. I took a moment to wipe the crumbs from the corners of my lips.

"Yeah. Why?"

"You seem...different. Did something happen at Charlize's?"

Deranged laughter erupted from inside me. Then food went down the wrong pipe, and I doubled over to cough it up. Papi slammed his hand against my back to help.

"Remember to chew, m'ija."

"I'm fine." I shrugged him off. Then I went back to eating.

Sunday was spent in a daze. Adrenaline and exhaustion took turns coursing through me. I was either passed out or on the edge of my seat. The two seemed to blur together no matter what.

"Are you sick?" he asked. It felt like the third time that day that he'd asked me, but I couldn't remember. I shrugged and slipped back into bed.

How long would I have until the police came to ask questions?

I was already linked to Charlize because of Cisco, and now she was missing.

Not that I could ever explain what had happened to the police.

I sighed and rubbed my temples. I had to cling to the hope that she wasn't dead—yet—even if I'd left her for dead, left her to fend for herself in the Echo.

Papi continued to stare at me as if he could read my thoughts. "What?" I snapped.

He furrowed his brow, clearly troubled. "We may have to stay away from the hospital for a while," he announced. "Whatever your mother has spread to two other nurses. They're not letting anyone into that wing just to be safe."

If I were feeling anything other than total exhaustion, I might have flared my nose or violently lashed out, but all my energy was drained.

"Okay," I said.

He didn't say anything else before he walked into his room, so I took that to mean that she was still getting worse. I hated when he couldn't be straight with me. How was he planning to break the news if had to plan a funeral?

The toll of the entire challenge and Mami's condition sank into my bones. I fell back asleep, and when I woke up several hours later, I was still groggy.

I looked down and stared at my phone. The screen was unlocked to a text I'd sent to Charlize just a few minutes ago.

You.

That was it. That was all I wrote. Just you. I didn't remember grabbing my cell phone, much less typing. I stared at the screen, trying to rationalize it. Maybe I'd briefly woken and thought the whole event was a bad dream. Maybe I went to text her, only to fall asleep again and accidentally hit send.

But Charlize was gone. She was gone and it was my fault, and soon enough Mami would be gone just the same. Everyone I cared about was slipping through my fingers, and there was nothing I could do about it.

I pressed my face into my pillow. It was wet with sweat. I shifted in the corner of the futon and spotted Charlize's scarf, tucked into my jacket.

The world around me blurred, and it wasn't until I wiped my face that I realized I was crying again. My chest shook with every breath.

Charlize was gone. I looked to my phone again, staring at my text. She didn't answer, of course. And she never would.

I tucked myself back under the covers. I didn't want to deal with the reality of Charlize being gone. Being awake was too much work. I just needed my brain to shut down for a few more hours.

THE NIGHTMARE
FOLLOWS

IT TOOK ME A LONG TIME BEFORE I REALIZED I WAS IN A dream. I was still lying down, but in a sleeping bag on hardwood floors instead of my usual bed. This was the memory of my soccer training camp. The wooden cabin walls were musty with the smell of light rain, and there was a draft that seemed to come from everywhere at once, making you constantly shiver. The only refuge from it all were the sleeping bags, but even then, I found myself wanting to curl up tighter as if to conserve body heat.

Charlize was right next to me. Her chest rose and fell with every soft breath and her lips were slightly parted. They looked just as soft as I remembered.

In my memory, I reached out to take her hand. Her palm was still soft and smelled of sweet berry lotion.

But in this dream, I turned away from her. I didn't try to reach out to her or grab her hand. I just rolled onto my other side and shut my eyes tight, willing myself to wake up or at the very least change the nature of the dream. The sweet berry that relaxed me in memory was now making me nauseous. Soccer was the one part of my life that made my lungs stronger, made the asthma attacks nearly disappear. Now, it was making it hard to breathe.

And I couldn't believe I had managed to forget about the resguardo *again*. You'd think I'd have learned by now.

The floor creaked under someone's weight. I slowly peeked out from under the covers, only to come face to face with Cisco.

He sat in the corner, rolled into a ball and rocking himself back and forth shakily. Black mold covered most of his skin and grew off him onto the wall behind, attaching him to it.

"Cisco?"

I jumped up and ran over. He barely looked at me or acknowledged I was waving a hand in front of his face. Mold and rot spread over his right eye, rising and falling like the spores were breathing. I was careful not to touch him, but I didn't want to leave him there alone. His voice came out in a whisper as he rocked.

"*Ch*-Charlize, I'm *so-so-so*-sorry—" he said, staring into thin air. "I'm *so-so*-sorry—"

He only repeated himself, oblivious to my presence.

"Cisco, I—" I opened my mouth to apologize but stopped. He couldn't hear me. There was nothing I could do for him in this state.

Suddenly he gasped and leaped to his feet. He ran through me like mist and went out the cabin door.

"Cisco, wait!" I followed.

The door opened to the same brick hallway as my earlier dream, with graffiti dripping off the walls and identical doors on each side. I closed the cabin door behind me and continued down the hall. Cisco stood farther down, staring up at something ahead.

When I finally reached him, I froze.

"T-the Slumlord…" he mumbled.

The man in front of us wore a suit. It was a casual look with no tie, but the blazer crawled like it was just a mass of thin, black worms. And it smelled rotten. He flexed his hands as his eyes bore into me. They were piercing blue with nothing behind them but the promise of death.

"L-leave Charlize alone," Cisco whimpered, clearly afraid but unwilling to back down.

"You know where Charlize is?" I asked, reaching over to him. My fingers grazed Cisco's shoulder, feeling him for the first time, but before I could say anything else, he screamed. The rot spread farther onto his face and down his neck, eating through it like acid. He crumpled to the ground with a gargle and passed out.

I looked back to the Slumlord. He didn't take his eyes off me.

I swallowed. "You can see me?"

The Slumlord took a step toward me, sending a shock of fear through my body. I took a step back out of its range of influence. It took another step. I took two steps backward. When it moved forward again, I quickly turned on my heel and ran. I tossed a glance over my shoulder, only slightly relieved to see that it was only following at the same slow pace.

But I still needed to wake up.

Wake up, wake up, wake up! I came back to the same cabin door and jiggled the doorknob. It was locked.

"Come on, someone open up, please!"

And then there it was—the unrelenting fear and panic. My heart threatened to jump out of chest altogether at the sight of his shadow happening upon me. His hands clamped down on my shoulders, calm but firm as if he only wanted to talk.

Then, his hands sent a flood of needles deep into my skin with just one touch, tearing a scream out of me. The pain spread down my arms, and when I looked, black mold was taking over my body. I struggled to push him off and kicked as hard as I could.

This is only a dream! It's a nightmare! Just wake up!

I thrashed against him, bringing my nails up to his face and tearing into his skin.

"Get off! Get—" My lungs halted as the needles reached into my chest cavity. The mold began to build up, choking me from the inside out, and no matter how much I hacked, it refused to be dislodged.

I fell to my knees, certain this would be it. If I wasn't going to wake up from the dream, I probably wouldn't wake up at all. Tears brimmed at my eyes as I lost all feeling in my limbs and fell back onto the door.

And it swung open. The Slumlord released me long enough that I took a breath, and when I did, I shot straight up on the futon, gasping for air.

I coughed loudly into the corner of the blanket until I spat something out. I pulled it into the glow of the moonlight and felt my insides grow cold.

Rot.

The Echo was inside me now.

LIBRARY DRAMA

On Monday, Aaron sat low in his seat with his head in his arms. From the gentle rise and fall of his body, I could tell he was taking a nap, but doing it during study hall was risky behavior when you had Ms. Mara checking in on everyone. She was the kind of teacher who wanted students to maximize their time as efficiently as possible—which really just translated to *no naps*.

I poked my pen in his side and waited for him to get up.

"What?" he said sleepily.

"Aaron, I need your help with something."

"*Mm-hmm*." He didn't look up. I resisted the urge to stab him with the pen. It seemed the violent thoughts were strongest when I had something in my hands, so I put it down and settled for the idea of beating him with my bare hands. Progress, I think.

"I'm serious—something bad happened." I leaned over. "Charlize and I did that challenge thing."

"Mm, how'd it go?" he mumbled, barely coherent. It was like a splash of red between my eyes. Irritation slipped in easy and so did the thought *What would it take for Aaron to be useful to me for once?*

While it wasn't as violent as my pen-stabbing impulse, it was still an undeserved sentiment. I sucked in a deep breath and cast the thought away.

Focus.

"Did you see Charlize at all today?" I asked, grinding my teeth.

"No."

"Exactly."

His eyes fluttered open, and he finally sat up.

"Wait...*what*?"

"After school. Hunts Point Library. I'll tell you then."

I spent the day trying to avoid sharp objects and people who annoyed me. Charlize's so-called friend Naomi was high on the list for gossiping incessantly behind her back.

"I just think she needs to get over it," Naomi said, standing right by my locker. A few of Charlize's other friends laughed like they couldn't believe what a dick Naomi was being. "Like, I'm sorry, but a missing family member does *not* make you more interesting."

"Oh, come on. She's allowed to be a *little* upset," someone said.

"Maybe for a day or two. But two whole weeks? Don't you think that's being a little dramatic?"

I thought about slamming my locker shut, hoping it would get the point across, but thought better of it.

Instead, I carefully lifted one of Naomi's braids into my locker and closed it. The lock slid into place easily, and I quickly walked away as the bell rang.

Even from down the hall, I could hear Naomi yelp. As

satisfying as it was, I knew the pain in my chest wouldn't be quelled as long as Charlize was still gone.

———

By the time Aaron and I got to the library, the table we normally used was already taken, but that was fine. We weren't staying long anyway. We turned into the nonfiction section and tucked ourselves into the corner.

"Yo...I think the cops are following you."

I froze and looked up at him. He pointed out the window, toward a pair of officers standing on the corner, waiting to cross the street.

This was the last thing I needed right now. I squinted. It was hard to make out the faces, but mannerisms and body type alone told me it was Officer Bored and Officer Quiet. Officer Bored gesticulated with his hands as he talked, while Officer Quiet nodded every few seconds, his own hands tucked deep into his jacket.

"How long have they been following us?" I asked.

Aaron shrugged. "I noticed them across the street from the school when we finally got out. I didn't expect to see them again here."

"Damn." I stepped away from the window. It looked like they were heading toward the library. "Come on." I grabbed his arm and dragged him farther to the back of the building. We slipped right between the manga and young adult section when the library door pulled open, letting in a freezing gust of wind.

"I can't deal with this," I said. "Aaron, do you think you can distract them?"

He shot me an incredulous look.

"Yeah, I know!" I hissed. "But they've been on my ass since

Cisco infected my mom, so you *know* this situation with Charlize doesn't make me look good."

"Oh, so fuck *me*, right?"

I let out a low groan and peered over the bookshelf. The officers were carefully scanning the room. I ducked back down when they turned in my direction. They were definitely looking for me. I swallowed and considered my options. The only other exit was the emergency exit, which would set off a loud alarm and put me in more trouble than I was already in. Even if I tried moving out of their sight, there were two of them, and they could easily corner me, especially when I was already technically cornered.

And the violent thoughts were already swirling the situation like piranhas. If I felt even a *little* threatened, I was going to lose it and commit a felony.

I mentally kicked myself for forgetting about the cops. They were going to jeopardize the whole operation.

Just then, a librarian cut around the corner of the bookshelf and disappeared behind a door marked FOR STAFF ONLY. I went to it immediately and slowly turned the knob. It was open.

"Hey!" Aaron whispered as I pushed into it. I closed the door behind me and slid down beside the glass wall. A poster hung over it, obscuring me just enough as I listened intently for the officers.

"Officer," Aaron mumbled a greeting.

"Hey, what's your name?" Officer Bored asked.

Aaron mumbled an answer again, but I was pretty sure he said *Mario*.

"Mario, do you happen to know a girl named Raquel Celestin?"

He didn't answer, but I knew he nodded. There was no point in lying since the officers already saw us together.

"Is she in trouble?" Aaron asked.

"Not yet," Officer Bored said.

Not yet.

I closed my eyes and exhaled through my nose. Charlize's mom definitely called the cops on me.

"Has she been acting suspicious lately?" Officer Bored continued. I glanced down to the floor, watching their feet. Officer Bored stood in front of Aaron.

And Officer Quiet was walking to the staff door. I looked down the hall. There was only one other door, and it was likely leading to the lounge where the other librarian was. I panicked. I wasn't going to get out of this easy. The doorknob turned, clicking as the door was pushed slightly open.

And then a static voice came on the officer's radio. A man repeated a code twice before the radio went silent. Then the door slowly shut.

"Okay, well, thank you for your time, Mario." The officer's feet shuffled away. I waited a few more seconds before standing up and reappearing. Aaron looked back at me, annoyed.

"Don't get mad at me, Mario," I said. He clenched his jaw and looked away.

"Whatever."

I followed him back to the window, where we watched the police walk up the block until they disappeared in the distance.

"Alright, so what happened to Charlize?"

"She's stuck in the Echo."

He was stunned at first. Like he wasn't sure if he heard that right. Then he gathered himself enough to speak.

"You're lying," he said. "That's not possible."

I stared at him, still twitching with anger. It was like lightning, constantly shooting through me.

"You're the one who found the subreddit *and* Olivia—you were there when we spoke to her. You *know* it's real!"

He thumbed at his nose and turned to the corner of the room.

"The Bronx's Echo is based off the Bronx's burning period in the seventies. Remember that dream I had? That was *nothing* compared to what I experienced. There were entire blocks just gone. Burned down, rubble, just nothing but dirt and ashes everywhere. And the people—" I shivered from the memory alone. "They were walking around like they didn't even know they were dead. Aaron, I saw a woman whose face was *literally* being burned off in real time, and you know what she did? She *hummed*."

I couldn't read his expression, but I had to make him understand that what we were dealing with was not just some internet challenge. When I glanced over his shoulder, he walked off and sat at the nearest empty table. I followed and sat opposite of him.

"Raquel? Tell me you're lying," Aaron said with a growl. I furrowed my brow, confused by his reaction. Why was he mad at me?

"I'm not." I swallowed and clamped my mouth shut.

"You just *left her there*?"

"What other choice did I have?" I slammed my hands into the table. The people around us jumped and sent over startled looks. I tried to find it in me to care, but my mind was cluttered with anger and guilt. My hands shook as my eyes swam with tears.

"She was gone, and if I didn't get on the train within the hour, I'd be gone too," I hissed. "Or is that what you want?"

"What?" He scowled at my accusation.

"Admit it, you would rather I *die* trying to save the girl you love—who by the way, has never even *thought* about you as anything more than Mario's brother."

He balled his hands into fists and clenched his teeth. "Take it back."

"You can't even look at her without getting tongue-tied. It's so pathetic, the way you pine after her," I said, unable to stop. The lightning was a roaring fire, burning so hot that I overlooked Aaron's sudden movements. He reached out, grabbed me by the collar, and pulled me to my feet. The librarian yelled in alarm.

"Hey! Take it outside!"

Even then, I couldn't stop.

"You know what's even more pathetic? The fact I *know* you're not going to do shit even if I told you we kissed."

And suddenly it was out there. Aaron's face twisted into something worse than rage and desperation. The light in his eyes dimmed with hurt.

"You kissed Charlize?" His shoulders fell as he loosened his grip. I felt myself reeling backward, trying to find a way to undo this mess.

Fuck! Why did I say that?

"Well, technically," I stammered, "she kissed *me*."

The look on Aaron's face told me that wasn't any better. In fact, it was worse. His biggest crush liking someone else who was unsure about their own feelings? Why would I think that would clear anything up?

Aaron stepped back and picked up his bag.

"Aaron, wait—" I grabbed his arm only to be shrugged off. He shook his head silently as he left the library. The people around me pretended not to care about the scene I just caused, but the shame was there all the same.

Not only did I abandon Charlize, but I hurt my best friend, too.

Out of the corner of his mouth, right before he walked away, he hissed, "Charlize may have kissed you, but *I* wouldn't have left her in the Echo."

PRISON WITHIN A PRISON

It was bad enough I left Charlize to fend for herself, but every moment I didn't go back to find her was another pound of added guilt. Seconds seemed to stretch to eternity, and there were times when I almost felt like I couldn't breathe, knowing she was out there. I had to make good on my promise to come back for her.

But I couldn't do it alone.

The knowledge of this was made worse by the fact Aaron clearly told someone about Charlize and me because by Tuesday morning, the news was out there: Charlize and Raquel kissed. Almost everybody was talking about it, and that was because the school was on high alert after Charlize was reported missing. I was the last one with her, and that made me prime suspect number one.

My stomach swung violently between nausea and guilt. Charlize's mom didn't necessarily blame me, but it was only a matter of time until she did.

And she'd be right to.

I went to the girls' bathroom and splashed cool water on my face between classes.

It woke me up for just a moment, but then the world around me swayed, and I could've sworn the ground under me lurched in one direction. I was dipping back into the Echo.

The next stop is...

I snapped my head up, jolting a younger girl to attention. She stared at me through her pink-highlighted bangs and sucked in a deep breath.

"Jesus..." She shuddered. "Are you okay?"

I looked around, forgetting where I was. The blue bathroom walls stood on all sides and the sound of a flushing toilet rang loud.

"Yeah," I lied. I swung my head back to the sink and splashed water a few more times on my face. My braids hit the porcelain, and the ends became drenched, but I didn't care.

I stared down at my hands. I hadn't felt the rot spreading in me, but I knew it was there. Waiting for something, waiting to choke me like when the Slumlord grabbed me. Every slight chest pain made me think back to the needles and wonder if they were growing again.

I should have brought the resguardo.

I should have brought it to the Echo, should have slept with it afterward, shouldn't have doubted its power... But did it really have any power? Who's to say everything wouldn't have gone exactly the same way if I'd had it in hand?

The girl shot another concerned look at me as I left, heading for my next class. I took careful steps down the stairs, waiting for the ground to shift under my feet again. I held on to the rail tight as I went, only stopping when I heard my name being called.

"Raquel?"

I looked up and met Mr. Wade's eyes. He waved over to me and smiled.

"Could I see you in my office for a quick minute?" His voice twisted up at the end, but it was less of a question and more of a command. I hated when he did that.

Resisting the urge to push back, I nodded. Even if I felt less cordial than before, I wasn't the kind of person who rebelled even a little. It was the rot that made me want to lash out, to cause nothing but destruction and pain to everyone around me. If I wasn't careful, I'd end up doing or saying something I'd regret.

And I needed to keep it together until I got Charlize back, at least.

I followed behind him at a distance, and when I turned the corner, I could see exactly why he needed to see me.

The cops were back. Officer Bored and Officer Quiet stood in front of his office with their hands in their pockets. Underneath their uniforms, they wore black turtlenecks, but their faces were still rosy red from the wind chill. Officer Bored glanced over at me, stopping midsentence, and then stepped forward.

Mr. Wade grabbed his office door handle and twisted it open.

Somehow, my feet wouldn't move. My spine rolled to its full length, and I stared up at Officer Bored with caution. He rose an eyebrow, expecting me to walk in first.

"Raquel?" Mr. Wade said. Whatever coiled inside me backed down, and I shuffled into the room with my head down.

Mr. Wade sat down. "Raquel, I'm sure you've heard the rumors about Charlize." He folded his hands together onto his desk, making sure to never break eye contact with me.

Officer Quiet stepped behind Mr. Wade. Even with his back turned, I could tell he was snooping through the bookshelves with no regard for boundaries.

Mr. Wade's eyes were gentle but firm, prompting me to answer.

"Yeah," I said, looking to Officer Bored. His lips were in a tight line, and he no longer seemed bored. He was alert and keeping his attention fixed on me.

Better tread carefully. He might get violent. Cops often did when something didn't go their way. I didn't know what led to shooting Hazel Boon fourteen times, but I knew damn well it couldn't have been because of a Popsicle stick. Just because I was in school didn't mean I could afford to be careless around them.

I needed to stay cautious, apprehensive.

"Is everything okay?" I said, softer.

Officer Quiet slowly turned and finally spoke. "No."

The word was rough. He had a slight Puerto Rican accent, and for some reason, that surprised me.

"Everything is not okay," he informed me. "As you probably already know, Charlize is now missing."

I blinked, waiting for whatever point he was trying to make. He raised an eyebrow, watching my reaction or lack thereof. I simply said, "Right."

The silence that followed was enough to make Mr. Wade uncomfortable, and when he cleared his throat nervously, I leaned back into my seat and folded one of my hands over the other.

"You don't seem to be upset by this, Raquel. Even though you were the last to see her," Officer Bored explained.

I pursed my lips, remembering the kiss we shared that night. I fought the strongest urge to throw everything off Mr. Wade's desk and set it on fire. But this time, the anger wasn't from the rot inside of me—it was from the injustice of having my own crush taken away just when I found out she'd felt the same. It was all wrong with a capital *W*.

Maybe if I weren't such a coward, I'd have known it all along.

I shrugged and swallowed the rising lump in my throat. "Like you said, I already know she's missing."

"Sounds like you two had gotten close recently. Several of your classmates say that leading up to her disappearance, you two were hanging out a lot. Her mother even stated that you two were having a sleepover at her house. Any reason why that might be?"

There was a smug tinge in Officer Bored's voice, bait he was casting out, waiting to see if I'd bite.

Oh, I'll bite.

"We used to be really close friends. On the same soccer team and everything," I said, keeping my stare steady. "Her mom doesn't remember me much, but I used to hang out over at her place all the time when we were younger. Did anyone tell you that?"

They didn't because it was old news. Not as exciting as problematic rumors.

"Did you notice anything strange about Charlize the night you last saw her?"

I shook my head, but I knew they were waiting to hear more about that night.

"She was the same as always. Worried about Cisco, sorry about my mom. We just sat around, ate junk food, and caught up." It was technically the truth, so I tried not to feel bad about it. Instead, I spoke with an eerie calm I didn't know I had. It probably looked effortless to them, but I was a dam of emotions that was very close to bursting.

"So what happened at the end of the night?" Officer Bored asked. "You just went home? Was Charlize there that morning?"

"Yeah," I lied. "I woke up early to get home and work on a project. She locked the door behind me."

A look passed between the two cops, and I felt a bit of panic surge through me. I didn't know what other information they were working with. Did they check the cameras at Hunts Point? No, they'd have no way of linking us to that location at that specific time.

Did Charlize's mom wake up in the middle of the night and discover us gone? If she did, I'd be having a very different conversation right now.

The cops never gave any indication that they were on to me, and I wondered if that was also just part of their song and dance. Make the suspect feel like they're home free just to see them crumble when new evidence is brought forth.

When it was obvious the cops had nothing else to say, Mr. Wade forcefully cleared his voice, reminding us of his presence.

"Do you have any further questions, officers?"

Officer Bored lips were pressed in a thin line, but he shook his head. "No. That'll be all." He stood up and pulled the chair aside as he walked out the door. I waited a few more seconds before exhaling with relief.

BAD APOLOGIES, STILL SINCERE

I CRUMPLED UP THE LETTER AND TOSSED IT IN THE TRASH can. It was the sixth apology letter I was trying to write to Aaron, knowing if I opened my big vicious mouth, I'd only end up tearing him a new one. But no matter what, I couldn't find the words I needed to say.

All that I wrote was *hey, I'm sorry* and then *help me find Charlize*, and that's when the words died inside me. I even tried to explain why I was so mean and irritated lately, but there was no way to write out *I think I've been corrupted by the Echo's influence* without sounding like I should have the cops called on me.

Speaking of the cops, I'd ordered pizza for dinner because I didn't feel like making another trip outside, knowing I was probably still being followed. Christ, they were useless, and they were only going to get worse the longer Charlize was missing.

Papi had left an envelope labeled *food money* and a note on the coffee table saying his shifts this week were going to be very late at night and he probably wouldn't be able to make it back until around 6:00 a.m. Strangely, it caught me off guard that Papi wouldn't be around for a while, but it also meant I'd have the opportunity to go after Charlize.

Even if I had no idea how to find her once I entered the Echo.

How long could she last in a place like that? Cisco was at his wit's end by the end of the week. If I were trying to get to her before she passed the point of no return, I'd have to get to her quick.

If only I hadn't fucked things up so royally with Aaron.

I lay back on the futon, clicking the TV on. I closed my eyes and breathed, my fingers closing around the small, blue resguardo next to me. The apartment was strong with the smell of camphor. Papi probably tossed a few fresh cubes in the corners of every room. I breathed it in and let it fill my lungs. I imagined it purging the rot the way Papi believed it cleared out bad energy.

But all I could think about was the smell of burnt flesh and charcoal.

"Back so soon?"

I jolted up, surprised to see I was no longer on the futon but on the same sleeping bag I used during the soccer training camp. The man in the corduroy jacket peered around the wooden cabin with a faint look of disgust.

"What *is* it about this memory that keeps calling you here?"

"What are you doing here?" My chest constricted with panic. "I was holding the resguardo when I fell asleep. I *know* I was!"

He didn't look at me when he answered. "Mm, only protects you against evil, I'm afraid."

"Are you trying to tell me that *you're* not evil?"

He *tsk*ed. "You already asked your three questions. Don't I get to ask something now?"

I started grinding my teeth as he paced. His movement seemed much more fluid at the moment. Instead of taking awkward steps, he looked like he was going on a pleasant stroll. The cabin light was dim, but I could still see him inspecting the place, stopping short of the side of the room where Charlize slept. I refused to look, and he smiled as if he knew.

"Fine," I spat. "Ask your questions."

"This memory." He tapped a finger against the wall. "You dream of it often. Why?"

My stomach fluttered with nervousness.

"I don't know."

"Ah, but you *do* know." He sighed.

Confusion twisted my face. "Why are you so different?" I asked. "You're usually so...scary. Angry." Like I felt, every moment of the day.

"There's something very calming about this memory," said the man in the corduroy jacket. "Besides, I'm not meant to always be scary. I'm meant to be a lure."

"Is that why you're here? To lure me back?"

His lips curled into a smile. "My turn to ask a question. What did you think of the Echo?"

"It's shit."

He laughed, but there was nothing funny about it. The Bronx Echo highlighted everything wrong with the Bronx. It somehow twisted even the graffiti into a colorless mess. The murals were supposed to add color, the people were supposed to be...well, not dead.

There wasn't supposed to be rot and mold everywhere. I mean, hell, where was the greenway? Where were the trees and the flowers that added more life to the Bronx? The whole place was sick.

"It's interesting watching you get so close to the answer and yet still remain so far," the man chided.

"You say that like there's a problem to be solved."

"There is." His eyes flicked to something behind me, and suddenly the room was filled with the smell of rotting flesh. I covered my nose immediately and twisted around.

"*Charlize!*"

Instead of being right next to me like she usually was, Charlize sat in the same corner as Cisco had been, not too long ago. Unlike him, she was still, sitting on the backs of her feet and leaning against the wall. She was covered in mold and rot just the same.

"Ra...quel...?" Charlize wheezed, eyes flitting open but unable to focus on me.

I ran over to her and rapidly started swiping at the mold. My hands went straight through it.

"Where are you...?" she asked.

"I'm—I'm right here." I knelt next to her. "Charlize, tell me where you are. Tell me where I can find you!"

She started to say something but stopped midway. Her chest shook violently in a coughing fit. Whatever was caught in her throat was thicker than normal phlegm, and desperate to help, I tried to pat her back to get it out. I still couldn't touch her.

"School is...safe..."

And then she dissipated like mist.

I couldn't hold it any longer. My rage boiled over, and I let out a loud scream as I willed her to come back.

The man laughed loudly at my grief.

"It isn't funny!" I cried. My chest was cracking, and I curled into a ball, holding it tight. Moments passed, but the rot in my chest didn't budge even a little. The man came forward and crouched in front of me.

"It's not the rot hurting you," he whispered. He almost sounded sympathetic. I looked up despite the pain and took in gasping breaths.

"What am I supposed to do?"

"Find the prison within the prison," he told me. "And find her."

A loud chirp ripped through the air, and I found myself lodged in the corner of the futon and the wall. The corduroy man had dematerialized completely. I moved to check the time on my phone and saw Aaron had texted me.

Aaron

> Meet me at my place in 30.

I stared at the text in disbelief, wiping the tears from my eyes. The pain in my chest continued to throb. Was Aaron trying to lower my guard before beating my ass?

I typed out a long paragraph about how sorry I was and how shitty it was of me to throw the kiss in his face, but then I stopped myself.

He deserved to hear my apology in person.

Slowly, I pulled myself together. I quickly deleted the paragraph and sent a simple *ok*, ignoring the wave of nausea that rolled in my guts. Time barely moved while I was dreaming. It wasn't as late in the day as I thought, but that just meant I needed to spend every waking second preparing for the next go around.

Charlize needed me—so I was going to do everything in my power to find her. I could only hope Aaron would help me.

PART FIVE

A GHOST IN
EVERY BRICK

I ALL BUT RAN TO AARON'S AS SOON AS I GOT READY. I DIDN'T want to waste a single second and wasn't sure if he'd been on the fence about contacting me. Considering how I acted, I wouldn't be surprised if he was, which was all the more reason to hurry before he changed his mind.

By the time I got to his house, I was sweating and my chest was throbbing with pain that I wasn't sure was from the rot or from my own out-of-shape lifestyle. Either way, I knocked on the door fast and loud and waited silently, catching my breath.

As soon as Aaron opened the door, I swallowed my pride and went for it.

"Aaron, I'm really, really sorry for what I said. You have to believe that it wasn't me, that I didn't want to hurt you, and that I was practically possessed with rage. Lately, that's all I am—angry and impulsive—and look, you're my best friend, and I would gut someone for hurting you just like you might want to gut me right now, and I don't blame you, okay?"

I paused to take in a quick breath. The words came out so fast and so quick, I didn't breathe the entire length of it. "I'm really, really sorry, and if you want, you can punch me in the back after this, but I *really* need your help—not just saving Charlize but also my mom."

Aaron's eyes twitched at the last mention of that.

"The hospital put my mom in quarantine," I wheezed. "Whatever she has—it's spreading." As if on cue, something rattled in my chest, and I coughed into my hand. I held it out to show him. It was faint, but it was there—small drops of black rot.

Aaron jumped back, and I wiped on the side of my jeans.

"You're really knee-deep into this, huh?" he said, looking down at my hands. They were shaking.

I nodded.

"Yeah. And it's bad." I took another breath. "I need to go back, but I need you to go with me. Please, Aaron. If I go in alone, I don't think I'll ever get back out. And if that happens, my mom will just die. I can't let that happen—"

"You won't," he said with a sigh. "And you can stop. I'll help you."

He turned into the doorway, letting me in. I followed him quietly into his house. The warmth of it was almost unfamiliar, and as we entered the living room, I noticed it was completely silent.

"Where's Mario?" I asked.

"Out with friends."

Out of habit, I sat on the couch and watched Aaron go into the kitchen to grab a bag of chips. When he returned, he tossed me my own bag of salt and vinegar chips. My favorite.

"Why?" I asked. My voice came out quiet, almost a whisper. I didn't have to elaborate what I was asking. Aaron already knew.

"Because, Raquel, you're my best friend. And even though I'm *pissed* at what you said, I don't want you to die over it. I just wish you would've been straight with me."

"I don't think that's possible."

He snorted.

"You know what I mean. I don't care if we like the same girl. I care that you *went behind my back* about it. Do you know what two dudes who like the same girl do? They each try their best, in a fair way, to get with her. You know, maybe a duel or weird contest. Winner takes all." Aaron leaned back into his seat and crossed his arms. "But you didn't. You didn't even tell me. *That's* what hurts."

"You know that's not how it usually works, right? Like, the girl usually has a say in who she ends up with—"

"Raquel!"

"Yeah, sorry. Go on." I mimed zipping my lips and placed my hands gently on the table. Aaron watched the motion with careful scrutiny and glared at me for a second longer before softening.

"Alright. I'll help you. But only if you actually give me a fighting chance to impress her."

I could give him a thousand years to try, and it still wouldn't happen. I nodded anyway, knowing the chance was all that mattered.

"Okay. Deal. It'll be our version of a weird contest to win the girl." I snorted as I said it. It felt a little awkward to put it that way, but once it was out there, it was done.

"Win the challenge, win the girl," Aaron said, and we shook on it. Then he grinned, as if he had an inside joke rolling around in his head. "Lucky for you, I've already been doing some more investigating on the subreddit."

I furrowed my brow and watched him jump to his feet. He ran straight into his bedroom and reappeared with his laptop in tow. The screen was already opened to the Echo Game forum.

"What's the point?" I asked, taking the moment to open the bag of salt and vinegar chips and pop one into my mouth. "I've already been there. I can just tell you everything I know."

He side-eyed me. "Uh-huh, except you don't really under-stand why you came out with a whole new personality."

"It's not just me!" I protested. "Cisco got really confused and—and remember Olivia? How anxious she was?"

"All the more reason to arm ourselves with a little more research. Knowledge is power and all that." He continued to scroll through the forum, opening a new tab for every post he deemed insightful.

"How much research are you planning to do?" I asked. "We can't leave Charlize in the Echo for too long. Her mind will get scrambled." Or worse—the Slumlord could've found her by now. "We're on the clock!"

I heaved a breath of frustration. The fact I had the same rot inside of me but not spreading in the same way filled me with guilt.

"Look, we can do it tonight if you want," said Aaron, "but we won't last two minutes if we do."

I started to argue when he opened a tab to a section on the kinds of monsters people had faced in their own Echoes. I didn't want to admit it, but it seemed like it would be good to know.

Aaron tapped the laptop as if he'd struck gold. "Read this," he said.

His finger rested next to a post by a theorist named xxrecklss69:

Aside from the obvious dead people, the creatures that spawn in Echoes seem to be a manifestation of some form of evil unique to the location—like Pyramid Head from the Silent Hill series.

"This mean anything to you?" he asked, though I knew it was obvious from the look on my face.

"Papi told me about something called a slumlord—landlords who just let buildings decay and fall apart."

"There are slumlords in the Echo?"

"Just one." I swallowed. "He's the reason Cisco and Mami are infected—the reason I'm infected."

Aaron sucked in a deep breath as that sunk in.

"Anything else?"

"Passengers. Victims who either died during the fires in the seventies or were trapped by the Echo." I wondered whether the first round of Fordham kids were trapped and Passengers by now. "And the giant bug monster."

"The *what*?"

"It looks like a giant centipede. All black and oozing—"

"Stop!" He shook his head with a look of disgust. "You don't need to describe something that gross. Anything else I should know about?"

I thought quietly about everything that had happened. There was so much that I never properly processed any of it. Like the memory the Passengers tearing apart the one girl I saw. "Wait!" I snapped my fingers. "The Passengers kept chanting something. 'Falsas promesas.' Is that something?"

I looked down to his laptop and scanned the page.

Aaron shook his head. "I don't think so. It might be one of those things that we need to know a little more history about to understand. Maybe more context."

I frowned, but I knew he was right. "I'll ask my dad about it," I said with a sigh. "The only thing was the tailor shop. You know the one around Banana Kelly?"

"The one that used to be a bodega?"

"Yeah, that one!" I nodded. "I came across it—as a bodega, I mean, and when I thought about the fact the bodega's not even there anymore, it just...changed."

Aaron furrowed his brow.

"What do you mean, 'changed'?"

"Like, the whole building started shaking and falling apart, and then was suddenly the tailor shop. All brand new."

Aaron pursed his lips and opened a new tab.

"So, you did something to change the landscape of the Echo? I never heard of anyone doing that..." he murmured, gears in his mind obviously turning.

"Well, not the *whole* thing. Just that one part."

"I'll look into it."

I watched Aaron scroll away, clicking on various posts on the subreddit until something caught my eye.

"Wait a minute—click on this." I pointed to a link.

PROTECTION IN CATACOMB ECHO?

The paragraph that followed it was a little hard to read since English wasn't the person's first language, but they went on to talk about the use of two little dolls that seemingly helped keep them out of harm's way.

"Nénette and Rintintin?" Aaron quickly googled the set of dolls. They looked like straw dolls, only made of yarn. One had a skirtlike line of yarn around its bottom half. I guessed that was Nénette, and the other that only had two thick branches of yarn tied off at the end was Rintintin.

"It's a protective charm," Aaron read aloud. "Apparently made a lot and distributed during World War I."

Groaning to myself, I leaned into the couch. "I *knew* I should have brought the resguardos!"

"Brought the what?" Aaron looked back at me with mild concern.

I continued to mentally kick myself and waved him off. "Don't worry. I'll bring them next time."

We continued researching in silence before Aaron spoke up again.

"You know what I can't figure out? Why the seventies?" Aaron asked. "And why does every Echo have to be based off the worst time period in any location?"

I opened my mouth to answer but struggled to find something.

"My dad said that he's always felt like the Bronx had a dark energy to it. 'A ghost in every brick,' he says. Maybe the Echo can only go so far back." I shrugged. "The Passengers didn't seem to know they were dead—or even that they changed. They just lose part of themselves over time. Maybe at some point they die again, forgotten. Until some new tragedy takes its place."

Aaron didn't say anything. We only sat in silence, reading as much as we could to be better prepared. Minutes passed without notice. Then an hour. Time slipped away from us, and it wasn't until I felt my cell phone ringing in my pocket that I was startled back to reality. I jumped.

"Paranoid much?" Aaron chuckled.

Shushing him, I picked it up. "Hello?"

"Hello, this is Dr. Yee from Lincoln Hospital. May I speak with Raquel Celestin?"

"Speaking." I sat up straight, hoping to get some good news for once. The doctor was silent, and I heard papers shifting around in the background. I held my breath in anticipation.

"Raquel, this may be very hard to hear."

Oh no.

"Your mother just...isn't doing well. We've put her on a ventilator and given her antibiotics, but it's only slowed the progression of whatever this infection is. Her lung function is at thirty percent."

All the life was sucked out of the room. "So what are you saying?"

Dr. Yee went quiet again, and I realized it was because they were bracing to tell me even worse news.

Aaron's brow crumpled as he watched my expression change.

"I don't think she has very long," said the doctor. "A week or two at most, but if this continues to spread, it'll only be a matter of time before she codes."

Codes. I didn't need Papi here to tell me what that meant. I blinked back tears and nodded.

"Okay."

"I'm sorry."

"Thank you for letting me know." I hung up. For a minute, I sat there quietly. This couldn't be happening. *Right?* I wasn't about to lose my mother at age sixteen. This just *wasn't* happening.

I began to shake.

"Raquel?" said Aaron.

My chest exploded in piercing pain. I couldn't stop the tears. This was it—this was my life. It was trauma after trauma with no end in sight. I was going to lose my mom, lose my crush, and eventually but not fast enough—lose myself. The rot and mold sat in my chest like a time bomb, waiting for the worst possible moment to drag me back into the Echo.

I wanted to scream. To throw myself into the cushions and thrash and punch until all the energy flowed out of me, salty and sticky like tears and snot.

The pain intensified until it was all I felt.

Then arms came around me. Aaron held me tight as if knowing I was close to physically coming apart.

"Who was it?" he asked. "What'd they say?"

"Hospital." I gasped for air. "Mami only has a week."

Aaron cursed through gritted teeth.

I pulled away long enough to lock eyes with him.

"Tomorrow," I said. "We have to do it tomorrow. I can't let Mami die, okay? So do whatever research you have to do, but I'm going *tomorrow*."

"Raquel, I—"

I pushed my face into his chest and screamed my heart out.

STAND CLEAR
OF THE CLOSING
DOORS, PLEASE

I DIDN'T GO TO SCHOOL ON WEDNESDAY. WITH MY ANXIETY ramping high, I wasn't going to deal well with any amount of classwork. Not to mention, our history project presentations were due soon, and I couldn't focus on that with a guillotine hanging over my head. I could work on it after I got out of the Echo.

So I stayed home and prepared.

Papi didn't seem to mind. He was dead tired from another late-night shift as an EMT and looked a little guilty about constantly being away from home. When I told him about the news from Dr. Yee, he looked like he took a punch to the gut but nodded and gave me a weak smile. He asked if I didn't feel like going to school, and when I shook my head, he said he understood before going to his altar.

He started picking off the longer beads. My mouth dropped open in shock. "Are you taking those down?" I said.

"No, I just…need something to hold on to, I guess." Papi stared down at the alternating red and black beads with a look that said he was hanging on by a thread. I could sympathize.

I shifted on the futon. "Does it help?"

"Most days. It's comforting to know there's something or someone out there protecting you. Whether it's a spirit or your own energy surrounding you, I like to believe these resguardos are amplifying it. Believing couldn't hurt, right?" He forced chuckle.

Maybe not, but… "What happens when it's not enough?"

"Honestly? There are a plenty of times when they aren't." He shrugged like it wasn't a big deal. "Back when the Bronx was burning, there were a lot of people who relied on prayer and goodwill—which is good and useful in certain circumstances—but those can only do so much." Papi clicked his tongue, eyes clouding over with memories of harder times. "Sometimes you need some more tangible help. People in your neighborhood, in your community. It's only right that we take care of one another. And yeah, sometimes we fail, but sometimes we don't. Alone, we might not be enough, but as long as we can reach out to each other and stand together, we can change a lot. Heh, make sure you put that in your paper." Papi clenched the beads as he made his way toward his room.

I opened my mouth to wish him a good, restful sleep but coughed instead. My eyes burned, and as I tried to take in lungful of air, I tasted charcoal and blood.

My vision swayed all around me.

Falsas promesas…falsas promesas…

"What's going on?" I cried out as the voices grew closer. "How is this happening?"

"You broke a rule, Raquel," the corduroy man hissed from behind me. "You have to know it's coming for you."

I was outside in an alley. A rush of air carried thick clouds of smoke, filling my lungs and choking me. There were crumbling buildings all around me, and decaying people stood oblivious to their own burning houses. I dropped to the ground to escape the smoke, but my loud coughing still caught the attention of several Passengers at the end of the alley. They slowly walked toward me.

Falsas promesas…falsas promesas…

I glanced back to see the man was gone, and I was cornered. I couldn't even scream without my lungs burning.

"Go away!" I coughed, holding my hands up over my face.

"Raquel!" A forceful pair of hands pulled me to my feet. The air immediately cleared, and I found myself back in Papi's apartment. I looked down at his hands and saw his resguardo pressed against my skin. His eyes were wide with fear.

"Papi?"

"Are you okay? You started screaming all of a sudden."

My eyes darted around the room, as if expecting something to be out of place, proof I wasn't actually at Papi's and was still being messed with by the Echo.

"Raquel?"

"*I*—I'm fine," I gasped. The air was still clear. "Sorry I—I don't know what happened. Thought the apartment was on fire."

Papi didn't flinch or question what I meant by that. He only held up the resguardo. "Want to hold on to this?"

"Yeah," I said, grabbing it. "Um, Papi do you know what the phrase 'Falsas promesas' might have to do with the Bronx burning?"

His face twisted in confusion. "I suppose…it could do with the amount of times the government broke its promise to provide financial assistance to rebuild the Bronx."

"That happened a lot?" I asked.

"More than you'd think."

My shoulders dropped. It was definitely more information, but it didn't sound like something that would help me in a pinch.

"You sure you're okay now?"

"Yeah, I'm fine. Just go get some rest."

He looked as if he didn't believe me, at least not at first. But he disappeared into his room, and I waited. It didn't take long before I heard the familiar sound of his deep snoring.

I took my time digging around the house, searching every corner for those little beaded resguardos. If there was ever a time that I'd need extra protection, it would be now. All the orishas and gods of the world owed me.

I dumped what resguardos I found in a little pile on the coffee table. There were five, and three of them were just bracelets. There was more than enough for each of us—Aaron, me, and Charlize when we found her.

Praying Papi wouldn't notice them missing, I tucked them into a pouch behind the futon. In the pouch was also my inhaler. With all the smoke and dust floating around in the Echo, I needed to make sure the one thing that didn't do me in were my own shitty lungs.

That'd be a really pathetic way to go.

I checked my cell phone for messages.

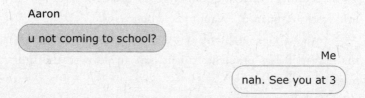

Aaron

u not coming to school?

Me

nah. See you at 3

I didn't have to clarify for him to know that I meant 3 a.m. By now, he knew I was serious. My mom was in trouble, so I was going in—with or without him.

And I was going to pay a visit to that piece of shit Slumlord.

My hands started to shake so hard, I dropped my cell phone onto the cushioned futon. It was a major surprise I hadn't destroyed it in a fit of rage, and I was grateful for whatever sliver of self-control I still had. *Hold it together, Raquel.*

Just a little longer now.

PART SIX

BEGIN AGAIN

BY THE TIME MY ALARM SOUNDED, I WAS ALREADY VIBRATING with energy. I texted Aaron and let him know I was going in and if he wanted any part of it, he'd meet me at Hunts Point Avenue by 2:45 a.m.

I traded my pajamas for a pair of sweatpants and hoodie. It was going to be a much colder night, and though I wanted to layer up, I knew I was going to have an easy time keeping warm where I was headed. The only layer I really *needed* was protection. Earlier today, while Papi was sleeping, I went home to find the shin guards I used to wear for soccer. Now, I slipped them on under my sweats before pulling on my boots.

I slid out my metal bat from underneath the futon. It was still in perfect condition, probably for the last time. Although I wasn't a sentimental kind of person, I hoped I'd still have it with me at the end of the challenge.

When it was all said and done, I'd need a reminder of what I'd been through—a physical one, proof I didn't just dream it all.

I lifted it up and brought it over my shoulder. There were no beer bottles to scavenge from the trash, so it would have to be my only weapon. After grabbing a pouch filled with some resguardos and my inhaler, I tiptoed out of the room and down the hall, careful to miss any of the weaker floorboards. The landlord might not have cared, but I didn't want to wake up the downstairs neighbors in case they were very familiar with Papi.

I checked my cell phone one last time for any messages from Papi. He would be working until six in the morning but said he would call me anyway to see if I was planning on going to school. He didn't say it outright, but I knew he expected me to go, if only so he didn't look bad in front of Mami.

He didn't say anything about Mami after we got the bad news. He didn't have to. I could tell he was trying to figure out the logistics if everything went south. Funeral costs, moving costs, even getting internet so I could reliably do my homework. I knew he was just trying to be a responsible adult and make sure he had all his ducks in a row, but it still hurt to see he didn't have any faith in the idea of Mami getting better.

Then again, he didn't know what I knew.

If Mami had been aware of what I was about to do, she'd be beyond pissed at me for putting myself in danger. She wouldn't even consider the fact that my involvement in the challenge was the only way to save her.

Sorry, Mami.

I needed to do this.

I came to the front door and quickly undid each lock. Then I was out on the street at 2:05 a.m., one hand deep in my pocket and the other clutching a metal bat.

The bus ride to Hunts Point was lonely without Charlize. The side of my body felt weirdly barren without something applying pressure. Instead, I focused on the resguardos, putting one of the bracelets on and holding the rest in the pouch.

If there were dead people in the Echo, then maybe I could count on the resguardos being a little more useful. Maybe the resguardos really *did* have a protective nature to them and would keep the Passengers away like crucifixes did to vampires.

To my surprise, when I got to Hunts Point, Aaron was already there, standing alongside Mario. They were facing each other, seemingly engrossed in conversation. Aaron stared at his brother with a vague look of boredom while Mario gesticulated.

I curled my fingers tightly into my palm, wondering why the hell Mario was invited.

"Hey!" the driver yelled. "You getting off or not?"

Aaron glanced up at me through the window. He mouthed my name, nodding his head in my direction. Mario turned around and lifted a hand to wave me over. The streetlight glinted off a shining pair of brass knuckles.

I let out a shuddering breath before descending the steps of the bus.

"Hey," Mario said. "Couldn't sleep?"

He said it playfully, but it still got under my skin. I shot Aaron a look that said, *What is he doing here?* and he gave me a look that could've been anything from, *Get over yourself,* to, *I've got a really annoying itch in my side.*

I turned on my heel and pretended to be more interested in the empty avenue. Just like last time, there was no one in the street. Empty buses would drive by sparingly, and there would be a few errant taxis carrying a passenger here and there, but other than that, Hunts Point Avenue was a ghost town.

"Oh, by the way—" Mario lightly tapped my shoulder— "Aaron told me about his lie."

I cocked my head to the side and glanced in his direction. I almost asked what he was talking about until I remembered the whole stint at Fordham.

"To be fair, I didn't really know anything about how you felt. I was just goofing off, but I'm sorry if I really annoyed you." He smiled.

"It's fine. I get it."

Except I didn't, not really. Mario was a jokester, and he prided himself on it. I knew he felt he had to be the comic relief because being serious was just too awkward at times. But I didn't get *why* he couldn't just shut up and let others have their serious moment. I wondered if that was part of the reason why Cisco and Mario had a fight. Cisco was always so sincere. Mario was the playful asshole. He couldn't give a genuine apology without putting his foot in his mouth.

Howling wind filled the space and silence between us until Aaron spoke.

"We're a bit early," he said, checking the time. "But we can use this time to make a plan."

"What do we need a plan for?" Mario asked, with a mischievous smile. It was obvious he didn't believe what we were doing.

"To make sure we all come back alive," Aaron said. "Raquel, tell Mario what you know."

"Okay, so we have to get around completely unseen. The Passengers and the other monsters in the Echo will attack us if they see us, and trust me, you do *not* want them to even get close to you. Stay hidden, move fast, and shut up." That last part was mainly for Mario's benefit.

I quickly described the bug-parasite creature and Slumlord and what to do if we came across them. It all came down to one thing: *run*.

"We split up but don't go too far. We have to make it easy on ourselves to regroup, so as a general rule, don't run more than two blocks away without turning back. Worse comes to worst, find the school and get inside. It's supposed to be a safe zone."

I didn't say how I knew this, but if Charlize thought it was worth mentioning, then I'd be damned if I didn't pass on that knowledge.

"You two are like, *really* into this, huh?" Mario said, looking between the two of us. God, I couldn't wait until he saw it all for himself.

"One last thing—try to keep yourself together," I said. "The Echo *will* get inside your head, and it *will* mess you up. Charlize thought she saw Cisco and went running out after him. We can't afford that happening to us."

Aaron nodded, shifting his hands in his pockets.

"So that's the plan?" Mario asked, staring into the distance. "We do the challenge, get off the train, and find Charlize. That sounds pretty easy."

He said this like he was checking off items on a grocery list. "It's not." I tried to keep the growl in my voice to a minimum. "We only have an hour, and the Echo—like the Bronx—is huge."

"What are you going to do if you can't find Charlize?"

Kill the Slumlord.

If he was the one who infected Cisco, and Cisco infected my mom, it stood to reason that getting rid of the Slumlord would get rid of the mold.

And if it didn't, well, I could at least avenge Mami. It was the least I could do for her.

"I'll keep trying," I said with an eerie calm. Mario snorted, and I was starting to feel like his obnoxiousness would get us killed within minutes. Hell, even *I* wanted to kill him, and that sentiment was there from before my first Echo experience.

With Mario involved, the whole operation was doomed before it started. I could almost hear the laugh of the man in the corduroy jacket.

"Why are you even here, Mario?" The question came out before I even realized I'd said it. For a moment, he looked taken aback. Then he cast his eyes to the ground and mumbled something.

"*What*?"

"It's what Cisco would've wanted!" he yelled.

We fell quiet, and even though his dark skin would show no sign of blushing, I knew his cheeks were heating with embarrassment.

"You two don't understand how close Cisco and Charlize were. It was like they shared some weird secret they thought no one would understand. If you guys are this hell-bent on finding his cousin, I might as well come along to make sure that happens."

"You're doing this for Cisco." It was a statement, not a question.

"I guess." He shrugged. "But that *doesn't* mean I believe in this whole Echo Game. I mean, hypothetically, let's say that this place *does* exist—"

"It does."

"And that these monsters *do* come after us."

I rolled my eyes. "They will."

"How are we supposed to fight them off? Oh, with a bat? A pair of brass knuckles?" He waved them in my face mockingly. I imagined Aaron had to beg him to bring those along and Mario only did so to humor him. Aaron sighed and rubbed his eyes. I hoped he could hear my voice in his head like a bell chime and saying, *I told you so.*

"If that happens," Aaron said, speaking up, "we'll kill them with this." He pulled his hand out of his pocket, gripping something sleek and black. I took a step back when I realized what it was.

"Aaron, *why* the hell do you have a gun?" I shouted.

"Hey, lower your voice."

"Ex*cuse* me?" I scoffed. I brought my voice down to a whisper and leaned toward him. "Where did you even get a gun? Is the safety on?"

"Don't worry about it," Aaron said, shoving it back into his pocket. I knew that answer. It meant he didn't know, but as long as he didn't accidentally pull the trigger, it should be fine. I glanced at Mario, but his face had gone slack. He didn't know about the gun either.

"Wow. Okay. Wow."

It was probably best I didn't address it at all. The more I thought about it, the more freaked out I was.

All this time, Aaron had access to a *gun*. The Bronx had its fair share of stereotypes about illegally carrying guns, but I'd never known a single person who actually did.

Suffice to say, it was jarring. Slightly less jarring than dealing with an underground cursed version of the Bronx, but it was jarring nonetheless.

I shook my head and tried to think about anything else. Looking down at my phone, I sucked my teeth and thought about the time. It was only 2:34 a.m.

"It's a bit early to start this challenge, isn't it?" Aaron asked.

We still had at least fifteen minutes before we could flip a coin, and my fingers were numb to the touch. I unstuck my fingers from the metal bat and switched it to the other hand. The weight of it felt less threatening.

"We only have to decide between one of two directions, so let's just flip the coin between uptown and downtown," I said. Neither of them could argue with that.

We turned up the street, right around the stone wall of the

subway station. The stairs dipped underground, and the harsh fluorescent light beamed at the last few steps. Mario took the first move towards it, and I followed. Aaron lagged behind us.

"What's on your mind?" I whispered.

He glanced at me and back to the station. "Just thinking about how stupid it is that we're running toward danger, not away from it."

I sucked in a sharp breath, unable to disagree with that. "Yeah," I said as I went in.

The underground train station was deserted, as expected. And it was much quieter. The wind didn't howl as much underground, which also made it easier to brave the cold. I dragged the metal bat on the ground and listened to the way it scratched the concrete.

We waited in awkward silence, and I stepped as much as I could down the platform without making it weird. The gun in Aaron's hand was startling for more than one reason. I'd literally felt the pain of people who died from gun wounds the last time I went into the Echo. It was a bizarre form of PTSD to be traumatized about something I never actually experienced for myself.

I checked the time on my phone then said, "Okay, let's flip," holding out the quarter. "Heads for uptown, tails for downtown."

We watched it soar in the air until it hit the pavement.

"Downtown it is."

The ground swayed under me, and bile ran up the back of my tongue. Suddenly, I was on the ground, and the bat rolled away from me.

"Yo, you okay?" Mario said, gripping my arm. I looked down at my hands, surprised to see them coated in dirt.

No, not dirt. *Soot.*

My hands were covered in ash and soot. Slowly, I stood up

with Mario's help. The station was still here but different. The green paint was peeling off the pillars even worse, and the tracks were loud with the squeal of rats searching for food and cover.

Smoke was thick in the air, and I coughed to clear my lungs of it. Mario slammed his hand against my back repeatedly. I ignored the pain that came with it and continued to look around.

"Why are we here?" I said, in between hacking coughs. But I knew. The Echo was coming to get me and all my friends, too.

"*Wh*—what's that?" Aaron yelled, pointing down the platform. His eyes widened, and before I could stop him, he pulled his gun out, aiming just over my shoulder.

"Hey!" I yelled. "Watch it!"

"He's got a gun!" a voice rang out.

I blinked, and we found ourselves back in our station. Standing down the platform were both Officer Bored and Officer Quiet, pulling out their guns and moving behind a pillar.

"Put the gun down!" Officer Bored yelled.

Aaron blinked, and the realization we were back dawned on him. His mouth dropped, and his hands began to shake.

"Don't shoot!" he shouted. "I'm sorry! *This isn't*—this isn't what it looks like!"

"We've got two Black men and a Black woman at the Hunts Point six train station, pointing a gun at two officers. We're going to need backup," Officer Quiet said into his radio.

"We're kids!" I screamed, taking slow steps away from Aaron. I held my hands up in display. Mario did the same but didn't budge from his spot.

"We're just kids!" I repeated, throat raw. "Aaron, put the gun down!"

"I'm so sorry!" Aaron's lips trembled. "I'm not trying to shoot anyone, but there's something behind you that I have to kill!"

My insides turned cold, and I looked to the cops. They held wide stances, focused completely on Aaron.

And oblivious to the thing that moved behind them.

"We're not going to ask you again!" Officer Bored yelled. "Put down the—"

He never finished that sentence.

His body arced backward and into the tunnel.

2:55 a.m.

THE COP'S SCREAM ECHOED THROUGH THE TUNNEL UNTIL it abruptly stopped. His partner swiveled around, turning his gun toward the tunnel then back to us, unsure which of us was the bigger threat.

"What was *that*!" Officer Quiet yelled. Spittle flew from his lips, and his eyes were large with fear. "What did you *do*?"

"We didn't do anything!" I screamed, voice cracking. I wanted to take a step back, but with the way the other cop's gun shook, I wasn't confident he wouldn't pull the trigger on impulse.

"Aaron, for God's sake, put the gun down!" Mario yelled.

"I can't *believe* you're still holding it!" I seethed, tossing back a careful glance. His hands were shaking just the same, which only doubled my anxiety.

"But what *is* that?" Aaron protested. The cop turned back.

"What is *wha*—" His voice suddenly cut out. Then he made a gargling noise, and a thick, dark stain spread through his clothes. His gun hit the ground. Then, all at once, his body crumpled.

"*Holy shit!*" Mario said.

I looked back at Aaron again and knew whatever he had seen was no longer there. His hand was steady on the gun. The trembling was replaced with petrification. My feet began to move forward on its own. Halfway to the officer's body, Mario shouted at me.

"Raquel, *don't*!"

I held up a slow hand to quiet him as I came to the body. I looked for any signs of life, hoping to see his chest still rising and falling. But there was no mistaking it. Officer Quiet was dead.

I nudged him over and gasped.

Blood ran down his glassy stare, and there was a dark hole piercing his chest. The wound was cauterized as if whatever shot through him was literally on fire.

I covered my face with the crook of my arm and tried not to imagine how it must've looked. The idea of something tearing into flesh and burning on contact should've disgusted me—made me *nauseous*—but it just didn't.

"Is he..."

I nodded and answered with a shaky breath, "He's dead."

"Shit." Mario sucked his teeth. "What the fuck do we do now? Should we call the cops or—"

"*You* wanna explain to them how this guy died?" Aaron sputtered.

"Well, aren't they on their way already? They called for backup, and you know whoever gets here first is going to check the cameras!"

I leaned over the cop's body and quickly grabbed his gun. Some part of me still recoiled at the sight of the weapon, so I hadn't absolutely lost it.

At least not yet.

Aaron and Mario continued to yell at each other, arguing

about our next move as I tucked the gun against my back in the waistband of my pants.

"Hey!" I snapped. "Stop arguing. You knew what we were going into when we started."

Mario's face twisted into a scowl.

"Who the fuck is *we*? I didn't sign up for *shit*!" His voice was pitched high, making it obvious how freaked out he was. Mario started backtracking, heading in the direction of the staircase, and I tightened my grip on the gun at my back in response.

"Where do you think you're going?" I said. "The minute we flipped the coin, we already started. If you don't get on the next train, you're next."

Aaron froze, considering the weight of my words.

"Is that a threat?" Mario said with a growl.

"No." I tapped the body of the dead cop with the tip of my bat. "*This* is a threat. I'm just translating it in a way you understand."

He didn't say anything after that. He only glared at me, shoving his hands into his pockets. His brass knuckles caught onto his zipper, and as I watched him angle it better to fit, I wondered if he still felt safe with it on.

Aaron stepped up beside me, looking deep in the tunnel.

"Is that...a person?" he said.

I could only see a brown pair of loafers connected to long, thin legs. Despite the consistent tunnel lighting, the darkness just about obscured the figure from the waist up.

But there was no ambiguity about that corduroy jacket.

The feet turned around and walked deeper into the darkness. Each light bulb he passed suddenly went out, and the sound of the wind completely quieted. The train station shifted again, and I knelt on the ground to keep my balance.

"He wants us to follow him," I said matter-of-factly. "What time is it?"

"It's two fifty-eight," Aaron replied, confused. The grip on the gun's handle left ridges in my back as I got to my feet.

"Let's get on the next train."

I turned my head to the opposite end of the tunnel. A quiet rumble made its way through, followed by the glow of a green numbered train. The six train whizzed into the station, slowed to a stop, and slid its doors open. The train car light was warm and inviting, but I could still feel the insidiousness of it behind the automatic voice.

This is a Manhattan-bound six train...

I took a step forward and felt a strong hand on my elbow.

"Wait," Mario said. I expected to see him full of doubt and anger, but when I looked back, his eyes were only full of concern. "Isn't someone on the tracks?"

"No," I said, getting on the train. "Now come on."

Without another word, the boys followed me onto the train, and the doors slid shut. I was exhausted and wired as I held on to the pole to my right. Aaron stepped behind me and grabbed an empty seat. His hand was still in his pocket, probably clutching his gun.

Mario sat across from us, staring through the windows intensely. He looked worried, like he was afraid something else was going to pop out from the darkness and gut him like a fish.

"Oh," I dug into my pocket for a pouch. "I forgot. I brought these."

Mario leaned forward and furrowed his brow at the sight of the small, beaded bracelets.

"What are those?"

I passed the only other bracelet to Aaron and gave Mario the ball-like resguardo with seashells.

"Resguardos. My dad said they're protective charms and used

to guard me against a ghost when I was a kid." I shrugged. "Doesn't hurt to have them."

Aaron put on his bracelet and then looked up at me. "Raquel, can I ask you something?"

"Go for it." It wasn't like there was anything else to do on this shitty trip.

"Why do you like Charlize?"

I felt my heart jump to my throat. That was unexpected.

"I don't know, man," I stammered, looking away. "Why do *you* like her?"

"She's pretty. And nice," he said with an ease I didn't think was possible. "She smells good, too."

"You're starting to sound creepy."

"At least I'm being honest."

Ouch. He crossed his arms and pouted, as if this were the most normal time in the most normal place to talk about crushes and *I* was making it weird.

"I'm just saying." Aaron tried to soften the blow. "At least I know why I'm into her. You act like you fell into it and don't have a clue what you should do about it."

I definitely fell.

"It's easy to say that when you're a guy," I muttered. "You don't know what it's like to like a girl *as* a girl." It was confusing and messy at best—and infuriating at worst. Girls were always so friendly with each other. How was I supposed to know if someone liked me back?

And worse, what if they didn't? What if they thought I was gross for getting my hopes up? What then?

"She literally kissed you," Aaron said. I briefly wondered if he could read my thoughts. "That's practically all the confirmation you need to just start a relationship."

He was right. The next thing I *should've* done was ask her out, but as always, I was too much of a coward.

"I can't believe you two like the same girl," Mario said. I almost forgot he was there. "This is pretty much me and Cisco all over again."

Aaron and I passed a look between us, having the same thought.

"You and Cisco fought over a girl?" Aaron asked.

"*Pfft*, yeah." Mario gave a weak smile to obscure the sadness in his eyes. "She played us both, though. Had us thinking she chose one of us while still hanging out with the other. It went on for so long, we were kind of embarrassed by it."

"Well, yeah, how the hell could you not know?" I asked, for once bewildered by something Mario said.

"She fed us some crap story about how the other was going to be too upset if we brought up her name, so we shouldn't mention her at all. It took three months and a mutual friend before we found out."

I glanced at Aaron and could see he didn't even know about it. It must have been a really bad fallout.

"We decided we needed space from each other, but then we started college and just...fell out of touch, I guess." Mario looked at the two of us before chuckling. "I thought we were pretty bad, but here you are, ready to put your differences aside and risk dying for this girl. Hopefully, Charlize doesn't do you dirty like Samira did us."

A spark of recognition flashed across Aaron's face. He probably met Samira once or twice and didn't know what she was capable of.

"Let's just hope we get out of this alive," he said, thinking twice about it. "And save Charlize if we can."

"Right," I agreed. "Finish the challenge, save the girl."

Aaron and I locked eyes, having the same thought.

And maybe even win both.

3:00 a.m.

"WAIT, SHOULDN'T WE HAVE...I DON'T KNOW, CHANTED something?" Mario asked.

I widened my eyes at him. "You actually read the rules?"

He didn't answer before the train came to a stop and the doors slid open. We stared out into the station. The edge of the platform visibly met the train, but beyond that, it was too dark to see anything.

"If we're going to break the rules anyway, we might as well start from the top," I said, carefully tapping my foot against the platform. It was solid. I wasn't sure what I expected. "Let's go."

We all stepped off the train as the automatic voice came back on, for the last time: *Stand clear of the closing doors, please...*

The train carried on, taking the only source of light with it. I grabbed on to Mario immediately, not wanting to get separated, and pulled out my phone. The beam of my phone's flashlight did nothing to the dark and only brought our attention to swirling dust particles.

"Both of you, hold hands," I barked. I could hear their coats shuffling as they moved closer together. Then I shined the flashlight ahead of us.

"I didn't know it would be this dark," Mario said.

"It wasn't last time I was here."

I held my hand out as we stepped forward together. The platform seemed to continue like a normal platform and eventually hit a wall. I ran the light over the wall, eyeing the familiar subway tiles. Eventually, it hit a sign that stretched out a few feet.

"Oh," I breathed. The sign read 149TH STREET, but it was cracked and oozed a clear liquid.

"What the hell?" Aaron said in exasperation. He reached out and lightly dabbed his finger into the substance.

I slapped his arm. "Why would you touch it?" I hissed. "You don't even know what it is!"

He gave me a look and then brought his finger to his nose.

"It smells like...gasoline," he said, holding it under my nose. I slapped his hand away quickly but still smelled the fumes. My mind spun, and I shook my head to clear it.

"We should get out of here," I said, pulling the line along the platform. "If we're on 149th, then there should be a way to the surface."

We shuffled along, carefully inspecting the ground before we took another step. Gasoline continued to drip through the wall, and the fumes became more powerful the farther we went. I knocked back into Mario a few times as my sense of balance faltered and mumbled an apology each time.

"Raquel, you good?" he asked, irritation in his voice.

"No." I tried to feel apologetic but could only come up with anger myself. "Let's just keep moving."

Eventually, we reached the turnstiles at the center of the platform. The metal was beyond rusted, and parts of it seemed to be scorched by flames. I brought my bat to it and pushed until I heard an audible click. It still functioned like a typical turnstile.

"Okay," I said, shifting my phone into my elbow. I turned back to Mario and nudged him to the other turnstile. He didn't argue. "You go there." Aaron followed the lead and went to the next turnstile.

I listened again for the usual clicks as we all passed through the turnstiles, but I only heard one. Panicked, I picked up my cell phone again and looked behind me. The flashlight gleamed off the rusted turnstiles, completely empty.

"Mario?" I called. "Aaron?"

They were gone.

A few things ran through my head. I thought about how we were literally in a hell version of the Bronx, and so things that were impossible and possible were already scrambled to begin with. I thought about how I was going to discreetly get the smell of gasoline out of my clothes before I got home, assuming I got home at all.

But most of all, I thought about how absolutely white it was to get separated from my friends during a dangerous game. After all, they were *right there*. We were literally *just* clinging to each other. In the few seconds we unlinked our arms, they were gone. And I was alone.

"I'm not allowed to make fun of white people in horror movies ever again," I said, trying to ignore my own rising goose bumps. In the distance, I could hear small feet scurrying and a light squeal. Something ran over my foot, and I jumped.

"Rats," I said, seeing the tail end of one. "It's just rats." I pressed onward until I came to a set of stairs. The darkness wasn't as thick at the steps, and toward the top, a red glow of light flickered.

"Mario? Aaron?" I called out. "Are you there?"

Slowly, I ascended the steps and listened closely for any movement on the surface. Sticking close to the wall, I peered over the street and felt all my blood pool at my feet. I had lived in the Bronx all my life. I watched hair salons turn into corner stores and vice versa. There were more cracks in the sidewalk than there was hair on my head, and there was constant train maintenance for as long as I could remember.

But even though I knew about the fires in the Bronx, I would've never imagined it like this.

The sky was thick with smoke, and most of the buildings were either on fire or already a collapsed pile of rubble and trash. Passengers filed in and out of them, completely oblivious to the flames caught on their clothes or their skin crumpling in the heat. A stream of blood poured from the fire hydrant, and there was a constant ring of a fire alarm in the distance.

Did things get worse since I last visited?

Because this was not 149th Street.

Where the hell was I? I squinted in the direction of the street sign, but it was too blurred to read. My stomach roiled once again. Now that I was here, I didn't want to be. But I had to do this—to complete the challenge. If not for Charlize, then for my mom. I couldn't explain it, but I knew I had find the Slumlord and kill him in order to save her.

Besides, I already came this far. Might as well see it through to the end.

I tucked my cell phone into my pocket and gripped the bat. The ridges of the gun pressed into my skin again, a constant reminder of what I had to do.

"Are you sure about that?"

I spun around, bringing my bat up onto my shoulder. The man in the corduroy jacket smiled a toothy grin.

I tightened my grip. "Where is Charlize?"

"Where she's supposed to be." He took a step forward. "But you don't seem to be in your place."

"I'm not going to become a Passenger."

He chuckled. "You seem awfully certain."

Why was he constantly showing up? It would be one thing if it were just tied to the burning—but even as a kid, he sought me out. Why?

"What's happened to you?" I asked, trying to get at him from another angle. Aggression came off him in waves. It was different from the last time I'd seen him. Was this what the Echo did to the dead? Or was he just emptied out again, a puppet for something trying to goad me into a trap? I beat down the rage, but it was building again, and my body felt live with excitement. "You were a person once."

"Still am." He smiled. "Just dead. Like you'll soon be."

"*No.*"

He took another step, and I jumped back. My palms were so sweaty, the bat slid under my grip. I made a move as if I threatened to hit him, but he didn't seem afraid. I had hoped that the resguardo I was wearing was enough to block the man out of my head. He seemed to be able to read my thoughts all this time, and right now would've been the absolute worst time for him to call my bluff.

"What is it that you think will happen, hmm? You think you can just traipse in here, find your little girlfriend, your friends, and walk out of here scot-free? You should know well enough what happens to those who break the rules."

"*Fuck* the rules!" I spat, trying to keep my distance. He only continued to get closer, and I felt my heart jump into my throat. "Now I want you to take me to Charlize and then to the Slumlord."

For a moment, his eyes shined with something that looked like glee. Then they darkened again, as if something took over his mind and forced his mouth open.

"And if I don't? What are you going to do with that big bat?" he said mockingly as he took a step forward with each sentence. "Gonna hit me? Better make it count. Better make it hurt. Better kill me in one shot."

His voice dropped low, sinister. "Hey, batter, batter..."

The whites of his eyes quickly turned red.

"*Swing*."

3:05 a.m.

I SHUT MY EYES TIGHT AND TWISTED MY HIPS WITH THE flow of the bat.

It connected with something dense then bounced right off. The motion reverberated back up my arms, almost cartoonish. When I opened my eyes, the man in the corduroy was gone.

Clicking my tongue, I looked around. It was getting really annoying to deal with several disappearing acts back-to-back.

I shifted the gun at my waist to keep it secure.

The Passengers in the area, besides being on fire and nonchalant about it, barely blinked an eye. I hugged the bat and jumped behind the nearest car before any of them turned in my direction, listening closely for the sound of approaching feet. It seemed like I managed to avoid their attention. The air was thick with smoke, and my lungs struggled to take in clean air. I grabbed my inhaler and took a quick puff. After a few seconds, I could breathe again.

From where I sat, the Bronx was a flat horizon of fire, dust, and toppling bricks. Broken glass and garbage bags littered the street. The smell of burning flesh and rubber threatened to make me gag, but I kept silent, if only to avoid attention from the Passengers.

I glared down at the resguardo.

"What gives?" I whispered to it. "You're supposed to protect me."

Of course, it didn't answer, which was just as well. It was a minor setback to my plan, but I'd have to find a way to work around it. I could only hope Aaron and Mario were together and keeping each other alive.

I knew they had to be somewhere in the Bronx—just in a different location. Losing them scared me shitless, but I tried not to worry—we all agreed to meet up at the school sooner or later. They would be *fine*.

For now, my focus was finding Charlize and then the Slumlord.

Rolling up my sleeves, I wiped the sweat from my forehead. I was right to dress light for the occasion. The fires and Passengers were keeping the area well heated.

The man in the corduroy jacket said Charlize was "where she needed to be," but that didn't make any sense. When I last saw her, she said the school was safe, which meant she had to be there.

But if it was safe and she was there, why was she still covered in mold?

I crossed in front of a boarded-up pharmacy. It reminded me a little of the tailor shop—and the hint the man in corduroy gave me. None of it made any sense either. I tried to focus only on what was in front of me.

Scattered pieces of glass littered the sidewalk, but something was still moving inside the building. A shadow scurried away from the door. The pharmacy was gated, but the lock had long since broken. I hooked my fingers into the grates and slid it up. It stopped short about halfway—just enough to crawl under.

"Charlize?" I whispered loudly, keeping a ready grip on my bat. "Who's there?"

The pharmacy was filled with rows of mostly empty shelves, pushed aside or toppled over. Pills decorated the floor under the small crevices of the shelves, and a rotten odor wafted in from the back.

I took a slow step forward, ignoring the broken glass under my feet, and squinted over a shelf. A figure scurried farther to the back and hid behind a desk.

Definitely not Charlize.

It was a Passenger or something else—I didn't need to waste time finding out. We only had an hour to get back to the train.

I turned back, crawling out from under the gate, then froze right at the entrance.

Oh no. Where the train station had been was all concrete now.

"No, no, no, no, *no, no, no*!"

I ran over to the spot and stomped the ground a few times, panic mounting. Nothing happened. The sidewalk was solid. No hint of a staircase that would descend into the subway. It was like it was never there.

"Noooooo!" I yelled again, slamming the bat against the ground. It was bad enough that the Echo was a shitty mimic of the Bronx, bad enough that friends and foes could disappear, but now the train stations could vanish?

If the stations could dematerialize at a moment's notice, how were we supposed to catch a ride out of this hellscape?

My arms twitched as I continued swinging the bat. A growl tore from my lips between every hit, relishing the momentum as the vibrations surged back up the bat. I only slowed out of exhaustion and looked down at my hands. Small cuts crisscrossed calluses.

Cálmate. Focus.

I sniffled and rubbed my eyes. Up and down the street,

Passengers were turning the corner, heading in my direction. None of them seemed in any shape to run, so I was lucky to have the advantage.

I booked it down the block.

Soon enough, I reached a deserted area.

There were spots of decaying body parts or broken bones left along the sidewalk in piles, a disturbing display of flesh. The walls of nearly every building were covered in murky-brown graffiti—a stark contrast to the actual Bronx, where the graffiti was bright and colorful. None of it rang any bells. If the Echo was a constant looping horror show of the '70s, then this was completely out of focus.

Which made me suspicious.

I upped my pace until I heard something even more off-putting.

Murmurs. People talking. And Passengers didn't talk so much as they hummed or attacked. There were living people nearby, and they were following me.

I gripped the bat in the other hand and pretended not to notice. The block I was on was starting to look familiar, even though it was supposed to be on a completely different avenue. Turning the corner down the street, I spotted an open alleyway behind a mechanic shop and ran for it. The shop was closed, but the garage hardly ever was, and it was filled with so many cars that there was decent cover if I needed to keep hiding. I ducked behind the large dumpster that sat in front of the door.

Then I heard the murmurs grow closer.

"She went down here, I think..." one of them hissed. The sound was gravelly, like it hadn't known water in weeks. Footsteps followed, and an intense body odor crept into my nose. It took everything in me to keep from gagging.

"Where'd she go?" a different voice asked. Judging from the footsteps, there were quite a few people. At least four, maybe five. Even with a bat and gun, I was outnumbered. I peered out for a quick glance and furrowed my brow.

Aside from the blood and dirt that stained their skin, the people were fairly pale. There were four of them: two girls with blond hair, a guy with a buzz cut, and another guy with matted curls. Their eyes were feral. They stuck closely to each other as if trying to hold on to the last shred of their humanity.

"Listen, I *know* she went this way, okay?" the girl said. She chewed her nails obsessively, ignoring how they bled. Her hair was thin and lifeless.

All at once, I realized who they were.

The Fordham kids. The original people who disappeared. They'd gone missing over a year ago, but the whole time, they'd been stuck here. Their clean, picture-day-ready faces that were shown on the news for weeks were essentially a *before* image to their now feral appearances.

Would that be me?

Nausea kicked into me as they stepped a little closer, and I almost rolled forward. Before I was exposed, a pair of hands grabbed me and pulled me back. Whoever it was put a firm hand over my mouth even as I thrashed around. With one free hand, I tried to jam the bat backward into their side, but the shock was absorbed by the thick winter coat.

"Raquel, can you chill?" Mario hissed. I let my body go slack before turning to him.

"Mario, what the hell? Where's Aaron?"

"Did you hear something?" one of the guys said.

Mario put one finger on his lips and gestured for me to follow him farther back into the alley. We crawled along the other side of a dumpster, where he removed a piece of cardboard on the wall and showed me a hole big enough to crawl into.

"Get in!" he whispered. "Trust me!"

I opened my mouth to argue, but he pushed himself all the way through. As I crouched, I watched him shove aside a wooden plank to reveal a broken ground window he then crawled through.

"Mario!" I hissed, only cut off by the sound of approaching footsteps.

"I heard it in this direction," said one of the Fordham girls.

I held my breath as I went in after him.

3:15 a.m.

I FOUND MYSELF IN A BASEMENT FILLED WITH HALF-EMPTIED portable gas containers. The smell was dizzying, and I had to lean against the wall closest to the window to get any air.

Mario stood on the other side of it, peering up through the window. It was too dark to see much of anything, but he didn't move for what felt like ten minutes.

Unfortunately, neither did the Fordham kids.

"Mario, what's going on?" I whispered between careful gasps of air. "Why are we hiding?"

"Shh!" he shushed me, but I got my answer anyway in the next few seconds.

"I want her face."

My jaw dropped.

"*I* want her fingers," the other girl said, petulant. "They looked nice and fat."

I looked down at my hands, disgusted before mouthing a question to Mario, "They want to eat *me*?"

He gave me a look that said, *I told you so*. I sneered, listening for more suspicious footsteps.

"No, we need to find out how she got here," one of the guys said. "She might know the way out."

If I'd been considering helping them, I definitely changed my mind now. The last thing I needed was to worry about cannibals plotting to eat me while I was looking for my friends.

I shifted away from the window.

Without realizing it, my bat swung lightly and hit the metal lining of the windowpane, letting out a soft ring.

"What was that?" the buzz-cut guy said.

Mario's eyes went round as he ushered me out of the basement. The hallway came to a dead end on one side, on the other was a set of stairs that rose to the first floor. Mario stopped me before I went any farther, suggesting we stayed in the hall until we knew for sure it was safe. It was sound logic, and yet we couldn't wait around too long, or we'd run out of time.

While Mario peered his head back into the basement room, I stepped off in the direction of the steps.

"Whatever," one of the blonds groaned, her voice echoing in the hall. "It's probably just one of those people again."

"We need to find the girl."

"Why don't we just eat them?" the blond asked, and I knew she was talking about the Passengers by the irritated sighs of the people around her.

"If you can even touch one without it trying to rip your throat out, I'll..."

Their voices continued to trail off as they shuffled away. Mario hissed my name behind me and raced to catch up.

"What is wrong with you?" He pulled my arm. "I thought you said we weren't supposed to split up?"

I shook him off. "I didn't *leave* you! You and Aaron disappeared on *me*. Where is he anyway?"

Mario twisted his lips before he responded.

"I don't know. He vanished just like you did." He let out a sharp breath. "I was just going to go straight to the school like we said—but then I ran into *them*." Mario jerked his thumb in the direction of the Fordham kids.

"Ugh, we're running out of time! Okay, you focus on finding Aaron, and I'll try to find Charlize—"

Just then, the sound of an explosion ripped through the air. It made me realize that the best place to search for someone wasn't from the ground—it was from the sky.

"Come on!" I shouted at Mario.

3:27 a.m.

MARIO CLIMBED THE STEPS TO THE ROOF AFTER ME. As soon as I slammed the door open, I was hit by the taste of ash in the air. I quickly gripped my inhaler in my pocket but didn't seem to need it. Instead, I rushed forward and skidded to a stop at the ledge.

"Don't jump!" Mario joked.

Down below, the Passengers milled about like zombies. Horrifying, undying, and unaware of it. Every so often they would bump into each other or trip over the crooked edge of a street corner, but they hardly reacted. I continued to scan the streets, hoping to catch sight of Charlize or Aaron. The Passengers' clothing was so dirty and tattered that it took me a while to see each one seemed to have come from a different time period.

"They're from the past," I whispered.

Bell-bottom jeans were the most prominent style, though they were mostly matted with blood and dirt or heavily scorched by flames. Colorful shirts had dulled over time, and any makeup on women was smeared, if not melted.

"What?" Mario came up next to me.

"Look at their clothes." I pointed at them. "They're dressed like the Jackson Five are still together. It's like we time traveled or something."

"Or something." Mario's lips curled into a frown as he gestured down to a stoop. A seemingly young Black boy sat there quietly.

The boy's movements reminded me of the man in the corduroy jacket, stiff and lifeless. He wore a sleeveless denim jacket with patches referencing old rock bands I'd never heard of. It was the cleanest attire I had seen since arriving here, and for a moment, I thought he was a normal kid...until he turned to face us.

A breath hitched in my throat. There were various holes chewed in the side of his face. The tail of a rat poked through and shifted, letting me know it was still alive in there.

I stumbled back a step. I thought I'd be able to find Charlize from up high, but I'd only gotten a better view of the horror.

"Do you hear that?" Mario furrowed his brow. I strained to listen.

"Is that a...helicopter?"

The *whomp-whomp-whomp* sound seemed to come closer and closer until we turned in its direction. All at once, we realized it wasn't a helicopter making its way toward us. It was the parasite creature. Its hundreds of legs slammed against concrete and metal as it zoomed over every abandoned car in the street. It was heading straight for us.

And it was pissed.

Next to me, Mario gulped.

"So," he began, voice hoarse. "This is the Echo."

I answered by pulling the gun out of my waist, testing the weight of it in my hands. I didn't know how many bullets this model carried, but I hoped that my aim in *Call of Duty* translated well into actual firearms.

There was a sharp uptick in my desire for violence as I gripped the sleek weapon. The Echo had ample time to worm its way into me, make me think of nothing else but lashing out and chaos. It was hard enough trying to keep myself from snapping at others; it was even *more* difficult to pull back the impulse for drawing blood. I gritted my teeth as if to keep it from spilling out—once I started shooting, I knew there'd be no going back.

Focus. I took in a deep breath. *Focus on Charlize.*

The creature had gotten to the building and was now skittering up the length of it.

Three.

Mario grabbed my bat and readied himself for the incoming attack.

Two.

The creature was closer now. My hands shook with rage, but suddenly my body remembered the feel of Charlize's lips against mine. I thought of how soft they were and how if I died here and now, I'd never get to feel them again. I thought of the peppermint scent of her hair as I planted my feet and took aim.

One.

And then something unexpected happened. Right as the parasite lunged to attack, a bright light shot out, shielding Mario and I on all sides. When the parasite's head met it, the light sharpened, and the creature screeched as though it had run into a high-voltage shock wire. Its hundreds of legs danced in pain as it fell backward and plunged down the side of the building.

The light started to fade just enough for me to see where it was coming from. Dangling from my wrist, the resguardo glowed faintly as the brilliant light retreated into each bead. A ring of warmth went with it, but unlike the heat surrounding us, the warmth had a calming effect. Even my violent thoughts had withdrawn for the moment.

"Holy shit!" Mario grinned widely. He glanced from the gun to the resguardo. "That thing is scared of a bracelet!"

But it wasn't just the resguardo. I remembered what Papi said about believing the resguardos could amplify energy and how the tailor shop sprung up from my own memories. If the Echo was a dumping ground of horrific memories and history, maybe the positive ones we carried with us could be amplified by the resguardo. After all, I'd been thinking of Charlize the moment the creature mounted the ledge of the roof.

Hands still shaking, I summoned the memory of Charlize's sleeping figure during the training camp and the feel of her palm when I held her hand.

The resguardo shone even brighter.

Mario cursed in Spanish. "Whatever you're doing, keep at it." As he looked back over the ledge, I could hear the creature's stomping legs drawing close again.

Charlize, think of Charlize!

I held my wrist out as the force field reemerged. I felt something try to push against it, but I refused to let go of my memories. The creature flailed again, pushed back each time the force field got bigger.

With a sharper screech, the parasite gave up. It jumped onto the side of the closest building, skittering down to ground level and along the avenue.

My knees gave out from under me as I took in a deep breath. The gun was still clenched in my grip. I took my finger off the trigger and watched the glow of the resguardo fade.

"Didn't know you were this powerful," I muttered, shaking out my wrist. I tucked the gun back into my waistband and took the bat from Mario's hand.

He was hyperventilating just the same from the shock.

"I can't believe you're willing to go through all this for Charlize," he said, locking eyes with me. "You must really like her."

I broke eye contact, my cheeks heating up. Then the image of Mami stuck in a coma flashed through my mind.

"Not just Charlize."

I cast my eyes to the landscape. The Bronx seemed to roll on forever, never meeting a river or tree that wasn't dead. Even the Sheridan Expressway was filled with cars pushing out smoke. What I couldn't see was Hyde High School. It was as if it kept moving.

Or being moved.

I scowled. If the school was safe, then there was no way the Echo would let us get to it. Not easily anyway. My gaze slid over to the juvenile detention center in the shadow of the Cross Bronx Expressway, looking more hellish than usual. Of everything that continued to shift and change, only the expressway remained static.

"It's like an anchor."

"What is?"

I pointed it out to him. "If the Echo is based on the past, the expressway is the starting point. Where everything went wrong."

I thought of the housing torn down just to make it, the hundreds of people who were made homeless over racist policies. The deliberate act of lowering it so much that people from the Bronx couldn't take buses to enjoy the beach. Even just looking at it, a chill crawled up my spine. It was bad news.

I averted my eyes long enough to catch sight of the tailor shop. A thick line of black rot ate along the sides of the building, chewing through the awning.

"That's weird," I murmured. The Passengers seemed to be avoiding the area.

"What are you looking at?" Mario said, breaking into my train of thought.

"The empty spaces."

"The empty spaces?" he repeated.

Suddenly it clicked.

Wherever there was mold and rot, the Passengers were gone. It was like they knew where not to be.

Find the prison within the prison, the man in corduroy had said. If the Echo was a prison, then did I need to go toward the juvie center?

"Alright, time for plan B," I said. With the Echo moving the school around, I couldn't be sure I'd be able to find Charlize before the hour was up, but I had a good idea of where the Slumlord was. And maybe if I managed to destroy him, I'd save my mom.

"Plan B? I'm still fuzzy on plan A. I don't—"

"Mario," I cut him off. "I need you to do me a favor. Find Aaron, find Charlize, and get on the next train by four a.m. *Don't* wait for me."

"Wait, what if that giant bug comes back?" He glanced at my own resguardo, looking skittish on his own.

"You still have your resguardo?"

He dug into his pocket and pulled it out.

"Good. Use that. And think happy thoughts."

"Are you shitting me?"

"No. Think of a good memory—*any* good memory." I turned for the steps leading down the building. We were running out of time, and I had to trust Mario to save his brother.

"Where are you going?" he called after me.

"To win the challenge!"

3:35 a.m.

My loud, thudding footsteps caught the attention of every Passenger in sight. They turned to follow: a chorus of feet, starting with a sudden swell and slow decrescendo the closer I got to the juvenile detention center. The sound of my labored breathing drowned out the dull roar of Passengers.

Quickly, I checked my watch. Twenty-five minutes left.

My chest burned as I struggled to keep my pace, but I pumped my legs harder with my eyes set on the black rot. The wind howled through the streets, bringing with it another lungful of smoke. I was confident my resguardo would protect me against the Passengers, but each time I accidentally brushed against one, I felt flashes of fire and pain from their lives.

Bullets tore into my body. I felt muscle spasms responding to violent hands that weren't there, and the memory of my head bouncing off the concrete was prominent and gave me a headache.

Find the prison within the prison.

I fought to keep my head on straight.

These weren't *my* memories. They were echoes of grief and trauma from the Bronx's past. The Passengers were dead, but they were still real people. They didn't deserve to be put through more pain in their afterlife—if that's what this was. The Bronx was more than this, more than just a long string of injustices against a community of people who did nothing but try to survive.

The ground underneath me didn't so much shift as beat with a pulse.

And the Bronx's synced with my own.

Carefully, I scanned the block I was on. Several memories passed through my head, a collection of illness and disease brought by a pale man with greed that filled him like sludge.

Of course. Where else would a Slumlord be but on a street with shitty housing?

I shook my head to clear it. I was on a narrow, one-way street. Rows of houses on each side were overgrown with dead plants, and the black gates that would've provided a barrier either swung open or were beaten into odd angles and shapes. The windows of the houses were both broken and boarded up, and the paint on the doors peeled in large patches.

At one house, the door hung off its hinges and several bricks were piled on the steps. Something about it felt different than the other houses. I cocked my head to the side and pushed my hand against the gate, swinging it open.

Nothing happened, so I walked up to the door and rammed my shoulder into it. The hinges squeaked, and the wooden door frame groaned as it was forced open.

The inside was definitely *not* a house. The walls were made of concrete, and the center of the large room was filled with rusted metal tables bolted to the floor. On all sides of the room, there were thick steel doors with peeling paint and a sliver of glass to serve as windows—all shattered, but windows, nonetheless.

Find the prison within the prison. The thought almost made me want to roll my eyes. *Right*. Terrible housing could count as a prison if you had nowhere else to go. Maybe the Slumlord had a taste for poetic irony, warping the inside of an abandoned home into a juvenile center.

Whatever the reason, there was nothing but cobwebs and rat poop scattered around the floor. Small holes were kicked into the walls, and the air was stale. It was an odd contrast from the smoke outside.

I narrowed my eyes and took one step into the building. Suddenly, I heard a creak.

"Mario?" I whispered. Had he been stubborn enough to follow me?

And then, a loud slam. I jumped and turned back to the doorway. It was wedged shut. I pressed my back into it, using my full weight to yank it open, but it wouldn't budge.

I was locked in.

A high-pitched squeal tore through the air behind one of the doors and heavy footsteps followed it. My hair rose on ends, and I froze in place.

The squeal came from a rat, I knew. Rats were predictable, even in this world. They ran when they saw you and went hunting for scraps when they didn't.

They squealed and crawled and made annoying pitter-patter sounds in the walls and ceilings. You could almost joke that rats were legal tenants in New York and paid rent just like everybody else.

Rats didn't scare me. No, it was what I heard after the rat. The heavy pair of footsteps, one after the other. I turned in the direction it was coming from, gripping the bat and checking to make sure the gun was still secure at my waist and my resguardo was still tied at my wrist. They were. A thick shadow fell over the door and then moved away.

The squealing continued.

I pressed myself against the wall and walked along it. Something wriggled out of one of the holes in the wall. The rat, still squealing, plopped down on the ground and skittered around haphazardly as if it had no idea where it was going. It moved so fast, it was almost hard to notice until it started slowing down.

Black mold, spreading from its tail to the rest of the body. Soon enough, the squealing became a short wheeze that stopped right when the running did. I carefully stepped closer to it and watched its small body stop moving. The mold covered every inch of it in seconds.

I clamped my hand over my mouth and stepped back—knocking into a table. It groaned in response, and my blood ran ice cold as the sound of the thudding footsteps came back.

My eyes darted around the room. I needed to find a place to hide, quick. I ran to each door one by one and pushed against them. Most of the knobs wouldn't even turn, and other doors refused to move. At the very last second, I managed to slip into a door that was just cracked open. The jagged edges cut into me and drew blood, but I held my breath.

I'd gone into a hallway, and I ran into the first door I saw. It seemed to be an office space with a wooden desk and several filing cabinets all in a row. I quickly crawled under the desk and waited. It was quiet for a moment. Then, there was a loud screeching sound as the Slumlord forced open the first door. I squeezed my eyes tight and clutched my bat. The footsteps drew closer to the office.

This is pathetic, Raquel.

The thought sneered at me in a way that let me know it was both me and *not* me. It was the part of me corrupted by the Echo. The angry part.

I clutched the bat in my hand, and the gun pressed into my skin from inside my pocket.

All these weapons and you're still too afraid to face the Slumlord.

Shut up! I yelled back at the voice in my head.

The office door creaked open, and the footsteps entered.

You're really going to let the man who attacked your mother walk? The guy who made her so sick, you couldn't even hold her hand?

My terror overwhelmed any bit of anger I felt. I wanted to save my mother, but who was to say killing the source wouldn't just kill her?

What if I only made things worse?

Excuses, tutted the voice.

The footsteps slowly stepped away. I listened to him walk the length of the hall and then back up to the original lobby. Still, I waited. Under his fearful influence, seconds felt like an eternity.

I shut my eyes and forced my lungs to take in slow breaths. A full minute just to calm my heart. The panic started to recede, and I crawled out from under the desk. My bat scraped noiselessly along the ground. I didn't hear or feel the Slumlord draw closer.

I had the element of surprise.

"Look who it is," a raspy voice drawled from behind me. I shot back a deadly glare at the man in corduroy. He wasn't as terrifying as the Slumlord. Taking him out seemed easier by a landslide.

But one thing at a time.

"I see you finally figured out my clue."

"Prison within the prison. Yeah, real clever. You couldn't have just told me?"

"No," he replied. "I *couldn't*." He sounded like he meant it. "The hunter won't let itself be the hunted."

"You are on a roll with the cryptic BS lately."

I peered out from the office door and ducked low when a shadow reappeared. The man in corduroy stepped forward and leaned over my shoulder.

"Gonna try and kill him for Mommy Dearest?"

"You are getting on my last nerve," I growled under my breath. I crouched on the ground and flattened my back against the wall. The shadow stepped away once again.

"Only the last one?" he said with a chuckle.

I didn't answer him. I pulled the gun out of my pocket and stared down at the stretch of it in my hands, then held it steady in a practice aim. The resguardo on my wrist stared back at me.

Hope you're not out of charge just yet, I thought. *This is when the fight really counts.*

I jumped to my feet and launched myself forward. The soles of my feet smacked the ground, and when I emerged from the hallway, I locked eyes with the Slumlord. He was clear across the room, giving me some space and a larger margin of error.

If Republicans were right about first-person shooters making people violent, I hoped they'd at least made me an accurate shot.

He stepped forward, and the terror immediately descended on me. It shook my heart and went all the way down to my hands. I realized the fear wasn't just my own—it was an emotional manipulation, coming off him in waves.

This had to be cheating.

He took another step forward, washing me in another wave of fear. I felt the crushing hopelessness of imminent eviction along with the uncertainty of survival. It was all I could do not to vomit out of anxiety.

There was something else I hadn't noticed before. The longer I faced the Slumlord, the more I felt my strength being sapped as if he was leeching off my life-force. My knees threatened to give out, but I forced myself to stand anyway. It was only a matter of time before I was done for, and I wasn't going down without a fight.

Focus. I breathed. *Think of Mami.*

I thought of the way her keys jingled throughout the house whenever she was just about to leave for work and how she hummed Spanish hymns while cooking dinner, as if blessing the food herself.

A glow formed around the resguardo.

I thought of the way she helped me do my hair—each strand carefully parted and detangled just before braiding. The soothing oils she'd massage into my scalp were a form of love itself.

As afraid as I was of the Slumlord, Mami didn't deserve to be in the hospital. She didn't deserve to die alone.

The Slumlord took another step forward, and I ignored the feelings he sent my way. He cocked his head, as if surprised. I blinked away my tears and took a deep breath.

And then I pulled the trigger.

The Slumlord jolted in place. His face didn't twist in pain like I'd expected. He didn't drop to his knees. He looked down at the bullet wound straight in the middle of his chest. His hand came up to the hole, and he probed it with two fingers, digging around until he found what he was looking for.

The bullet fell to the ground with a single ping.

"Tsk, tsk." The man in corduroy appeared beside him. "The Slumlord has been around longer than you've been alive. Infecting so many people with sickness and ailments. Draining them of their life-force—their resources. His mark on history can't be erased. And you should know you can't kill a memory."

The Slumlord's eyes were full of rage, more than I'd ever felt. He unhinged his jaw and let out the same guttural scream I heard in my dream, then stomped toward me.

I inched back until I hit a wall and closed my eyes.

Come on, resguardo, I prayed. *Do your thing!*

A hand gripped my shoulder. Like before, painful, needlelike sensations forced their way into my skin and spread rapidly. It was only mildly pushed back by a short memory.

"I'm not raising my baby girl in an apartment full of asbestos and mold," Mami yelled through the phone. *"So you can either get off your ass and fix this, or I'm taking you to court."*

The memory was muddied by my young age. I couldn't have been more than six or seven, but it was the first time I'd heard Mami yell and the first time she cursed in front of me. The needles slowed in its progression, and I leaned hard on the memory.

"Cálmate—"

"Do not tell me to calm down, Samuel!" Mami slapped Papi's hands away as he tried to comfort her. *"It's been months that we've complained about the mold in the kitchen. And they still haven't done anything about it..."*

The memory began to wane, but it was enough. I opened my eyes and looked down at the resguardo, only faintly glowing but still pushing back the needles and replacing them with a deep sense of relief.

I finally peeked up at the Slumlord. The fire in his eyes dulled to a confused simmer, and as he pulled his hand away, a crack began to form on his skin.

The Slumlord was a near-constant presence in the Bronx, doing nothing but preying on vulnerable people.

But that didn't mean we couldn't fight back. It had been so long since Mami and I dealt with our own slumlord back home. Mold in our apartment triggered my asthma, and Mami refused to just accept the threat to my health. She absolutely demolished the slumlord in court. Most of the settlement money was placed in a college fund for me, and the rest went toward paying off Mami's loans.

The Slumlord couldn't take anything from us without paying the price.

I picked up my bat and curled my hands around it tight.

"You know, I don't care much for baseball," I said, body in a ready stance. My thoughts shifted to Papi's loving playfulness in that moment. "But I heard this period was an *amazing* time for the Yankees."

And then I swung. My hips twisted with the motion, making it a stronger hit. The bat connected flawlessly with the Slumlord's head. The cracks in his face spread, and when I looked into his eyes, I recognized the unique look of powerlessness from someone who was so used to causing it.

A light screeching in the air turned into a piercing ring so sharp, I felt it in my bones. I covered my ears. The house around me began to shake as though I were at the center of an earthquake. Tucking my bat under my armpit, I made way for the front door and found it easier to open.

I jumped onto the sidewalk just in time to see the home shake the rot off its frame. The black mold dissipated into the air until none of it was left.

I stared up at it in awe.

3:45 a.m.

BLACKENED PIECES OF GLASS—WHAT USED TO BE THE Slumlord—scattered around the sidewalks. A pile of fuzz with spores collected on it, floating up with any slight wind and dropping back down. I carefully stepped over it.

The man in corduroy came out of the house and stood next to me, staring down at the glass. "He won't stay dead, you know," he said. For once, he was unamused. His lips were in a taut, straight line, and he narrowed his eyes as he measured me up.

"I know," I said. The Slumlord was a memory, not a real thing. He couldn't be erased for good. But hopefully killing for him now meant the mold spores would be erased from my mom, the way they were from the house. And maybe he'd stay dead long enough for me to find Charlize and get the hell out of here. "You." I pointed the end of my bat at the man in corduroy. "Take me to Hyde."

To my surprise, he nodded. I secured the gun at my waist again and clung to my bat. The man in corduroy shuffled ahead of me with stiff movements. Every so often, his head would jerk backward and I'd jump into a defensive staff, ready to swing. But then nothing would happen. If he knew how nervous his erratic movements made me, he didn't show it. No mocking laugh, no cryptic hints, and definitely no distracting comments. The only sound that came from him was the swishing of corduroy sleeves on torso.

The nearby expressway was lined with crashed cars, still smoking as if ready to blow. We passed them by without incident and headed onto the ramp.

The Passengers standing on the cracked sidewalks didn't spare us a glance.

"Why aren't they attacking me?" I asked, watching them intently. A pregnant woman with her literal guts poking out the side of her stomach looked in my direction but wasn't too interested in what she saw.

"Because I'm here," he said. I snapped my attention back to him. The back of his head was indifferent to my questioning stare.

He'd said he needed me for a reason he couldn't remember. Was that why he was protecting me?

Soon enough we came to the top of the expressway. I glanced over the edge of it, taking in the sight of torn-down buildings, rising smoke, and garbage everywhere. Rats ran from one trash can to the next. Roaches were crawling all over each other in a pile. Just the sight of it made me itchy, so I looked away and grimaced at the top of buildings.

Even the graffiti was...worse. It was completely illegible, chaotic. The colors melted into each other into a rusted brown and the line work was sloppy. If this was supposed to be the Bronx during the '70s, the graffiti definitely didn't match it. The Point had photos and documentaries about how it actually looked—all bright colors, sharp lines, and clever imagery. History could call them vandals all they liked, but the people were artists so brilliant, even Cisco tried to emulate them in his sketchbooks. I'd only seen a few of his personal works, but I remembered how the pages seemed to come alive with his creativity.

Compared to that, the Echo's graffiti was a graveyard.

The man in corduroy stopped dead in his tracks. The horizon blurred with the length of the expressway and smudges of burned buildings. Old Cadillacs formed a semicircle pileup, with fires coming up from the engines, and others half teetered over the edge of the expressway.

I jutted out my chin. "What's the matter?"

"This is as far as I go. The school is just ahead."

"Why's that?"

"Can't go to the future, can I?" he said. I furrowed my brow. *The future?* "But first you need to get past that." He pointed behind me, and before I could pivot to look, I heard it: quick feet, in rapid succession. Almost as if there were more than one pair.

Goddammit. The corduroy man vanished, but the parasite was back.

The monster's leg scraped against the ground, drawing closer.

A loud chirping pierced the air. Insect-like. Sharp and high-pitched. I ran to the nearest nonflaming car and crouched beside it, tugging at my resguardo. A few seconds later, the noise stopped, only to be replaced by the sensation of something thick and hairy running over my legs.

On instinct, I grabbed my bat then brought it down over and over on the squirming mass that was the creature's torso. I thought of all the times I had stomped on a roach or a centipede, and my resguardo shot a light into the bat, strengthening it. With every hit, the parasite seemed to screech louder, but I didn't stop until the midsection was as flat as it could be, with a distinct black goo oozing out of the sides. The legs wouldn't stop wriggling, and it wasn't until the two sides pulled apart that I realized I had just made the situation worse.

"No, no, no, no, *no*—"

The creature was now in two. The goo reformed into a head on the second body, and as both skittered around toward me, I could tell it was angry and about to launch an attack.

Okay, forget the bat! I tossed it aside and opened the car's door. I jumped in, hoping to put some distance between the two creatures and me. They both slammed into the door and shook the car.

I made my way to the other side of the car, but that door wouldn't budge. The hinges were stuck, and no matter how much weight I threw against it, it refused the pressure.

Come on, come on!

One of the creatures stuck a long appendage into the window behind me and pulled the entire door off. The sound of the metal scraping against the ground only partially blocked out its screech, and I gave up on the other door.

The broken window would have to be good enough.

I pulled my sweater sleeves over my palms before gripping the outside of the door's window. Glass crunched under my grasp and weight as I began to pull myself through the opening. Another loud chirp bounced in the car as the creature crawled in, snagging my ankle in its insect mandibles.

"Aaaah!" I screamed. Pain flooded my foot, and my grip weakened where it pulled at me. I kicked at it with my other foot and used one hand to grab the gun in my pocket. It thrashed me around the car, attempting to loosen my grip.

"Ugh!" I groaned. My head connected with metal and glass several times. The last time was hard enough for me to feel vertigo.

Aiming wildly, I hoped I wasn't about to literally shoot myself in the foot. That would be embarrassing.

"*Piss! Off!*"

I pulled the trigger and shots rang out. The creature shrieked in pain and finally let go. I took the moment to hoist myself up onto the broken window. Glass cut into my knees and thighs, but adrenaline kept me going. I dropped onto the concrete on the other side, wincing with the pain before getting up.

The loud screech of the creatures was replaced with weak occasional chirps. I could even hear one of its legs trying to gain strength, pushing itself up only to be brought back down. One of its legs connected with the steering wheel, and the Cadillac honked.

Cautiously, I peered into the wreckage of the car. Black goo oozed out everywhere and I stared in horror as it began to form little spiderlike creatures.

"Are you fucking kidding me?" I muttered. At least the Slumlord had the decency to shatter—this thing just kept coming and coming like the pest it symbolized. I took in slow breaths as I watched how easily they materialized. There seemed to be hundreds, and for a few seconds, they were clumsy. Their legs awkwardly felt their way out of the parent's corpse with loud chitters that sounded like high-pitched static.

The last thing they formed was teeth. Large, sharp pincers just like the parents had, and once I heard the same wet snapping sound, I knew it was time to go.

Shit! I took off and yelped. Pain radiated in my ankle, and my thigh was struggling with glass shards still in its meat. The adrenaline was wearing off, but I had to keep going.

Come on! I shook my resguardo.

"What happened to the force field?" I muttered.

It stared back at me, muted as if it had completely run out of charge. Distracted, I tripped and dropped onto the concrete. The wet snapping sound was drawing closer, but I didn't have it in me to look back.

I dropped on the ground, unable to take another step.

"Help!" I yelled through my tears. "Someone, *help*!"

I had heard about other people's near-death experiences. They always said something about their life flashing before their eyes. They talked about it like it was a profound experience, like they learned something from it. They learned they needed to treat the people in their lives better or that they were insignificant and humbled by the thought of death on their doorstep.

But no one told me that facing it was so terrifying.

I shut my eyes, getting ready to feel the sensation of being eaten alive.

"Raquel!"

Hands grabbed me at the waist and pulled me up. A glaring light fell over me. I gasped with relief and wrapped my arms around the person.

"Aaron?" I swallowed, squinting in the glare to meet his eyes. "Aaron, you're okay?"

He was better than okay. He was alive. Scabs formed in patches around his face, but his eyes were still lit with recognition. Our resguardos were matched in their glow, keeping the small creatures out of our lit radius.

Aaron pulled my arm over his shoulder, holding my weight.

"Less talking, more running." He gritted his teeth, glancing out at the goo monsters. Just like their parent, they refused to enter the field of light. Instead, they scattered.

I took the moment to catch my breath and took a few puffs of my inhaler. Instant relief flooded my lungs, but once the dust settled, I heard the familiar sound of shuffling feet as a crowd of Passengers came into view.

"Oh no."

Aaron cursed under his breath. He pulled my arm tighter

over his shoulder and moved us along. I looked around, recognizing our current location. The random disorganization seemed to place Garrison Ave just around the corner.

"The school." I coughed. "We need to get to the school!"

Aaron didn't argue with me.

We pumped our legs faster, and I ignored the searing pain in my own, but the Passengers continued to follow, creating a barrier to our only escape. We were trapped.

"Fuck," Aaron hissed.

"Wait!" I pointed ahead. "The post office!"

The redbrick building sat behind a tall black fence that opened on opposite sides. The Passengers hadn't filed in there, leaving us with just one exit.

Aaron and I hustled faster until I saw stars in my eyes and pain blocked out almost every other sense. We passed through the first gate and closed it but weren't able to make it to the next side without another mob forming.

"Close it!" I yelled, falling to the ground. I watched Aaron lock the other side as well, keeping the Passengers out but also keeping us in.

"What the fuck do we do now?" He huffed, jumping away from the gate. The Passengers reached their arms out to grab him, and he only narrowly escaped before helping me up. "How are we supposed to get to the train?"

We looked back and forth. Aside from the gates, we were shut in by brick walls. Aaron would be able to scale it no problem, but every small step I made resulted in a near blackout.

"Aaron, did you find Char—"

"Hey, it's that girl."

I froze. From the corner of my eyes, the Fordham kids poured out of the post office and stared at us with malicious smiles.

3:55 a.m.

A GUY WITH A BUZZ CUT CAREFULLY LOOKED ME UP AND down before glancing over to Aaron.

"And she's got a *friend*." There was a snarl in his voice, and it made me consider running as fast as I could.

"Who the hell are they?" Aaron muttered. We took a half step back toward the gate as they came forward and surrounded us.

"It's the Fordham kids that went missing," I whispered to Aaron.

"From a year ago?" he asked as a girl with nail-less fingers leaned in far too close for comfort. "They've been here all this time?"

She grinned in a way that could've been a sneer while the other girl leaned in close and sniffed his neck long and hard.

Aaron ducked his head between his shoulders. The timid reaction was a surprise to me, but when I saw him recoil even more, I knew the Echo was changing him, too.

The Fordham girl wrinkled her nose. "He smells weird."

"He's bleeding," Nail-less said, raising a finger to Aaron's cheek.

"Hey!" I yelled, slapping her hand away. "Don't touch him."

They all stared back at me, and I lifted my nose to them. I tried my best to look intimidating even with a bleeding leg and shaky breath. Contrary to what most people thought when they saw me, I had actually never been in a fight in my life. The idea of it scared me, and the few times a fight broke out at school, they would be broken up by the time I could get close enough to see anything. I didn't know how to punch or how to block or what to do if I got shoved to the ground.

But Aaron was here, and he wasn't in any position to fight. The Echo was getting to him, and it was getting to me too, filling in my muscle memory and instinct on what to do next. I ignored the pain and widened my stance, getting ready for any action.

I just had to remember not to lose myself completely.

The girls sent dagger stares my way, but I didn't budge.

"Hey, hey, hey!"

The curly haired guy jumped in between us. He waved his hands, bringing our attention to him.

"I'm really sorry about my friends, we've just been here too long." He spoke quickly and swallowed. "I'm Westley and—"

"I know who you are," I cut him off. "You're the kids from Fordham. You've been missing for over a year." I wasn't sure how much to tell them, so I left it there.

"It's been...a *year*?" Westley said. His face fell, and he turned to look back at his friends. They barely took their eyes off me. Nail-biter reopened a wound in her finger, and fresh blood dripped down her chin.

"Jesus Christ..." He ran his hand through his hair. "Well, do you know how to get out of here?"

I narrowed my eyes at him. He was thin and gangly to the point where his eyes were sunken and his cheeks were gaunt. My shoulders slowly fell as I took in his appearance. Of the entire group, he seemed the least threatening.

"The train." Aaron suddenly spoke. His voice wavered, deeply

afraid of the predicament we were in. "Just get on the next train..."
He trailed off, weakly pointing beyond the gate. I wondered how
the hell he managed to save me from the parasites when he couldn't
even raise his voice to the cannibals in front of us.

I opened my mouth to answer but froze when I saw what was
on his wrist—the resguardo bracelet. The glow was dim, but it was
still doing its best.

I looked down at mine and suddenly had an idea.

"What does that mean?" The guy with the buzz cut said. He
put both his hands on Aaron's shoulders and shook him roughly.
"What does that *mean*?"

A second later, Buzz Cut was flat on his ass. Adrenaline shot
through me for what must have been the third time that night,
siphoning every bit of strength into my fists. The guy lightly
touched his swelling cheek, glaring at me.

"I *said*. Don't. Touch. Him." I took a step forward, movement
blurring at the corner of my eyes.

"Don't move!" Westley pointed the barrel end of Aaron's gun
at me. "Get back!"

I glared at him but listened and even lifted my hands up to
show how empty they were. The action pissed me off, and the
anger coupled with the adrenaline felt really dangerous, but I
didn't dare move.

Westley wouldn't stop fidgeting. He shuffled his feet from
side to side, and his hands shook. He hadn't made up his mind
about whether to shoot me or not.

Which now made him the most threatening person here.

"How the hell did you manage to lose your gun?" I hissed at
Aaron.

"You don't know what I've been through, okay?" he snapped
back at me. "Besides, where's *your* gun?"

I didn't answer. I only clenched my jaw and scanned the area.

Both gates were still blocked from end to end with Passengers. They reached out, clawing the air and pushing against the grated metal without even a hint of awareness about their own decaying bodies.

"He smells fine to me, Jules," she said, sniffing Aaron deeply. "Barry, come on over and smell her."

"Can you three *stop* being such cannibals for three seconds?" Westley yelled. He shot them a glare over his shoulders before training his eyes on me. "*You*. Talk."

If this were a movie, this would've been the Moment.

The moment where I summoned every bit of charisma in my body and tried to sweet-talk my way out of this. I would have used what I knew about this guy to do it. He was clearly the only Fordham student who managed to salvage some of his humanity given the circumstances, and wasn't that just so hard? We were two and the same, weren't we?

And we had exactly what the other needed to survive. I had information about how to get out of this place, and he had experience of surviving in it. I would say all this, and he would put the gun down and convince his band of merry cannibals to join my friends and me before booking it out of this plane of existence forever.

This would have been the moment to do all that. Except for the fact that I was not charismatic or charitable. I was a petty Black girl, and he just made the crucial mistake of waving my friend's gun in my face.

"Huh?" I blinked, playing dumb. "What do you want to know?"

"Do you know *anything* about where we are right now?" His voice cracked.

"Stop yelling at me!" I said, curling into my shoulders. I made my lips tremble and pushed out the tears I'd been working so hard to hold back. "I really don't know! I'm just as lost as you are!"

Westley glared at me, unsure if he should believe me. I fought the panic rising in my throat and pushed it down.

"Fine," he said, putting his gun down for a second. "You'll just have to be our bait."

"What?" I yelled. His friends grabbed Aaron and me, twisting us around. We were forced to face the Passengers as Buzz Cut came to the lock on the side. The Passengers reached out to him, but he swatted them off before they could grab anything substantial.

"This isn't personal," Westley said as if he believed it.

"Westley, no!" I struggled weakly. "Don't do this!"

"With your wounds, you won't survive long anyway," he explained. "Think of this as putting you out of your misery. Barry, open the gates!"

Buzz Cut managed to unlock it without another scratch before sprinting back into the post office. His friends followed him but not before pushing us into the open crowd of Passengers.

"Aaron!" I yelled, grabbing his arm and pulling him in. He buried his head into my shoulders, and I whispered loudly in his ear, "Remember last year's Fish Parade?"

The memory caught him off guard, I knew, but once it caught fire, it didn't stop. Our resguardos' light intensified as the memory surged through me—and him, I could tell.

The heat of the sunlight was nearly scorching, but the light breeze helped pull back its sting that summer day. Aaron sat still as a face painter applied a light blue with dots of yellow on his cheeks. He pretended to be embarrassed by it, but I knew better. It was one of those days when he was living in the calmness of the moment. There was nothing urgent to do and nowhere to go, so he relished every sensation, from the smell of a churro cart to the feel of grass under his feet.

"Hurry up, Aaron," I said, sitting back on my bike. "The parade is almost there."

"How am I supposed to hurry up?" He laughed, almost messing up the face painter. They didn't mind. It was just face paint and any mistakes were an easy fix. When he was finally done, he hopped on his bike, and we rode to catch up with the parade. Familiar faces laughed and cheered along the way. We greeted everyone we knew and those we didn't.

"This is our community," I said, knowing the Echo was listening. "And we don't hurt each other."

The high-pitched ring faded with the flashback, and we slowly peeked up around us.

The Passengers stood a few feet away, blinking and rubbing their eyes in bewilderment.

"Aaron, let's go," I said, pulling him along with me. We inched along through the crowd and only stopped any moment they seemed to fix their eyes on us. Their expressions would twist in confusion for half a second until they looked away and found something more interesting to follow.

Unfortunately for Westley and his friends, it was them.

"Uh, West?" Barry said. The glass door they hid behind was locked but slightly cracked.

The mob was closing in on Westley's group. The Passengers cocked their heads to the side and grinned, showing their rotting teeth and bleeding gums.

Westley's wild eyes met theirs, and he cursed under his breath. He raised the gun toward them and pressed the trigger.

Click.

His eyes widened, and he pressed it again and again.

Click, click, click.

"It's empty!" Westley suddenly turned desperate and let out a short whimper. His eyes met mine, pleading.

"Please!" Westley said. "You can't leave us here!"

I flipped him off as I turned the corner. The last thing I saw of them was the horrified look on Westley's gaunt face.

3:59 a.m.

MARIO OPENED THE GLASS DOORS OF THE SCHOOL AND waved his arm out at us.

"Mario!" I breathed, stumbling alongside his brother. He bolted out toward us and pulled my legs out from under me.

"We don't have time for this!" he said, carrying me as he ran.

I'd forgotten how long Mario's legs were. He extended them fully in a haphazard sprint, getting me to the school in a matter of seconds. Aaron closed the door behind us and jumped away from it. The Passengers closed in around the school, and yet they didn't touch it.

Suddenly I realized what the man in corduroy meant about not being able to go to the future. Hyde was built way after the '70s—which meant not even the Passengers could go inside.

"Now what do we do?" Mario asked, facing the glass door.

My mind swirled, but I tried to keep my eyes focused on Mario's figure. I wiped the sweat off my brow in a dizzy attempt.

"Let's go find a room to barricade ourselves in," I said. "We'll figure everything out afterward."

My leg was numb with throbbing pain. I sat on the floor while Aaron tied a piece of cloth around it and propped it up on a chair.

"You're bleeding real bad," he said. "This should help staunch the blood flow."

I wasn't worried about the blood, though. Mario stood by the window, looking out over the street. He didn't have to say it, but I knew the mob was still there, encasing the school. By the way his face paled, they were also staring back at him.

I scanned his body. Parts of his clothes looked like they had caught fire, and even the side of his hair was singed. I wondered where he ended up after we parted at the turnstiles and was tempted to ask.

But that could wait.

Charlize was still nowhere to be found. I was fighting to stay conscious, hoping she would make an appearance soon. My head lolled forward even as I tried to keep it upright. Aaron said something to my right, but my mind couldn't even begin to string apart the garbled words, much less process them.

Aaron scanned my face with the kind of concerned look that would've made me feel embarrassed under normal circumstances. "You okay?"

"Yeah." I shuddered and swallowed. "I'm okay." I looked around the classroom, finally taking it in. The sinks built into the tables had grime lining the grooves, but the sight of it didn't set me on edge. That was just how the sinks actually looked in school.

"Did you do all of this?" I said, forcing myself to stand.

"No, actually." Aaron looked to Mario even though Mario had never been inside Hyde before. He shook his head as well then said, "I thought you did this as some sort of landmark. You know, for when we got split up—just head to Hyde and meet up there."

I stumbled then stopped with both hands leaning on a table. My bad leg barely had any feeling in it, which made walking an extra adventure. Aaron came to my side immediately and offered his arm.

"What are you doing?" he said, keeping me steady. "You're going to hurt yourself even worse. You should lie down—"

"I'm just trying to *think*," I said, waving off his concerns. I thumbed the resguardo around my wrist, trying to make sense of it all. The Echo was supposed to be a hell mirror of the '70s, and Hyde didn't exist back then. The school building definitely didn't exist. It was an empty plot of land before Hyde came along and should have stayed that way in the Echo.

So, if I didn't rebuild Hyde, and Aaron and Mario didn't do it...

"Let's go down to the cafeteria," I said. The two of them shared a look of confusion.

"Uh, why?"

"Because I have an idea of where Charlize is."

Mario followed silently as Aaron helped me down the steps. He offered to help carry me down, as it was a very time-consuming endeavor, but I refused.

"I'm pretty sure I passed out the first time because you kept moving my legs when you carried me."

He looked offended but said nothing else until we reached the first floor. Aaron shifted next to me, holding his arm out to the double doors of the cafeteria.

"You ready?" he asked, casting a look of uncertainty to me.

I matched his arm with my own on the other door, and together we pushed through. The short hall leading into the cafeteria was spotless and led to the sight of round tables spaced equal distance apart.

We carefully moved forward, step by step, surprised but not disarmed by the initial look of the room until we turned the corner and froze.

It was a sea of black rot.

From the high ceilings, partially covering a window, and scaling down to the floor and tables was nothing but a black, pulsing goo. I felt Aaron deflate beside me, and Mario yelped a sound of surprise as he followed our line of sight.

"Raquel?"

"Yes, Mario."

"What the hell is this?"

There was no way to answer that without making it sound like we were fucked.

I don't get it, I thought. *I fought him. I won.*

And yet, just because one little house shook off the rot didn't mean that all the Echo was free of it. Did that mean Mami was still doomed?

I looked away and saw a glint of light bouncing off the tile wall.

"What is that?" I stumbled toward it. My resguardo had long since dimmed and so had Aaron's, but that light was coming from somewhere. I scanned the room intensely, ignoring the pain in my leg when I tripped over the side of the table.

That was when I saw the knife.

"Raquel, what are you doing?" Aaron ran to help me up. I shrugged him off long enough to reach down and grab it.

"Look!" I said, holding the long blade up. "This is the knife I gave Charlize!"

The blade was bent and had rusted blood over the serrated edge, but it was still here, which meant my theory was still right.

Charlize was here in the school.

"Okay..." Aaron said, flinching when I held it up. "So what? She might have run out of here a long time ago."

I turned away from him and pulled out the last remaining resguardo from the pouch. Focusing my eyes on the thickness of the goo, I knew she had to be there. Somewhere underneath the blanket of mold and rot, she was there, and she needed help.

I stepped toward it with the knife in one hand and the charm in the other.

"Raquel—don't!"

I jumped in, slashing every way I could. Maybe I couldn't save Mami after all, but Charlize still needed me. The rot creeped up to my feet and was pushed back by the light of the resguardo. The farther in I went, the deeper the goo became, but I pushed forward and sliced everything that got in my way. Sharp pain dug into my leg, and for a moment, I thought it was just the glass until I looked down and saw a rod of mold sticking out of it.

"No!" I yelled, pressing the charm against it. The other end bit into me, and I felt it surge through my veins. It was like burning acid, drops of fire consuming every inch of me. I saw sparks and faltered.

"Raquel!" Aaron screamed. I turned and watched Mario hold him back from running in after me. His face was twisted in agony, thick lines of tears mixing with snot as he struggled against his brother.

"Let go!" He screamed again. Mario refused, pulling him away from the rot.

Thanks, Mario.

And then I slashed once more.

The knife bounced back, running into something stubborn and solid. A light of white was exposed, and I knew I'd hit a table. I slashed the knife in the center of the table and slammed the resguardo down. Piercing light shot out and cleared the area of all rot.

"Charlize!" I gasped as she appeared next to me. She sat still, with her arms flat across the table as if she were just having lunch.

I pulled her closer. Her skin was dull, but she was still warm to the touch. I pressed the resguardo into her hand and clenched it.

"Charlize, please," I cried, still feeling the rot needle into my muscles. "Please come back, Charlize. I'm so sorry about everything—"

I was sorry about snapping at her the last time I'd seen her, sorry I kept my distance from her all those years. I was downright ashamed at my unwillingness to face facts. I mean, it was obvious, wasn't it? How far I went to save her. I could've stopped at destroying the Slumlord, I could have come back another time for the parasite. But I didn't. And now I was here, holding the hand of the girl I loved most.

"Please, Charlize." A tear fell over my cheeks. Despite the piercing agony in my joints, I reached up and turned her face to me. Her eyes fluttered open, but the light inside them was still dim.

Desperate, I brought her lips to mine.

A rush of warmth flooded my body along with memories. Memories Charlize was holding on to. The first time we'd met and I played with her. The time I defended her against the kids down the street who made fun of her braids. The time we spent together on the soccer team, both in public and alone.

The soccer training camp, when I reached out and held her hand as she slept, only she wasn't sleeping. She only pretended to sleep and was overjoyed but frozen with indecision when she felt my skin touch hers. She pulled my hand closer to her face, flush with her warm cheek. We slept all night like that, and when morning came, neither of us wanted to wake up and pull away.

I could see all the times she noticed me walking by, hoping I would turn and talk to her. The disappointment when I didn't. The excitement when I did, even if it was only for a moment. The conversation she had with Cisco, coming out and telling him she had a crush on me. She was scared that she would be disowned by her family, but he promised he would never turn his back on her.

That promise gave her hope.

I could see all the support and advice Cisco gave her to try and talk to me. The nervousness that ate her up inside when she tried to and the regret when she couldn't.

The flutters she felt when I came over to check up on her. The security she felt when I said I believed her. Every bit of memory between us, mixed into something tangible, something very real. Something she had to hold on to, otherwise she'd be just another drop in the ocean. Diluted.

The last two memories I was all too aware of.

"I have this friend that, uh. I kind of like. And I say kind of because we haven't spoken in a long time. Not deeply anyway, not since we were kids."

She'd tried to tell me.

"And I just don't know if they're into me. Like, maybe I'm misreading all the signs because lately they've just been so nice to me and going out of their way for me."

She'd been so nervous.

"But what if they're only being nice to me because of the whole situation with Cisco? I don't want to mess up the opportunity to get to be friends with them again by assuming they have any feelings for me."

And so afraid.

She was so afraid to tell me, so she skirted around it, hoping that I'd be braver. But I wasn't, and so she'd kissed me, and I still couldn't say anything. When she ran off the train, it was more than just Cisco.

She just wanted to know I liked her.

I do, Charlize.

I like you, too.

Just like with the resguardos, a bright light fell over us. I felt the rot inching backward, being pushed away by the luminescence, and in my mind, I felt something grow like a seed. A thought, a feeling, an existence—it rooted itself in my mind, and when I opened my eyes, Charlize stared back with the same curious look, as if she felt it, too.

A link.

We didn't have time to explore it as the weight of the world suddenly fell onto us.

"Ugh..." Charlize groaned as she stood up, clutching her head with her free hand. Looking around, I realized the black rot was completely cleared out of the cafeteria. The only piercing pain I felt was from the glass still embedded in my thigh. I winced every few seconds, but compared to everything I just went through, it was manageable.

Mario and Aaron sat next to us, somehow looking worse off than either of us.

I glanced at Mario and gave him a weak smile.

"You look like shit."

"Ha," he mocked, before looking away. "What are we supposed to do now?"

"It's way past four a.m.," Aaron confirmed. "The train's already left. We're stuck here."

The truth of the matter sank into our bones. We were covered in sweat, grime, and dried blood. One hour in the Echo took a hell of a toll on a person.

"Did you ever find Cisco?" I asked. Charlize shut her eyes tight and exhaled.

"Yeah," she said, voice hoarse. "Follow me."

She quietly led us to the side exit of the school. It opened to an alley with a metal fence, but it was obvious the Passengers couldn't get that close anyway. As soon as I turned to the side, I saw him laid flat against the building. Cisco's arm was folded over his chest, which looked like it had caved in and filled with more of the black rot.

Mario made a retching sound as he turned away.

"I found him over by the expressway, half-passed-out, half talking nonsense. I saw that the school was safe, so I dragged him as far as I could, but then the Passengers got close, and he told me to leave—to save myself." Charlize hugged herself and hung her head. She sniffled as she continued, "I didn't want to, but I was so scared. By the time he managed to crawl all the way to the side door, I was already losing my own mind."

I gripped her shoulder knowingly. The way the Echo could get inside a mind and twist it was something I wouldn't wish on my worst enemy.

"I didn't want to believe he'd died, so I went back into the school and sat down, hoping it was a bad dream."

Mario fell to his knees beside Cisco's body. His hands shook as he reached over, as if unsure about whether he wanted to touch him. The black goop bubbled up, causing him to yelp and jump away, but the grief on his face never left.

"We have to bring him back."

I almost didn't hear him. Mario jumped up, and before I could react, he tore something from my arm and did the same to Aaron.

"Hey!"

I watched as he piled the resguardos in the palm of his hand and gripped them tight. He closed his eyes and whispered something insistently. He didn't stop until the resguardos reacted, glowing bright as they usually did before tossing them into Cisco's open chest cavity.

"Mario, what are you doing?" I shrieked. But it was too late. The resguardos sank into the black rot until not even the light was visible. I slapped him on the back of his head.

"That was our only protection!"

"Raquel...*look*!" Aaron gasped.

It was like watching Cisco become pure light. His body radiated with a glow that pushed the black rot out of his chest and brightened until it was painful to look at him. Unlike how the resguardo dulled, Cisco's light exploded, forcing us to jump back in fear. Once it was over, we carefully looked up and froze.

"Huh." Cisco's eyes touched down on his now-translucent hands before looking up at us. "So this is what being dead is like."

None of us knew how to answer. I stared at the center of his chest, where a collection of resguardos seemed to be floating in place. I remembered Papi's words about how he felt the resguardos worked.

Spirit.

The resguardos were amplifying Cisco's spirit.

"Y'all gonna say something, or should I just assume you can't hear or see me?"

He gave the same lopsided grin he had since birth, and though he was dead, his eyes had never been kinder.

Charlize took a few steps forward and placed a gentle hand on Cisco's shoulder. It went clean through, and she cried out in frustration.

"Hey, hey!" Cisco tried to grab her, but of course, he couldn't touch us either. "Hey, it's okay. Don't cry. I'm fine."

He glanced over to me as if to say, *Can you please hold my cousin for me?* and I obliged. Charlize buried her face in my neck and shook while Cisco looked on with a wistful smile.

Until Mario coughed awkwardly.

"Mario. You're here."

"Don't 'Mario, you're here' me!" Mario snapped. And then all at once, his tough demeanor fell. "You're fucking dead, you asshole..." Fat tears and snot rolled down his face. He stood there, half sobbing and half cursing Cisco out for dying so suddenly.

"Yeah, I know," Cisco said in a whisper. "I'm sorry."

It was another few minutes before the shock wore off and we could talk without sniffling in between sentences. Despite not being able to touch Cisco, Charlize and Mario stood as close to his spirit form as possible, soaking up as much interaction as they could from him before we had to go. I tried not to feel jealous about the sudden switch. He was, after all, her cousin.

I hung back against the wall with Aaron, who was also awkwardly watching while the three of them talked.

"I can't believe we actually did it," he mumbled. Then he looked at me, eyes weirdly calm and understanding. "I can't believe *you* did it."

My cheeks burned and I looked away.

"Hey, I wouldn't have gotten this far if you didn't tell me about the game in the first place," I said, holding out a fist bump. "Thanks for coming, by the way."

"Are you kidding me?" He fist-bumped me. "I can't leave my best friend hanging. You'd die without me around."

"*Pfft.*" I couldn't help but laugh as I considered the truth of that statement. The most I'd ever been able to handle on my own was starting the challenge. Surviving it wouldn't have been possible if I didn't have the memories of my mom, my friends, and my community.

Papi was right. Alone we could only do so much, but when we were together, we could change a lot.

"Oh. Wow, I'm such an idiot." I pinched the bridge of my nose.

"I agree," Aaron said. I jammed my elbow in his side. "What?"

"Hey, I have an idea, but we have to get to the train first if it's going to work."

The other three fell silent.

"You want to *leave* the only building that keeps those things out?" Mario blinked, incredulous. "Are you sure you didn't hit your head somewhere along the way?"

I scowled at him until Aaron answered.

"I'm in," he said, shrugging. "The last idea you had saved Charlize, so..."

"I guess it's official, then," Charlize said, beaming at me. "Let's head out."

4:15 a.m.

FOR MILES AND MILES INTO THE HORIZON, ALL THAT COULD be seen were collapsed buildings and smoke. The Passengers were few and far in between, but many still stumbled around, with wide grins and unblinking eyes. Some began to groan, as if only then understanding the depth of their wounds. Some looked at us and then at Cisco. After a long pause, they went on as if we weren't there. I led the group down the street. With the exception of Cisco, our arms were locked together as we marched.

Once we crossed the Bruckner Expressway, I stopped. The ground where the train should've been was covered in concrete, just like the one at 149th Street. But that was okay.

"Okay, guys, I need all of your help in this."

And then I explained. Without unlinking our arms, we closed our eyes to remember the exact outline of the stairs leading into the platform. Charlize imagined the steps, Aaron imagined the turnstiles, and Mario imagined the train tracks that would take us home.

Redbrick pillars poked out of the ground and staircases paired with black handrails descended into the platform. The ground beneath us shook but eventually stabilized.

I trudged forward with Charlize's hand in mine until she pulled back.

"You're not coming?" she asked.

I knew what she was talking about even before I turned around. I could hear the rising grief in her voice.

"You know I can't," Cisco said softly. "But don't worry. Just because I won't be around doesn't mean you'll be alone." His eyes fell over me. "You'll be in good hands, Charlize. Besides"—he turned around, and it was at that point I realized there was a dark figure drawing close—"I never got to throw hands with this asshole."

From the shadows of the expressway, the Slumlord reemerged.

The lines in his face were reminiscent of broken glass, and every move he made came with a crunching sound, as if his own jagged edges were scraping against each other. His eyes burned with a cold hatred I could only assume meant we were in for more trouble.

"What's that sound?" Mario muttered and I listened close.

"Falsas...promesas...falsas promesas..."

The consistent sound of shuffling feet came with the united chanting. A crowd of Passengers appeared on all sides, pinning us to the entrance of the Hunts Point Station. I felt exhaustion sink deeper into my soul than I was prepared for.

And then, a spark of righteous anger.

"Seriously?" I breathed. I stepped forward, just a few feet in front of everyone else. "You're *still* after us? Because of what—the rules of the Echo? The ones that *keep you here*, still burning and dying over and over again? It can't do *anything* for you. It never has! All these promises you might have been told, the broken ones that you keep chanting about? Do you even remember *who* made you those promises? Not us!"

I stepped along the semicircle of Passengers closing in. They were now silent in their march, but I wasn't done.

"This *Slumlord* has been around here, still feeding on you, still making every second of your afterlives miserable! Just like he did when you were alive! *He's* the one who made you false promises. *He's* the one you should be tearing apart!"

Despite their faces being bloodied and burned, not a single one of them even twitched with a reaction.

"Well?" I roared. "Answer me!"

The crescendo was slow but clear.

"*Falsas...promesas...*"

I almost screamed in frustration until I saw the distinct change in their march. They weren't coming for us.

They were coming for the Slumlord.

His eyes darted around in panic, but before he could think to run, they descended. The sound of clothes tearing apart gave way to another sharp crack of glass and bones and meat. The four of us tried to look away as the Passengers gave a whole new meaning to the phrase *Eat the rich*.

In the carnage of it all, Cisco urged us to go on.

"Before it's too late."

He locked eyes with Charlize, and though she teared up, she nodded and turned into the station. Aaron followed close after, and I made my way halfway down the steps before I heard the last thing Cisco would say to Mario.

"We deserved better than Samira."

Mario soon stepped into the subway station with a hardened look. I'm sure he meant to look apathetic, but more than anything, it looked like he was trying to keep himself from crying.

The tunnel was dark and unforgiving. We moved along slowly, careful with our every step so we didn't trip.

I breathed in deeply and noted the way the gasoline smell fell away to cooler air. There was a calm breeze, something I hadn't noticed was absent from the tunnel before.

"You sure about this, Raquel?" Mario asked. "I mean, this is a pretty weird way to—"

"Mario, shut up." I strained my ears. The tracks under my feet were sturdy, but every so often, I could hear something creak and crack.

"Don't tell me to—"

"Shh!" I said loudly and paused to listen. I heard another sudden crack and whispered, "There's something in the tunnel with us."

"Please tell me it's just a rat," Aaron whispered back.

We stood still as it came in wisps. The smell of smoke and a low cough. I recognized it fairly well.

"Guys, you go on ahead," I said, pulling Charlize forward.

"What? *Why?*" She flailed until she caught my wrist again, but I forced it off.

"Just trust me." I kissed her on the cheek. "Get off the tracks as soon as you can and call an ambulance."

They were quiet as they considered my words but wouldn't budge.

"Just go!"

And then they slowly picked up the pace, begrudgingly—but still. The sound of sneakers kicking against gravel grew faint.

"Raquel, if you don't bring your ass back alive, I'm going to kill you!" Aaron yelled. The threat made me snicker even when the coughing grew louder.

Then it fell silent.

"You okay?" I asked, softly. The man in corduroy stumbled forward, another crack under his foot.

"I'm fine." He coughed, lying. "Just dying for the last time."

He said it like it was no big deal, like it was easy to die over and over without being able to hold on to his sanity.

"That was a very interesting speech you gave," he said. "You almost remind me of someone."

At first, I didn't answer him. I only took a careful step forward. "You could have just told me you wanted help to move on."

A movement in the tunnel told me he was shaking his head.

"It was too hard to keep everything straight up here." He tapped his temple. "When you've died as many times as I have, you barely remember your own name, much less what you want. Being used by the Echo didn't make it any better."

I nodded, understanding the truth of his words. I hadn't died, but I experienced so many people's deaths in the two trips through the Echo, and that alone drove me mad. Lures were still victims through and through. Maybe I couldn't stop the Echo from taking people, but now I knew how to get them back.

I held my hand out and waited until he gripped it. His own coughing became a horrible wheeze, and I felt his body fall to the tracks.

"I hope this death finally gives you peace," I said, holding on to him. And soon enough, he stilled. The smell of smoke went away with the coarseness of his hands as he disappeared for the last time. The tunnel breathed with a rush of air that sounded suspiciously like the man's echoing voice.

Thank you, Raquel.

——————

I walked onward, a cool breeze skating over my forehead and my own labored breath loud in my ears. Then came the sound of an argument from the platform.

"...coming back?"

"I don't know!" the voice hissed. It didn't take me long to know who it belonged to.

"Mario? Aaron?" I rose my voice. "Charlize?"

A head poked into the tunnel, squinting into the dark. Hope and relief swelled in my chest as I finally came to the end.

"Raquel!" Aaron yelled. He reached his hands out toward me, and I grabbed hold of him. I was now mostly dragging my bad leg and wasn't sure how much farther I could go on my own.

"That shit worked?" Mario asked, seeing me emerge from the tunnel. He was incredulous, I knew, but I didn't care. We were finally out. That's all that mattered.

"Yeah." I said, breathlessly.

"Now help get me off the train tracks before a train runs me over."

PART SEVEN

LAUGH IT OFF

WHEN WE EMERGED FROM THE HUNTS POINT TUNNEL, crawling out of the tracks, bleeding, beaten and scarred, the first thing we did was call an ambulance. The pain in my leg was dulled, but so was any feeling in it whatsoever, and I knew that wasn't a good sign. Aaron helped me sit on the sidewalk with my back against the redbrick pillar. Charlize sat next to me, pulling my hand into hers.

"So...you like me, too?" She nudged me, playfully.

I smiled and rolled my eyes.

"Only if you like me back."

And she laughed.

The conversation with the emergency operator went about as awkwardly as I expected. After we explained we needed an ambulance at Hunts Point Avenue, the operator asked how we got our wounds.

"We're...not sure," Mario said, eyeing me like a deer in headlights. I shrugged, knowing I wouldn't have come up with something better anyway. The operator would either think we were on drugs or that we were trying to cover up a crime, but either way, we'd get the help we needed.

There was a brief pause after Mario spoke.

"Okay," the operator finally said. "An ambulance is on its way."

It snowed while we waited. Half an inch of white covered the streets, pristine and pure everywhere except where we sat. Our dirt, sweat, and blood mixed with the white and turned into slush. I sat with my leg flush to the snow, using it to numb the pain.

"Hey, Aaron." I spoke up, figuring this was the time to ask questions. He looked over at me with curiosity. The blood on his face was crusting, and the open scabs were closed again.

"What happened? Like, after we got separated?" It almost felt like he cheated his way in getting an easy meeting with the Echo. Meanwhile I fought tooth and nail through all of it.

Still, I was happy he was okay.

Aaron bobbed his head in a short nod.

"To tell you the truth...I don't know. I remember getting over the turnstile, and suddenly I was alone. I went aboveground and freaked the fuck out before hopping from building to building. I thought as long as I kept moving, I could stay alive." He reached up to his face, lightly touching it as if he couldn't believe it was there. A brownish-red dust collected deep under his nails. It almost blended into the dirt, but there was no mistaking blood. We had already seen too much of it.

"And you, Mario?" I said, leaning just enough to catch his eye. "What happened when we separated?"

He shook his head and looked down. He opened his mouth for just half a second before mumbling a response.

"I don't want to talk about it."

I leaned back against the pole, letting him keep his secrets. The last thing Cisco ever said to him had to do with a girl who hurt both of them. I wondered if it bothered him, if he regretted letting someone get between them, or if he just wanted reassurance that Cisco didn't hate him after all.

Whatever he felt, I hoped he at least got some closure out of it.

I shut my eyes instead and listened to the howling wind. Few cars passed us by, and it was only a few more minutes until I heard the whirring alarm of an ambulance.

"Hey!" Aaron yelled. I felt him stand up next to me, hopping up and down as if waving for attention. "Over here!"

The alarm got closer and eventually stopped altogether when it pulled up in front of the curb. The slam of the metal door came next, and then the sound of boots squelching in the snow.

I slowly opened my eyes, meeting the paramedic's face. He didn't seem much older than us, but the harsh look in his eyes told me otherwise. He wasn't even fazed by a group of bloody teenagers.

Weirder things happened in New York, and much stranger things in the Bronx.

His partner got out from the back of the ambulance and scanned us all. They were clearly looking for the most injured person to send first and focused their eyes on me. Then they called for backup, clearly planning on splitting us all up.

"Hold on, it's just these two," Aaron protested, pointing at Charlize and me. I narrowed my eyes on him and opened my mouth to speak.

"He's got a concussion. He was just vomiting earlier," I lied. Aaron glared at me, and I ignored it. A good chunk of his memory was missing. The least he could do was get his brain checked.

"Yeah," he said, cutting his eyes away from me. "Right. I forgot about that."

The paramedics took one look at each other and shrugged, calling for backup again. Moments later, two other ambulances showed up. Mario refused to leave Aaron's side and just rode in the same one with him.

I didn't want to leave Charlize, but I didn't have a choice. We were both bleeding and needed to be tended to separately.

We locked eyes just as the stretcher she was on was being loaded onto the back of the ambulance. Her eyelids drooped, and her face was still pale, but I knew she would be okay.

"I'm going to ask you a few questions, okay?" the paramedic said, strapping me onto the stretcher. I winced when he pulled it tight over my legs.

"Does that hurt?"

I quickly nodded. He loosened it as the ambulance rolled off.

"What's your name?"

"Raquel Celestin."

He continued to ask the standard questions for any battered victim. How old I was, did I know what day it was, did I know where I was, who were my parents or guardians...

"Wait, you're Samuel's kid?" He looked disbelieving but kept with the pace of questioning that was necessary for doing his job.

Until it came to the one question I knew I couldn't answer.

"Can you tell me what happened out here?"

I laughed.

There was really no way to answer that without being sent to a psych ward. I shook my head and closed my eyes. He didn't ask anything else, taking the hint that I didn't want to talk about it. Once I was fully strapped in, he shut the back doors and yelled for the other paramedic to drive.

Eventually I dozed off, with the rumble of the ambulance lulling me to sleep.

———

"Hello, yes, I'm here to see my daughter." The voice echoed loudly through the hall, and I groaned under my breath. I thought about pretending to be asleep, but I knew Papi would just shake me awake anyway. There was no way to get out of what was coming.

Might as well get it over with.

A nurse mumbled a response, and feet slapped against the floor down the hall.

"Sir, please don't run," the security guard said, but he didn't listen.

Papi's ragged breathing announced his appearance even before his face did. He slid around the corner of the door frame, nearly slipping and crashing into the sharps container before regaining his balance and facing me.

His eyes were bloodshot, angry.

And they shined with tears and a shimmer of relief. I was alive.

"I cannot *believe* you would sneak out of the house!" he said, sharply and under his breath. His eyes darted toward the cloth curtain that separated me and my roommate. She was an old Ecuadorian woman still healing from a discectomy or something. I couldn't remember as my brain fogged over details at every turn.

"And for what? To play a stupid game at three a.m.? How did you even get this injured?"

"Papi, please." I coughed. "I just got out of surgery."

His face went slack for a moment, and he looked down at my leg. I was covered in blankets, but he could easily see the ankle brace keeping my foot aligned. His voice became a whisper, a fast stream of Spanish curses and prayers. I hoped this would be the end of the interrogation—at least for now. But I was wrong. His eyes went back up to mine, now twice as angry.

"Do you know how upset your mother will be?"

"Is Mami...okay?" I held my breath. My eyes were half-lidded and struggling to stay open. My own painkillers were fighting me, but I struggled to stay awake long enough to hear the news.

Papi slowly blinked and sighed.

"Yes," he said, walking over to me. He plopped in the chair right by my bed, exhaustion drowning him with ease.

"Your mother, thank God, has somehow started recovering. The...the fungus started to recede. The doctors don't know why, but at least it's happening."

My chest shook with relief.

Thank God.

AS GOOD AS
IT COULD BE

I SAT ON THE LEDGE OF MY HOSPITAL ROOM WINDOW. IT WAS snowing again. The top of every building and car was a sheet of white and continued to pile on with every falling snowflake.

I watched the scene quietly. I wondered if everyone else was also just a little on edge. Every night, when the nurses would come to check my vitals, I could almost hear the raspy laugh of the man in corduroy, bouncing around in the back of my head.

But it was just my imagination. PTSD or whatever. I read somewhere that traumatic experiences can cause that, and what was more traumatic than jumping into a hellish dimension on a whim?

I should probably get therapy.

Part of me expected to blink and see fire again. I expected to wake up, drenched in my own sweat and jumping into a fighting position at the ready. Or to *really* see the man in corduroy with another cryptic answer to a straight question.

But he hadn't shown up once since I left the tunnel. He was really gone. And for once, it was unnerving.

I couldn't help but laugh. Really, who was I going to share that with?

The window was locked, but the cold continued to filter in through the cracks. I pressed my temple against the glass and breathed in the relief.

No fires. No angry impulses. No fever.

A cold Bronx was the opposite of a burning Bronx, and though I'd never been a fan of coldness before, I was grateful for what it brought.

An end.

I looked up toward the television. The news went through its usual cycle, from the weather to city events, and coming right back around to any recent crimes that took place. Suddenly, the TV flashed with the faces of Officer Bored and Officer Quiet.

"The NYPD is continuing their search for the missing officers, Stephen Batista and Manny Quiñónez. The two were last heard from calling for backup at the Hunts Point station before they disappeared. Unfortunately, video evidence could not be recovered as the cameras had been shut off before they stepped inside…"

I stared at their pictures with a vague sense of discomfort. Part of me still felt awful for the way they were taken. They weren't meant to get all caught up in the challenge, and had I known they were still following me, I might have taken a less direct route to the station.

I turned off the TV before the anchorwoman finished the report. There was nothing I could do for the officers now.

A light knock at my door brought my attention away from the screen.

"Raquel, are you ready?" a nurse asked. Right behind her were a new set of officers, who I affectionately called Officer Glum and Officer Smokes.

"Yeah," I said, leaning away from the window.

I carefully brought my leg down and then reached for the crutches. My leg was carefully wrapped and stitched up after needing surgery to remove all the embedded glass. Luckily, I didn't break a single bone, but I'd still need help getting around for a month or two.

The nurse came over to help me as soon as I stood on my good leg. I waved her off.

"I need to get used to this," I said, awkwardly stepping over to my bed. I turned my back to it and lifted my ass on it first. Then I shimmied into a comfortable position and rested my hands on my lap. The nurse looked from me to the officers and smiled.

"I'll be out there if you need anything."

I nodded, though I wasn't sure if she was even talking to me.

Officer Glum took the nearest seat and sighed loudly. It was something she always did at seemingly random times, like she *wanted* you to hear how tired she was. And her facial expression never did anything to help her. Her eyes always looked far off when she spoke, and I wondered if she was having an out-of-body experience each time.

"Okay, so we spoke to your other friends."

I nodded, happy to know they were okay. Aaron and I called to talk whenever we wanted, but it was still a relief to know others could see him, too. The scabs on his face were peeling off with the help of some ointment he swore would take care of scars. He offered to bring me some the next time he and Mario visited, but I declined.

"Your friends Mario and Aaron are still giving conflicting stories regarding each one's disappearance, what happened to your leg, and how you found Charlize. Charlize won't say a word, and you still insist you were sleepwalking and woke up just getting out of the tunnel."

I nodded again. We didn't think to get our stories straight before the ambulances picked us up, so we chose what was most convenient to us and stuck with it. That was the important thing.

My eyes cut to Officer Smokes, who was trying to jiggle the window open. He was fidgeting in a way that let me know he was having an intense craving.

"Uh—" I pointed to Glum's partner. "You're not allowed to smoke in a hospital."

He dropped his hands and clenched them into fists.

"Right," he said through gritted teeth. He turned and took long strides past Glum and out the door. "I'm going to go have a smoke."

Glum didn't react. I looked back to her and struggled to keep a straight face. Her eyes sparked with resignation that deepened when he stepped out.

I made a sudden shift in bed and cleared my throat loudly to bring her back to attention. She sat up and opened her mouth to continue.

"And you're sure you didn't see your assailants at all?"

I blinked before I shook my head. I had forgotten they assumed someone attacked me with a broken glass bottle. I was just shocked they didn't immediately assume I did it to myself for a bullshit reason. It was odd to have the police actually treat you as a victim rather than a criminal.

Even if they were technically wrong somewhere in that line of thought.

I quietly thanked God for two boring cops who hated each other and their jobs too much to care.

"Okay," she said, getting to her feet. She took a moment to

dig into her pocket before pulling out a card. "Well, here is my number. If you remember anything at all, you can give me a call."

"Thank you, I will," I lied. Glum was immediately out the door. She couldn't handle what I knew.

———

The day I was discharged, I demanded to visit Mami. Papi insisted that I rest, but I knew I wouldn't be able to until I could finally see her face to face.

"Please, Papi?" I whined. "Pleasepleasepleasepleasepleasepleaseplease—"

"Okay!" He threw his hands up in defeat. "But don't pout if she isn't awake yet!"

The ride from Montefiore to Lincoln Hospital was objectively short. A twenty-minute commute was *always* short in the Bronx. Except, in this case, every minute stretched on to eternity. I couldn't keep my good leg from jiggling anxiously with every street we passed. Papi filled the silence with small talk, mostly to the cab driver. When he turned to talk to me, I almost completely missed it.

"What?" I asked.

"I said, let's wait until your mother is healthy and discharged before we tell her about your latest stunt, okay?"

I nodded.

Soon enough, the cab driver slowed to a stop, and Papi helped me out of the car.

"You go on in, I've got to make a stop somewhere else first," he said. I didn't argue. I went as fast as my bad leg allowed. The sign-in with security was a blur of throbbing pain and well-meaning offers of accommodation.

"You sure you don't want a wheelchair?" a nurse asked as she watched me struggle to the elevator.

"No, thank you."

It took me a few minutes to mentally collect myself before entering her room. I knew Mami was up and awake—I could hear her murmur responses to the doctor. I knew she was fine because they let me get this far without needing to put on a hazmat suit. Mami's room was no longer under quarantine, and the people who moved throughout the hallways were no longer concerned about whatever she was infected with making its way to them.

And yet, I was still afraid. Everything that had happened had been so absurd I half expected the rug to be pulled out from under me.

Eventually Dr. Yee exited the room, and with a reassuring smile, she nodded and let me know I could go in.

I staggered awkwardly with my crutches into Mami's room and locked eyes with her.

"Raquel?" Her eyes were half-lidded, and she looked weak—but she was alive. The black rot on her arms was gone, and although her voice was extremely hoarse, I was told the mold on her lungs had completely receded. "What happened to you?"

I almost didn't answer. The relief I felt was so overwhelming, I forgot to breathe. Eventually, I made my way to her side and squeezed her hand.

She could hardly squeeze back.

"My muscles atrophied," she explained. "Two weeks of being comatose will do that to you, apparently. Now are you going to tell me what happened to your leg?"

"Had a little accident," I said, wiping tears from my eyes. "I'll tell you once you feel better."

"Hmph." She pouted. She didn't like having secrets kept from her, but she had no strength to protest. I just sat by her side and held her hand. She closed her eyes. After a while, I thought she'd fallen asleep. But then she spoke.

"I had the oddest dream about you..."

"Hmm?" I massaged her palm out of habit.

"You remember that old apartment we used to live in? The one with all the mold and asbestos?"

I pressed my lips in a thin line to keep from smirking.

Eventually, Papi arrived with a bouquet of tulips for Mami. They were her favorite kind of flowers, and even though she tried to pretend she was only tolerating his presence, I could see her eyes softening every time she looked at the bouquet.

"Are you the reason my baby's out here walking with a limp?" She tried to say this with as much of a serious tone as possible, but it was hard to take her seriously when she sounded like Darth Vader.

Papi's face fell. "Why are you assuming it's *my* fault?"

Mami couldn't stop her lips from quirking upward.

"Because Samuel, I'm out of the picture for only *two weeks*, and as soon as I come to, my baby's leg is all messed up."

"Why do you keep saying *your* baby? She's my daughter too!" Papi pouted.

"Then you should be more careful!" Her voice cracked, and her chest shook as she struggled to clear her throat. "You're lucky I can barely hold a pen right now, otherwise I would be wringing your neck!"

Even in her extremely weakened state, Mami wouldn't pull her punches, and she argued fervently with Papi. The Spanish that was thrown back and forth sounded like daggers—sharp and precise. It was so fast, I couldn't for the life of me understand what they were saying.

Papi's shoulders fell, and like waving a white flag, he sighed in exasperation.

"You just woke up from a coma—how are you already so energetic?"

It was a fair question, one even I wanted to know.

"You should know by now there isn't anything I wouldn't do for my baby girl."

Blood filled my cheeks, and I blinked away tears.

Me too, Mami. Me too.

THE LEGACY
OF THE BRONX

I STEPPED OFF THE BUS, AWKWARDLY BALANCING HALF MY weight onto the crutch. I aimed it for the spots in the sidewalk where the snow was most melted and ignored the memory of blood and viscera that tried to overshadow it.

"You doing okay, m'ija?" Papi asked, helping me along. His hand was positioned on my shoulder, light enough to not add any extra weight but firm enough that he would catch me if I slipped even once. "You know you don't have to get back to school so soon. You can take another few days to rest, if you need to."

"No, it's okay," I said with a shake of my head. "Besides, my teacher said he'd give extra points for anyone who presents their term paper early." For a moment, he looked shocked, like he couldn't believe I was more concerned about my grades than I was about my leg.

"Your presentation!" he finally said. "I forgot!"

He patted down his pockets and pulled out something that looked like an old photograph.

"Here, maybe this will help. A real piece of history." He grinned, handing it over.

I furrowed my brow but turned to the school as I looked down at it. Then I froze. The photo was of a host of people hanging together in front of a newly built garden. I could easily point out the younger versions of Papi and Xiomara, but just a few feet away, there was someone else that I recognized.

"Papi? Who's this?"

He pouted and followed my finger down to the picture.

"Ah! That's Johnson." There was a hint of sadness in his eyes as he clicked his tongue. "He was such a trickster. You couldn't make pians with him on April Fools' because he would always try and pull a fast one. Wouldn't stop trying to tell you riddles either."

"What happened to him?" I asked, keeping a straight face.

"Died, unfortunately," he said with a shrug. "Had to have been what, twenty years now? It was the most asinine thing, too. There were tons of gangs where he lived, and he'd survived so many shootings, and you know what did him in? Asthma."

I stared down at the face of the man in corduroy. His smile was wide, and his eyes seemed hopeful. It was hard to imagine this was the same man who had been following me around the last month and even harder to imagine him as an actual person.

Papi kissed me on the cheek. "Anyway, you go on in before you end up late."

The security guard held the door open for me as I walked into the lobby. I could feel the other students watching me. I kept my head down, pretending not to see any of them as I headed to the elevator and took it to the third floor.

I kept my breath deep and even until I got to my locker and emptied my bag into it. Even though the crutch was padded for my comfort, it still dug into my armpit uncomfortably.

"Heard you were going to present today," Aaron said, turning the corner. Trailing behind him was a group of guys I had in my classes but never really clicked with. They dispersed when they saw he had moved on from their conversation. "You are *such* a nerd!"

I smiled and rolled my eyes. "I might as well, since I finished my report. Why? Want my help with yours?"

He scoffed. "For *your* information, I think I've got enough sources."

"Playing the game does *not* count as a source," I said, closing the locker door.

"It should count! I risked my life!"

"*Sure.*"

I watched Aaron shimmy his bag off his shoulder as he went straight to his own locker.

"Cut me some slack, okay? I did *just* lose the contest. Though I guess it wasn't much of a contest. You had a head start and all." He emptied his bag out. It was so full of textbooks, I only hoped it had to do with why he hadn't spoken to me in the last few days.

Once he rearranged his locker with what he needed for the day, he bowed to me in a mock Victorian fashion.

"But I am nothing if not a man of my word, so I concede. Good day."

"You know the idea of 'winning' a girl from a contest she has no say in is just a little misogynistic—"

"I said, good day!" He snapped his fingers and twisted on his heel. I shook my head, laughing as he walked away. Not only did he take all the cuts and bruises in stride, but he took Charlize's decision in stride, too.

He told me not to, but I felt bad about it. Aaron was my best friend, and I knew cracking jokes was his desperate attempt to keep things lighthearted.

"Raquel!"

I smelled the mint before I even turned to look at her. Charlize made a beeline to me, eyes focused straight ahead as if she were still in a tunnel. She pulled me into a hug and giggled even under the stare of the entire hallway. Students eyed us with curiosity and smirked knowingly at the display of affection.

I resisted the urge to push her away for a few seconds and instead hugged her back.

Is Aaron still being weird? Charlize asked in my mind. Our new closeness was bittersweet because of how it had come about. Our connection to the Echo thankfully ended when we left the tunnel, but we kept our connection to each other.

Yeah. I don't blame him, though.

We would have to sit down and talk about what happened in the Echo one day. But for now, I would just have to give him time.

My balance faltered when I felt a small peck on my cheek, sending me spiraling backward.

"Careful!" I said, grabbing my clutches.

"Sorry." Charlize grinned as she pulled back. "How's your leg?"

"Well, it's not bleeding anymore," I said. I followed her to her locker, where she undid her scarf and peeled off her hat.

"I should be able to walk on my own again—" I stopped, mouth agape. "Charlize...your hair."

The Shirley Temple curls that had been part of her signature look for years now were gone. She had shaved all of it off. She reached up and idly touched the base of her head. Her eyes were still a little dim, but there was a spark in there when they met mine.

"Is it...bad?" She pouted.

"No. It's just...different."

A group of students spilled into the hallway, only to stop long enough to gape at Charlize.

"Holy shit, Charlize!" They laughed. A few surrounded her, brought their hands up to her newly shaven head, and rubbed in circles. She looked around at them with an embarrassed smile until they walked off. Then Charlize pulled my hand into hers as though they never interrupted us.

She squeezed it and gave me a small smile. "Can I walk you to class?"

───

"Okay, Raquel, you have the floor." Mr. Chan stepped off to the side while I brought up my PowerPoint.

Clearing my throat, I looked out at the classroom.

"Right. So. When I thought about the most vital part of Bronx history, the most Bronx thing I can imagine is community organizing."

The presentation opened with a picture; it was group of marching protesters, slightly blurred but still clear enough to read the signs they held. NO MORE TRUCKS was the most prominent one, and I turned to face the class with my laser pointer in hand.

"A prime example is the annual Fish Parade. It started as a protest against the incoming fish market, which would certainly bring in more trucks, increasing pollution and rates of asthma among the community." I clicked to the next slide, a clearer picture of a much larger group, marching for a different reason.

"Although the fish market ended up coming anyway, the protest inspired the residents to come together and celebrate their community. Several grassroots organizations in the Bronx take part in this event, bringing performances, vendors, and information on resources any resident may need."

I flipped to the next slide. It was a closeup of a small Puerto

Rican girl, twirling two batons in synchrony while wearing purple and green mermaid scales and colorful makeup. Though I didn't know the girl personally, I saw her a few times a week as part of an after-school program.

I glanced over to Mr. Chan, who nodded, before I clicked to the next slide, where a map of the parade was outlined in red.

"The parade occurs every June, usually the last week of school, and goes from Riverside Park all the way to Barretto Point Park, where the vendors can be found and where you can enjoy a great view of the Bronx River."

The longer I went on, the more my own anxiety quieted down. When Mr. Chan first introduced this project idea to us, I was certain I'd breeze through it with no effort involved. Most people only had the worst ideas of the Bronx—ideas that shaped the Echo and the experience of it.

But the Bronx has more good to it than anyone could think.

I clicked to the last picture. A line of lush green curving along a paved walkway. Two people sat on a bench overlooking a huge body of water. In the distance, Manhattan skyscrapers and bridges both stood tall.

Beneath the picture was a caption in white:

You don't have to move out of your neighborhood to live in a better one.

I thought about Aaron and Charlize: my best friend and my new girlfriend. Things would never be perfect, but that didn't mean they couldn't get better. I knew that now—all the makings of a better neighborhood were right here.

It wasn't just in resguardos or altars.

It was in ourselves, and no matter what happened, that would always be part of our legacy.

Author's Note

In all honesty, the best places to start with learning about the Bronx are the grassroots organizations found in various places throughout the borough. Some of them were mentioned in this book, and if you would like to help make a difference, here are some places to donate to:

The Point CDC
thepoint.org

Bronx River Alliance
bronxriver.org

Rocking the Boat
rockingtheboat.org

Pa'lante
palanteharlem.org

Bronx Defenders
bronxdefenders.org

Acknowledgments

There's way too many people to acknowledge the creation of this book. I could start with God for making me, my mom for birthing and raising me. Then to all the people who directly inspired and encouraged me in my writing, like my best friend, Desiree Johnson (on God, we gon' get you that brownstone!), my soul mate, Kay Peebles, for always giving great feedback and putting up with my breakdowns. I could never forget the people at The Point like Danny Peralta, Irene Perez, Teresa Rivera, Dania Abouzied, Sasha Diamond, Maya Davila—all people who had a hand in the most formative time of my life. Really could not forget about my mentor, Aubrey Mike, for all his help in keeping my spirits up through rough points in my life.

And then there all the people who really were deep in the trenches of getting this book out: Kristina Pérez (agent), Eliza Swift (editor), all the way through to Cassie Gutman (production editor). Reading your comments on my book gave me so much life.

There's not much else I can say but thank you for every step it took to get me here.

About the Author

Vincent Tirado is a nonbinary Afro-Latine Bronx native. They ventured out to Pennsylvania and Ohio to get their bachelor's degree in biology and master's degree in bioethics. They have had short stories published in *Desert Rose* and *FIYAH* magazine. Visit them at v-e-tirado.com or on Twitter @v_e_tirado.

FIREreads

#getbooklit

Your hub for the hottest young adult books!

Visit us online and sign up for our
newsletter at FIREreads.com

 @sourcebooksfire

 sourcebooksfire

 firereads.tumblr.com